Never Planned on You

Also by Lindsay Hameroff

Till There Was You

Never Planned on You

A NOVEL

Lindsay Hameroff

ST. MARTIN'S GRIFFIN
NEW YORK

This is a work of fiction. All of the characters, organizations, and events portrayed in this novel are either products of the author's imagination or are used fictitiously.

First published in the United States by St. Martin's Griffin, an imprint of St. Martin's Publishing Group

www.stmartins.com

Designed by Gabriel Guma

The Library of Congress Cataloging-in-Publication Data is available upon request.

ISBN 978-1-250-90294-8 (trade paperback)
ISBN 978-1-250-90295-5 (ebook)

Our books may be purchased in bulk for promotional, educational, or business use. Please contact your local bookseller or the Macmillan Corporate and Premium Sales Department at 1-800-221-7945, extension 5442, or by email at MacmillanSpecialMarkets@macmillan.com.

First Edition: 2025

10 9 8 7 6 5 4 3 2 1

For Jordana, my firecracker, whose breadth of talent is rivaled only by her enormous heart. Never settle for anything less than everything.

Never Planned on You

Prologue

EIGHT YEARS AGO

"Moment of truth. Someone's life is about to change." I peer over the edge of my playing card, narrowing my eyes as I stare down each of my competitors. Across the table, my flatmate Morgan groans.

"Give it a rest, Ali. We're playing Kings, not hustling for a ticket aboard the *Titanic*."

I shrug, then tip my chin toward Morgan's boyfriend, Theo. He's got the sickly green pallor of a man who's just realized this ship may sink and there definitely aren't enough lifeboats. "You alright there, Theo?"

Theo opens his mouth to reply, then snaps it shut, clutching a fist over his lips. Our favorite pub is busier than usual tonight, the buzz of voices and clinking glasses undoubtedly muffling a whimper behind his hand. He swallows, then nods wordlessly.

"Okay, then. Alfie, start us off?" My friend Alfie flips over his card, revealing a six of clubs.

"Six is dicks," Morgan declares. "Drink up, boys."

Alfie and Theo raise their glasses. But before he can take a sip, Theo bolts in the direction of the bathroom. I shake my head as I take another sip of beer.

"Men," I say. "The weaker sex."

Morgan stares longingly at her unfinished lager, then rises reluctantly. "I'd better go check on him."

"Seriously?" I protest. "That's half the players at the table. I can't play with just Alfie!"

Alfie smirks. "Sure you can. One-on-one competitions are where I shine. Especially contact sports."

I throw my cards down on the sticky wooden tabletop. "Gross, dude. I'm out."

"Well, in that case, I win by default," he says.

"Excuse me? How on earth do you figure?"

His grin widens. "I paid for the pints."

A spark kindles in my belly. It feels a lot like the time my older sister, Sarah, told me I was too young to watch *The Ring* with her and her friends. Sure, I might've slept with the lights on for a month. And refused to rent movies from Blockbuster (RIP) for years after. And maybe I still occasionally get freaked out when I spot preteens with long black hair and pale skin. But I didn't back down then, and I'm sure as hell not about to back down now. I shove back my shoulders and lift my chin.

"Over my dead body. The game isn't over until it's over—and we still have a few cards left. Let's find another player so we can end this properly."

Alfie cracks his knuckles. "Fair enough," he concedes, and I can't help but grin at the way he pronounces the word "fair." I've spent the past three months in London for my semester abroad, but I'm still not over how pleasing certain vowels sound with a British accent.

"My flatmate Graham is over at the bar, probably nursing some grumpy old man drink befitting his grumpy old man nature. I'll see if he'll rally."

"Your flatmate?" I raise an eyebrow. "We've hung out almost every night this semester, and I still haven't met this alleged flatmate. I was starting to think he was imaginary."

Alfie shakes his head. "Wanker hardly ever comes out. He's been revising at LSE and spends most of his time holed up in his room, bent over an Excel spreadsheet or something equally depressing."

With a groan, Alfie shoves out his chair and heads over to the bar. He taps the shoulder of a sandy-haired man who's sitting alone, nursing a tumbler of dark liquor. Alfie whispers something in his ear, and the guy glances over his shoulder at me. A wrinkle forms between his brows as he meets my eyes. Then he shakes his head and swivels back around. A hot flash of indignation spikes through me. *Seriously? Who does this guy think he is?*

I'm about to go over there and give him a piece of my mind, but Alfie claps a hand down on his friend's shoulder and forcefully guides him toward the table. A moment later, they're both standing in front of me.

"Got our replacement player," Alfie announces. "Ali, this is Graham." My eyes flit over the other man, who I am now fully prepared to despise, and *oh*.

Graham is taller and leaner than Alfie, with a mop of golden hair that contrasts with Alfie's dark curls. There's a sprinkle of freckles across the bridge of his nose. Above it, bright blue eyes regard me curiously behind a pair of tortoiseshell glasses. He pushes them up with his index finger, an expression of annoyance painted across his face. Also of note: he is wearing a cardigan. In a bar.

Alfie was right; this guy is definitely giving off These Neighborhood Kids Keep Stomping on My Hydrangeas vibes. But in like, the hottest way possible.

I clear my throat. "Right. We're playing Kings. It's the last round, but we need someone to carry us to the finish line. Have you ever played?"

Graham blinks, as if trying to comprehend the concept of recreational drinking. "Party games aren't really my thing," he says after a moment. When I roll my eyes, he quickly adds, "But I'm a fast learner."

He slides into Theo's vacated seat while I explain the rules. "Theo was up next, so you can take his turn," I say. Graham nods and flips over the card that was lying face down in front of him.

"Eight is for . . . mates?" he asks tentatively. His accent is more subtle than Alfie's, just a hint of the British influence bringing a lyrical quality to his voice. I wish this fact made me swoon any less.

When Alfie nods, Graham flicks his gaze toward me, and something sparks to life behind his eyes. Something I recognize immediately as a challenge. "Shall we?"

We stare over the edges of our drinks, eyes locked like we're two Real Housewives forced to endure the reunion episode after months of shit-talking each other in our confessionals. We chug for one second, two, and then . . .

"Finished already?" I ask, wiping my mouth as he slams his glass against the tabletop. "I didn't realize this was amateur hour."

Graham's mouth crooks into a half smile. "Going easy on you felt like the gentlemanly thing to do."

With effort, I tear my eyes away from his lips and scoff. "Trust me, I am the last person you will ever need to go easy on."

Graham's eyes widen a fraction as the subtext dangles in the air between us. Then Alfie clears his throat, dispelling the tension.

"Aces," he says, holding up his card. "Waterfall."

We throw back our drinks again. A few seconds pass, then Alfie slams down his half-empty pint with a loud belch. Graham and I keep going until both our glasses are drained, then set them down in perfect synchronicity.

"Well, I always enjoy a good pissing contest," Alfie says. "Although I guess I must declare this one a draw."

My head snaps in his direction. "A *draw*? How is that fair? He just sat down!"

Graham crosses his arms. "I'd be down for a tie-break."

He tips his chin toward the dartboard across the room. "How about a friendly game of darts?"

Alfie and I grin at each other conspiratorially. I've been honing my skills on that board all spring and haven't lost a game in weeks. "You're on."

Ten minutes later, Graham and I are somehow evenly matched, and we each have one dart left.

"Are you sure you don't want a stool?" Graham appraises me with a sidelong look. "I imagine it's difficult to see the entirety of the board from your eye level."

I roll my eyes. I've been the shortest kid in my class since the first grade and have been called every nickname in the vertically challenged catalog. So, if this guy thinks heckling me about my height will distract me, he's going to need to get a lot more creative.

"Please. You're going down like a Fourth of July hot dog."

"Americans," he says. "Always so eloquent."

"Of note, you are suspiciously good at darts for a person who doesn't spend much time in pubs."

Graham smirks. "We have a board in our student lounge. It's a nice way to blow off steam between classes. Now are you ready, or do you require more time for stalling?"

"Don't get your britches in a bunch, Benedict. I was born ready."

"Benedict?"

I shrug. "You have the essence of a Benedict. Might have to do with the posture. It's so . . . rigid. Have you ever considered applying to the Buckingham sentry?"

Graham's lips twitch in amusement, his eyes lingering on mine for a long beat. The intensity of the prolonged eye contact sends a pleasurable shiver down my spine. I grab my beer off the table, taking a long sip before he can fully derail my concentration with smoldering glances.

"In fact," I say, once I've recalibrated. "Why don't we make this interesting?"

"Interesting, huh? What did you have in mind, Polly Pocket?"

"Loser buys us both chips at the food stand across the street."

Graham's eyebrows shoot upward. "That's your best offer? Frankly I pinned you as a bit more innovative."

I scowl at him. "Okay, how about this? Loser gets a tattoo. And the winner gets to choose it."

I know I've got him now. There's no way in hell this dude's going to agree to a tattoo. Because again, *the cardigan*. But then he grins at me and—in the most shocking twist since Marissa's untimely death on *The O.C.*—replies, "Okay. You're on."

I squint one eye, aim, and toss the dart. It arcs gracefully through the air, following the precise trajectory I envisioned. And with a satisfying *thunk*, it lands directly in the inner circle. Black six. Finally, my otherwise useless pursuit of dart supremacy has paid off.

"You're getting inked tonight, Benedict!"

Graham ignores me, his eyes trained on his own dartboard. "We'll see about that," he mutters. He aims with a worrisome sense of ease, shoots, and . . . *son of a bitch*. His dart lands in the exact same spot mine did.

"Mother*fucker*!" I exclaim.

Graham crosses his arms and grins. "Guess this ends in a deadlock."

I scoff. "In your dreams. Tie means we're *both* getting tattoos." Shit. That sounded smarter in my head. Did I just agree to getting a tattoo? *Shit.*

Alfie, who's been spectating from a stool in the corner, chooses this moment to chime in.

"There's a tattoo parlor just 'round the corner," he offers helpfully. *Fuck you too, Alfie.*

I straighten my shoulders with resignation. *Fine.* I've made my bed, and now it's time to lie in it with this hot British man. Which, when put in those terms, doesn't sound half bad. It also doesn't matter, since there's not a chance in hell Graham will go through with this. Because again, *the cardigan.* The only way to win this thing is to call his bluff.

I pick up my purse. "Ready when you are."

Graham gives me a broad smile as he gestures to the door. "After you."

Ten minutes later, we're standing inside a dimly lit spot called Cloak and Dagger, thumbing through a sticky binder of tattoo images while an enormous dude named Ivan stares us down, his own heavily inked arms crossed.

"Let's see," I say, flipping through the book. "My friend Benedict here is looking for something that really captures his essence. A pair of ballet slippers, perhaps, or maybe just a butterfly with an accompanying Mariah Carey lyric."

Ivan raises a questioning eyebrow at Graham.

"I'm not actually called Benedict," he says quickly. Then he points to an image in the binder. "There. That's the one she's getting."

I peer over the side of his arm and physically recoil. Staring back at me is a unicorn's head. On the body of a pig. A uni-pig. A pig-icorn. It looks like something straight out of a Tim Burton fever dream. In other words, it is perfect.

"He'll have the same," I say, snapping my binder shut. "On his hip bone. I'll go easy on him and pass up the opportunity for a tramp stamp."

I grin triumphantly at Graham. This has to be it, the moment he breaks. Instead, he narrows his eyes, fixing his gaze on mine with an expression that's equally resolute.

Ivan rolls his eyes. "What a thrill. Who's first?"

"I'll go," Graham volunteers. He slides into a chair and then unhooks the button of his trousers, sliding them down an inch to reveal a sliver of taut, tan skin. My mouth goes dry as I stare at the exposed flesh, utterly transfixed. Up until this moment, I've never noticed how sexy a man's hip bone could be.

I don't realize I'm staring until Graham lifts his head and lets out a low chuckle.

"It's not too late to back out," he says, and I realize he must be mistaking the look on my face for fear. "There's no shame in surrender." He's staring at me with that penetrating gaze again, the one that blurs everything else in the background, and my heart spikes.

"In your dreams," I manage to choke out. Then I take a deep breath and settle into a leather chair to await my turn.

"I can't believe we actually did that," Graham says. We're strolling down the street, passing a greasy takeaway bag of chips back and forth. "The one night I take a study break, I end up getting matching pig tattoos with an American girl. I don't think I've ever done anything so reckless in my life."

"I can't believe you did it either, Benedict," I say. "Though admittedly, it was a very in-character move for me." My brain queues up a memory from earlier in the semester, when my friends and I spent an evening in Notting Hill. On a whim, I'd attempted to scale the gate at Rosmead Garden, Julia Roberts–style. Only instead of scoring a kiss from Hugh Grant, the night ended with two badly scraped shins and a tense exchange with Garden Patrol.

We come to a stop outside our apartment building. Graham shoves his hands into his pockets, shifting his weight from one foot to the other.

"So," he says after a beat. "How have you been enjoying London?"

I suppress a smile at his adorably awkward transition, pleased that he's as reluctant to end the night as I am. "Well, the curry is amazing. But I've also lived here for three months and have yet to spot a single member of One Direction, so, you know. Peaks and valleys."

Graham grins as he shakes his head. "How is it possible that we've been living in the same building for three months, and I've never run into you? Of all life's injustices."

I shrug. "According to Alfie, you never leave your room."

Graham exhales a conceding laugh. "Yeah, it's been a tough semester. But I just took my final exam today, so my schedule should be freeing up a bit. Maybe I'll see you again?"

"Afraid not. This is my last night in London. My study abroad is over."

Graham's shoulders deflate. "Oh. Right then. Shall I walk you to your flat?"

I grab hold of his hand and give it a little squeeze. "Or I could walk you to yours."

Graham stares down at our interlocked fingers, clearly startled by the boldness of the gesture. But then, I've never been shy. When I see something I like, I go for it.

His hand is still interwoven in mine when we arrive in front of his door a few minutes later, and I'm suddenly aware of how reluctant I am to release it.

"Well, Benedict," I say, hoping my voice doesn't sound too reluctant. "It's been a pleasure."

Graham uses his forefinger to push his glasses up the bridge of his nose as he stares down at me. Conflicting emotions brew behind his eyes. Caution, mixed with something else. Desire.

Taking a step forward, I place a hand against his stomach. I skate my fingertips under his shirt and over his skin, pausing when I reach the top edge of his bandage.

"Does it still hurt?" I whisper. Graham swallows, his Adam's apple bobbing as he shakes his head. Then his eyes drop to my mouth, and I hear his sharp intake of breath. The sound is the green light I need. Before I can overthink it, I lift onto my tiptoes and press my mouth to his.

For one long, horrifying second, Graham doesn't move. But then his body relaxes as his warm lips melt into mine. He reaches one hand forward to cradle my cheek, lifting my face toward his to deepen the kiss. The pad of his thumb brushes gently against my cheekbone, and I release a sigh into his mouth as our surroundings fade to a blur.

When his tongue parts my lips, I reach a hand up the back of his shirt, dragging my fingertips against his skin and leaving behind a trail of goosebumps. He groans as he tightens his grip on my hips, pulling me flush against him. My legs turn to water, and I'm grateful for his strong hold, the only thing keeping me upright.

I'm not sure how much time passes before he breaks away. He takes an unsteady step backward, his chest rising and falling with jagged breath as he stares at me wild-eyed. My head spins as I come crashing back into reality. *Holy shit.*

"Do you want to come in?" he asks finally, his voice low and raspy. Then he blinks a few times and clears his throat. "Or we could just say goodnight. After all, it's not like we'll see each other again."

Desire tightens its grip on me as I take a step forward, closing the space between us.

"We'll never see each other again," I agree. "Which is exactly why we shouldn't let an opportunity like this go to waste." And with that, I yank him into his apartment, slamming the door behind me.

1

NOW

"So, just to make sure I have this right," I say, glancing up from my notes to look at our client's earnest face. "You're going to be dressed as Princess Fiona, your husband is going to be Shrek, and your bridal party will be dressed as . . . ?"

"A fairy-tale character of their choosing!" she finishes, clapping her hands gleefully. "I'm not one of those crazy bridezillas who's going to force her friends to all wear the same gown! They should be free to choose an outfit that embraces who they really are: the Gingerbread Man, a little piggy, or even Donkey!"

"Well, let's hope no one makes an ass of themselves," I reply. Asha, our company's lead wedding planner, kicks me under the table.

"I think your guests will adore it," Asha says. She tucks a glossy strand of black hair behind her ear and gives the bride a megawatt smile. "And I love that your wedding theme is so personal."

The bride beams back at her. "Felix and I met three years ago at a Halloween party. I was dressed as Fiona, and he was Shrek." Her expression turns dreamy. "As soon as our eyes met across the room, I knew I'd met the man I'd spend the rest of my life with. I guess you could say I was head ogre heels!"

She lets out a little giggle, then lowers her voice conspiratorially.

"Shrek says ogres are like onions, but I've always found Felix to be more of an eggplant."

I bite down hard on my bottom lip and Asha discreetly nudges my water bottle toward me. I snatch it, taking a long gulp to keep the retort on the tip of my tongue from erupting like lava.

"The Visionary Art Museum is the perfect venue," I say, once I've recovered. "Such a creative space for a wedding that is so . . . whimsical."

The bride bobs her head enthusiastically. "So, what's next on our to-do list?"

Asha consults her iPad. "We still need to book your hair and makeup trial, and then schedule a cake tasting. Are you good to meet again next month?"

After Asha schedules the bride's upcoming appointments and escorts her to the exit, she returns to the conference room, crossing her arms and giving me a pointed look.

"What?" I ask. "I thought I exhibited exceptional self-control, all things considered." She rolls her eyes in exasperation. I just shrug. I'm right, and we both know it.

"Although," I add, "I think it's safe to assume that the groom's costume will be anatomically accurate. They seem like the sort of couple who pays attention to detail."

Asha groans.

"Do you think when she lay awake in bed as a teen, fantasizing about her wedding night, she imagined it would include getting railed by a green penis?"

"Ali!"

Asha massages her temples as she slides into the blush pink chair next to me. "Remind me again why a person as cynical as you wants to become a wedding planner?"

"Because, despite my withered heart and hopelessly bleak outlook, the creative process thrills the sliver of soul I've got left," I remind her. "And you'd be jaded too if you'd spent half a decade dating in New York."

"That would suck the romantic out of anyone," Asha concedes. "Tell me again about that mime who didn't break character during sex?"

"The point is," I continue, "my cynicism is hard-earned, so kindly leave me to my disillusionment. Not all of us find true love on the first day of college like you and Nadia did."

Asha's eyes soften at the mention of her wife. I can't blame her. The two of them are the epitome of couple goals.

"Speaking of true love," she says. "Now that you've moved back home, maybe you can rekindle things with that kid you dated in high school. The one who was a bit of a pyromaniac?"

It's the way that she says "kid" that reminds me how long Asha and I have known each other. She and my older sister have been best friends (and occasional rivals) since middle school. Growing up, she spent so much time at my house that I think of her as a bonus sister. On the one hand, it's nice to have grown up with so many people who cared about me. On the other, it means that part of her still sees me as the reckless teen who needed to be picked up at a house party after drinking too many Smirnoff Ices and peeing in a birdbath.

Also, it's not my fault that my ex had a fascination with fireworks that bordered on pathological.

"On that note," I say, standing up. "I'm going to grab some lunch. Want to join?"

Asha shakes her head. "I'm good. Nadia packed me lunch today."

"Of course she did." Asha's wife is one of Baltimore's most successful ob-gyns. When she isn't working crazy hours running her own practice, she somehow finds time to be an amazing home chef. I've been trying to get my hands on her baba ghanoush recipe for years.

We learned how to make the dip back when I was in culinary school, but it's nowhere near as good as hers. "I'll be back in twenty."

I breathe in happily as I step out of our office and onto West 36th Street. As much as I miss New York some days, there's a reason why Baltimore is called Charm City. There's something undeniably enchanting about the office's Hampden neighborhood, with its array of thrift stores, antique shops, kitschy boutiques, and hip restaurants. The fact that Baltimore, unlike New York City, has never needed to appoint a municipal rat czar doesn't hurt either.

My gaze drifts across the storefronts as I pop in earbuds. Even though the mid-September air is still sticky with humidity, most stores have already started decorating for the season. Their windows are lined with artificial leaves and plastic pumpkins, spiderwebs and decorative crows. It's a Halloweentown fantasy brought to life.

My favorite window display features an Edgar Allan Poe lamp. And whatever you're picturing, I promise it doesn't hold a candle to the real thing. A bust of Poe's head serves as a base, with a hyperrealistic raven lampshade, its wings spread in glorious splendor. But the cherry on top is the anatomically correct heart encompassing the bulb. This city never lets its patrons forget Poe's Baltimore legacy. Especially around spooky season.

My reverie is interrupted by a sudden vibration in my purse. I check the name that flashes across the screen: Babs Cell.

"Hello, Mother," I say, as I pick up the call. In the background, I hear the whir of her KitchenAid mixer and the faint murmur of voices drifting from the television. Even without being able to see her, I can picture her in the kitchen, busying herself with her Friday morning ritual of baking challah while blasting reruns of *Grey's Anatomy*.

"Hey, Al," my mother yells over the mixer. Because why move away, or better yet, call after she finishes? "I just wanted to remind you to stop by the wine store on your way home and pick up a bottle of white for dinner. But make sure not to get that stuff in the blue bottle. It gives your father gas."

I suppress a groan as I round the corner and head toward Spruce, my go-to lunch spot. My mom has hosted Shabbat dinner every Friday night since I was a kid, and growing up, I absolutely loved it. The attention she put into curating every detail of the meal is one of the reasons I fell in love with cooking. As I got older, I adored the weekly ritual of preparing the food alongside her and adding my own creative touches. Family dinners are less thrilling, however, when you're a fully grown adult who's just moved back in with her parents.

Oh yes, did I neglect to mention that at age twenty-eight, I'm once again sleeping in my childhood bed? Because after five years in New York, I decided to abandon the years I'd put into culinary pursuits and venture into event planning. It seemed so exciting at the time. So long, brutal restaurant hours! Goodbye, arrogant, masochistic chefs! I'm off to live out bigger and better dreams. That is, until I realized that most companies require internship experience, and quitting my job as a hotel line cook to become a professional fetcher of coffee meant I could no longer afford the rent for my Murray Hill studio. Moving home was the only option.

Luckily for me, my bonus sister, Asha, is a senior planner at Antoine Williams Events, one of Baltimore's most well-respected event planning services. She got me a gig as an intern, and I've enjoyed every minute of my past three months with the company. But if I'm ever going to move out of my parents' house and get a place of my own with a shred of my dignity still intact, I need to land a full-time gig—and fast.

As I step through Spruce's doorway, the air is braided with the overlapping scents of coffee and freshly baked bread. An espresso machine whistles loudly in the background. The small space is stuffed to the gills with the noon lunch crowd as I step into the line, which is so long it nearly extends to the dining area. Still, it moves quickly as I busy myself sorting through emails, and before I know it, there's only one person ahead of me.

He approaches the counter and orders a flat white and a croissant. At the sound of his voice, I glance up. Pleasure flickers through me as I clock his British accent. It's been eight years, but the sound of it sends me straight back to my study abroad semester in college.

Heat floods my cheeks as I remember one Brit in particular. My right hand subconsciously drifts to my hip, brushing over my permanent souvenir from that fateful evening.

A strange sense of déjà vu washes over me as I stare at the man's back. From behind, he sort of resembles my Brit. He's even got the same mop of dirty blond hair and that rigid posture, like he's forgotten to take the coat hanger out of his jacket. In fact, he looks a *lot* like him. It's kind of unsettling. It's also ridiculous because that man lives in London. And last I checked, there's no wave of British tourists flocking to see the sights of downtown Baltimore.

That's why it isn't remotely plausible that he's currently standing a foot in front of me, ordering coffee at my favorite café. Yet the longer I stare at the back of his peacoat, the more the sense of certainty seeps into my pores, until it's no longer possible to deny the six feet of reality standing right in front of me.

The barista stares up at the man in front of me and asks, "Can I get a name for the order?" at the exact same moment I hear myself say, "Benedict?"

2

The man in front of me freezes. My mouth goes drier than the Sahara as my heartbeat echoes in my ears. Then, slowly, he rotates his body, turning toward me. My jaw drops open as I stare up at a face I never expected to see again.

It's not that I haven't thought about him over the years. No matter how many dudes you sleep with, it's hard to forget about a guy when a permanent reminder of the night you spent together is literally branded on your skin. Especially when that reminder is a half-pig, half-unicorn that still scares the hell out of you every time you catch a glimpse of your post-shower reflection in the bathroom mirror. Eight years have done nothing to temper that jump scare.

No. I haven't forgotten about him. In fact, I've thought about him so often that I've sometimes wondered if I've built him up in my memory. Maybe he wasn't half as attractive as I remember. Maybe ninety percent of his appeal was his accent and that inexplicably charming cardigan. But the face staring back at me negates every lie I've told myself in the past decade.

I let myself stare. Gawk, even. My eyes drink in every feature. Pink, pouty lips. A smattering of freckles across the bridge of a well-shaped nose. Cornflower blue eyes, wide with disbelief behind those same thick glasses I remember. *Fuck, why are his glasses so sexy?* Have I somehow gone my entire life not knowing I have a spectacles fetish?

"Ali?" he finally asks. His eyes have gone wide, but the hopeful tone of his voice conveys something more than surprise. Is it possible that he has thought about me too, that he's wondered what might have been? Speechless for once, I simply nod.

"Sorry, did you say your name is Benedict?" the barista interrupts.

He shakes his head, the spell broken as he turns back to the register. "No, sorry, it's actually—"

"Graham." I finish for him.

Graham whips back around, the shock still evident in his face.

"What are you doing here?" he asks after a beat.

"What am *I* doing here? What are *you* doing here?"

"What are any of us doing here?" a voice says from behind us. Now we both turn to see a short, balding man giving us a death stare.

"Personally, I'm trying to get lunch, so if you're not going to order anything, maybe you two could take this little reunion elsewhere."

"Oh, right. Lunch." I'm so disoriented that I've completely lost track of where I am, and what I'm doing here in the first place. Swiveling back to the counter, I order on autopilot. It's the same lunch I've had nearly every day this month: a pumpkin spice latte with a grilled gouda and apple sandwich.

"Pumpkin spice, huh? I guess everything they say about Americans is true." We slide down to the other end of the counter to wait for our food.

"First of all, it's September, which means it's my prerogative—nay, my *responsibility*—to consume as many artificial gourd flavors as possible. And second, um, hi? Care to explain why you've gone so far out of your way for coffee?"

"I could ask you the same thing."

"I live here. My office is a few blocks away. I come here for lunch a few days a week. Now you're all caught up. Your turn."

Our orders slide across the countertop. Picking up our trays, Graham and I find a two-seater table close to the back of the restaurant. Once we're settled, Graham takes a small sip of his coffee.

"I moved here about three months ago to help my grandmother with the family business. She and my grandfather managed it for over thirty years. After my grandfather passed away last November, it fell into a bit of financial trouble."

"Oh, I'm sorry to hear that."

"It's okay. I'm fortunate to be able to help her. My grandparents have done a lot for me over the years, and it feels good to give back."

"I'm sure your grandmother is happy to accept the free expertise of her grandson, the London School of Economics alumni."

Graham's lips quirk. "Something like that." He fixes his eyes on mine, and we stare at each other for a long moment, a current crackling in the air between us. My stomach cartwheels. I clear my throat, dispelling the tension.

"Well, I'd love to catch up. Want to grab a drink tomorrow night? I know all the best spots in the city, so you really don't want to pass up this opportunity."

Graham feigns a look of horror. "A drink with you? Sounds dangerous." His eyes drop to where my tattoo hides, and his cheeks go pink. My skin ignites beneath the fabric.

I mask it with a laugh, reaching forward to give his forearm a good-natured shove.

"You'll be fine. The post-cocktail belly button piercings are completely optional."

Graham's gaze shifts to my hand on his arm, and I watch as something indiscernible crosses his face. For a long, mortifying beat, I'm positive I've misread the situation. I double-check his left hand for a ring. It's bare. So why the hesitation? Am I misremembering the chemistry we had eight years ago? I mean, I'd been drinking that night, but I didn't think I was *that* wasted.

With a tangle of mixed emotions in my chest, I realize I'm desperate for him to say yes. Worse yet, I'm terrified he isn't going to.

But then the darkness clouding his face passes, and he smiles. "Sure," he says warmly. "A drink sounds great."

"Damn, that must have been one strong latte." Asha raises her eyebrows as I storm into the conference room. "Your face is redder than the time your dad found that stash of shirtless Taylor Lautner photos under your bed."

"I just had one of the most surreal experiences of my life," I say on an exhale, collapsing into the chair across from her.

Asha presses her elbows into the table and leans forward, eyes alight. "Go."

"I was in line at the coffee shop, and I ran into this guy I haven't seen since college."

Asha raises an eyebrow. "A guy? I'm intrigued. Tell me more."

"It was the weirdest thing. We met on the last night of my study abroad semester. Just once. I never expected to see him again. Because, you know, England, Baltimore. Not exactly close. Plus, it's been eight years. And then bam. Out of the blue, he was just standing in line at Spruce like he'd been shot out through a time portal."

Asha doesn't bother to mask her unbridled glee. She leans forward on her elbow, propping her chin in her fist. "Is he hot?"

"Beyond. Think Jude Law in *The Holiday*. But it's more than that. It's like there was this weird energy between us. A literal spark. It sounds ridiculous, I know."

Images from our coffee shop rendezvous flash across my brain.

Graham's lips curling into an amused smile. His blue eyes dancing behind his tortoiseshell glasses. The way my name sounded in his velvety accent.

Ali.

For better or worse, I've had plenty of dating experience, but I can't remember the last time a man has had this effect on me. A memory stirs, conjuring the image of Graham stripped to the waist, his lips trailing down the column of my neck, and I go breathless.

"Have you ever met someone, but the timing wasn't right? But then they show back up again, and it just feels like it's a sign? Like things are finally falling into place?"

I look up at Asha, then sigh. Of course she doesn't know what I'm talking about. She and Nadia have been together for two decades. She has no idea what it's like to go on dozens of crappy first dates and never feel anything close to chemistry.

"Negative. But I also haven't dated enough people to make up the cast of three *Bachelorette* seasons. You have. And I've never seen you act like this about any of them. Your pupils are basically cartoon hearts."

With a dramatic sigh, I slide farther into my chair, flinging out my arms like a Victorian damsel suffering a swooning spell.

"We're going out for drinks tomorrow night, Ash. And I know my outlook on dating is more *Tortured Poets Department* than *Lover*, but it feels like this guy is different. Like maybe he's . . . Someone."

"You know what they say. When something is meant for you, it always finds its way back. It's fate," Asha shrugs, a small smile playing on her lips. "I just found my fate a little faster."

I give her a tiny smile.

"I don't know if I believe in fate. But what you and Nadia have? That certainty in each other, in your life together? For the first time, I feel like maybe I could have that too."

Asha taps the tips of her fingers together gleefully. "Oooh, I am loving this!"

"What do you love?" A deep voice reverberates behind us, and we both turn to see the hulking figure of my boss filling the doorway. Antoine Williams is an absolute icon in this industry. He started planning parties for family and friends when he was in high school, and over the past twenty years, has become one of the most sought-after event planners in the mid-Atlantic region. I've known hopeful brides to reserve dates with him before they even have a ring.

His six-foot-four frame is cloaked in one of his signature kimonos, which fans out behind him like a leopard-print kite as he breezes through the doorway. I've never met anyone who can pull off a kimono quite like Antoine. Come to think of it, I've never met anyone else who can pull off a kimono. It's unclear if he has them tailor-made or if it's just his general aura that makes them look so elegant. Either way, he's looking positively regal this afternoon.

"Ali met a guy," Asha says. Her brow furrows. "Or I guess, re-met a guy?"

"How fabulous." Antoine rests the stack of binders he's carrying on the white laminate conference table. "And speaking of fabulous, we have a prospective client meeting in half an hour." He leans forward, then adds conspiratorially, "And it's a big one. The bride is engaged to the grandson of Trudy Dyson."

Asha and I look back at him with blank stares. I rack my brain. *Trudy Dyson . . . Trudy Dyson . . . Should I know that name?*

"Trudy Dyson is the owner of the Black-Eyed Susan," he fills in. "And yes, she wants to host the wedding there. You can imagine the budget we'd be working with on this one."

My eyes go wide. The Black-Eyed Susan is one of Baltimore's oldest and most famous hotels. So famous that it's a registered historic landmark, as much a part of the city's fabric as Camden Yards and the Inner Harbor. Meeting its owners feels akin to encountering royalty.

"Asha, I'm putting you on this account," Antoine continues. "A client of this caliber requires something chic, chic, chic, and you're our best bet."

"What about me?" I blurt out. Antoine swings his gaze toward me, eyebrows raised in surprise. *Whoops.* That's not how I meant that to come out.

"Er, I mean, I would love to assist Asha with this wedding. I'm eager to develop my skills and join your team as a full-time planner. And who better to learn from than Asha?"

Antoine purses his lips, considering. I hold my breath. I know it's a gamble, making such a bold request. So far, I've only been assigned to help with smaller affairs. Which makes sense. I've been interning here for three months, and I'm still not sure if Antoine likes me or just . . . tolerates me. What if I've overstepped and rubbed my boss the wrong way? But then he nods, and relief floods through me.

"Mrs. Dyson is a pillar of the community, and I'm betting the guest list will be substantial. An extra set of hands might be helpful. Plus, I like your pluck."

He pauses a moment more. "In fact, let's consider this your final audition. Do well, and I'll bring you on as a junior planner."

A wave of excitement ripples through my chest. This is it, the big break I've been waiting for. An actual, permanent job with Antoine's company could grant me entry into the world of event planning. Plus, it comes with a real paycheck, which means I can finally afford to move out of my parents' house and get a place of my own.

Most importantly, it will show my family I'm no longer the job-hopping flake who's changed careers three times in less than a decade. That I am, in fact, a fully functioning adult who can stick with something and succeed. And nailing this big account will be the first feather in my cap.

We spend the next thirty minutes prepping a vision board and powering up the deck for our new client meeting. By the time Antoine's assistant opens the conference room door, ushering in an older woman with a sharp silver bob, and a younger woman with fire-engine red waves, we are ready for action.

"Welcome, ladies!" Antoine glides across the room with the speed and elegance of an ice dancer. He clasps the older woman's hands in his.

"Mrs. Trudy Dyson," he coos. My eyes widen as I take her in. The best way to describe this woman is if Chanel N°5 became a person. She's wearing a long pink cardigan with a black trim over a crisp white button-down, which she's paired with black cigarette pants and quilted loafers. The overall look screams, "Pardon me, but I can't remember where I parked my yacht."

"And this"—he looks toward the younger woman—"must be our blushing bride."

"I'm Claire," she says. Her face splits into a warm grin as she gives us a little wave. "Nice to meet you all." She's not what I was expecting, considering the family she's marrying into. No aristocratic blue blood with a string of heirloom pearls and a DAR card. Instead, she's dressed in a bright green sweater, wide-leg jeans, and sneakers. I like her immediately.

Antoine, who is known for many things but not his patience, especially when there's a sizable deposit involved, clears his throat. "Yes. Let's get started." The two women sit down as Antoine's assistant carefully places five glasses and a bottle of Perrier on the table.

"So, Claire," Antoine says. "Tell us about yourself."

"Well, I work in comedy. Humor columns, stand-up, that kind of stuff," she says. "And I just landed my dream job writing for *The Cash Castillo Show*!"

"Wow, he's my favorite late-night host!" I exclaim. "Well, other than Samantha Bee, of course. It'll be tough to ever top *Full Frontal*."

Claire's face lights up.

"Thanks! It's still kind of surreal that I'm getting to do this. They don't have late-night shows in Canada, so working in a writers' room always felt like a completely out-of-reach dream."

"How fascinating," Antoine says, though his gaze is already starting to flicker impatiently to his laptop. "And how does one get into that?"

"I got a spot in the NBCUniversal Page Program while I was in grad school. When it ended, I submitted my late-night packets alongside everyone else in my improv group, but I never thought it would lead anywhere. Honestly, I sort of assumed I'd spend the rest of my life waiting tables and filming reels with my cat. Which is unfortunate, since Carol Purnett has made it clear that she's not enjoyed her forced participation thus far."

"Carol Purnett is your cat?" Asha asks.

Claire nods. "She's orange," she says, as if that explains everything. Which, in fairness, it does.

Trudy clears her throat. "Claire is very funny," she says, although she doesn't look particularly amused by her future granddaughter-in-law. Then her expression softens. "She always made my husband laugh."

Claire gives her a tiny smile. "I've got a respectable social media following," she continues. "And a few of the things I've written for *McSweeney's* have gone viral. Once men start sending you death threats and screaming in your DMs about how women aren't funny, that's when you know you've made it."

There's a long, uncomfortable beat while Claire smiles confidently at us all, and it's clear neither Antoine nor Trudy knows how to respond. Luckily, Asha swoops in, gracefully steering the conversation back into charted territory.

"So how did you and your fiancé meet?" she asks.

"Oh, right." Claire's eyes soften. "Teddy and I met at NYU. I was getting an MFA in Creative Writing, and he was working on his MBA. He was in the audience at one of my improv shows and was the only person who laughed when I made a Monty Python joke. I knew then that we were destined to be best friends." She smiles wistfully at the memory, and even my ice-cold heart isn't immune from melting a tiny fraction. *But wait, did she just say "friends"?*

Claire blinks a few times before quickly adding, "Who would've thought we'd end up falling in love?"

Ah, a friends-to-lovers romance. Classic.

"My grandson wasn't able to slip out of work today. He's very busy," Trudy says, with a slight air of satisfaction. "Although he will be happy to join us for the next meeting if we decide to work with you."

"Of course," Antoine says. "And speaking of which, let's talk details. Do you have a date in mind? What about a guest list? A preferred color scheme? Mrs. Dyson, I know you'll be hosting the affair at your beautiful hotel. Who could pass up such a gorgeous venue?"

"We don't have too many specifics worked out yet. But I'm cool deferring most of them to the experts," Claire says, looking at us expectantly. "I'm going to be pretty busy with work—being part of the writers' room means I'll be spending most of my week in New York—so I'm happy to give your team full creative direction." She smiles as she throws her hands up in mock surrender.

Something about Claire's nonchalance strikes me as odd. Sure, not every bride comes in with a curated Pinterest board, predetermined color scheme, and strongly held opinions about orchids. But Claire seems unusually laid-back. Almost disinterested, even.

"We were thinking early January. The show will be on break, so that's when I'll have the most availability," Claire continues.

Antoine's brow lowers as far as his Botox will allow. "That's only four months from now. A much shorter planning period than we usually advise."

Trudy's lips twitch. "I'm sure you're more than equipped to handle a challenge. After all, your reputation precedes you."

At this, Antoine's expression shifts, his eyes lighting up. Words of praise are the man's love language—and the surest way to hook him. Trudy's got him in the bag, tight deadline be damned.

"It would truly be an honor to work with you," he says with a conclusive smile. "Now, let's talk about some of the packages we offer."

3

The rest of the meeting goes smoothly, and Claire signs a contract before she even leaves the office. By the time I'm on I-83, heading north toward my parents' house, I'm positively jubilant for the first time in months.

Moving back home has not been the easiest of transitions. I left behind not only my career and the life I'd built for myself in New York, but also my two best friends, Lexi and Chloe. Although if I'm honest, things were changing for all three of us even before I left. After two miserable years of working on the line, Lexi ditched restaurant life to start her own business selling comfort-food care packages with another chef friend, Mia. When she's not working, she's traveling the globe with her rock star fiancé, Jake. My other best friend Chloe met Riley, a fellow celebrity publicist, at Polo Bar a few months back when they both took over their clients' reservations, and now she spends half her time visiting her in L.A. The three of us have gone from talking every day and getting together for happy hour once a week to hosting bimonthly FaceTime calls and sending each other Reels. But I guess this is the nature of friendship when you are on the cusp of turning thirty. Life is changing and everyone is in different places, literally and figuratively.

But now, with the promise of a new job on the horizon, I'm finally starting to feel settled. The whole family will be coming over tonight for Friday night dinner, making it the perfect opportunity to announce my big news.

Sarah's minivan is already parked in the driveway when I turn down our parents' court. I don't even have to look through the windows to know that the interior is immaculate, despite the fact that my sister uses it to shuttle around her four kids. Everything about Sarah is always immaculate.

My sister is ten years older than me and fits the firstborn personality profile to a T. After graduating top of her class at Penn, she married Jordan, her high school sweetheart, earned a CPA, and popped out her first kid—all before her twenty-fifth birthday. She worked in finance for a few years, but once she had the twins, she needed more flexible hours. So, she repurposed her business skills to start a home organizing business. She now staffs half a dozen employees and has become a social media influencer, best known for posting videos of her serial killer–level organized home on TikTok.

At twenty-eight, the only thing I've managed to create is an exorbitant amount of student debt.

When I push open the front door and step into the foyer, I'm hit with the familiar smells of freshly baked challah and spiced chicken, followed by screams of "Aunt Ali's here!"

I miss a lot of things about living in New York, but it's impossible to deny how nice it is to be close to family. And there's something genuinely comforting about returning to the house I grew up in. Because no matter how many other things change, this place is frozen in time. The family portraits of us clad in matching denim still trim the staircase, and the same faded entryway rug awaits guests at the front door. Our elementary school artwork is still adhered to the fridge with magnetic photos of me and my sister, toothless and donning ill-fitting softball uniforms. The outside world is fast and ever evolving, but a childhood home, if you're lucky, is eternally steady.

Olive and Emme come barreling toward me, still dressed in their crisp day school polos and matching plaid skirts. Their little brother, Benny, toddles behind them, a giraffe pacifier dangling from his mouth as he drags his tattered gray blanket behind him. Jackson, the oldest, is nowhere in sight, but I feel reasonably confident he's made himself comfortable on the living room sofa, locked in a Roblox battle.

The girls tackle me, and I pull them close, inhaling the sweet scent of their shampoo. Sarah comes up behind them. Per usual, she's dressed like a model for a Suburban Mom Starter Kit. Knit pullover? Check. Lululemon leggings? Check. Lifestyle sneakers that retail for more than my paycheck? You know it. The only thing she's missing is a fanny pack and a Stanley tumbler.

"Hey, lady!" she says, before pulling me into a hug. As much as I adore my sister, the sight of her reminds me once again that our differences extend far beyond our personalities. Everything about Sarah is tidy, from her narrow, toned frame to her naturally pin-straight blond hair. I'm a head shorter, curvy with big boobs, and in possession of the type of dark, frizzy curls that are constantly serving the Ashkenazi special. Despite coming from the same gene pool, she looks like a shiksa goddess while I perpetually look like a buxom Mia Thermopolis (*before* her makeover sequence).

I make my way into the kitchen, where the rest of my family is gathered. My mom, Barbara, stands behind the island, carefully arranging a platter of appetizers, while my dad, Howard, puts ice cubes into glasses. Bubbie, my maternal grandma, is perched on a barstool, doing what she does best: supervising and giving unsolicited feedback. She's dressed in one of her favorite velour tracksuits, her platinum blond hair teased and hairsprayed to within an inch of its life.

"*Bubbeleh!*" she calls when she sees me, her eyes lighting up behind her enormous glasses. The left lens is perpetually fogged over, and one of the great family mysteries is whether she can actually see out of it. She slides carefully off the stool and wraps me in an embrace. Then she licks her thumb and rubs it against my cheek.

"Hang on, honey, I schmeared you," she says, swiping at what is undoubtedly a raspberry-colored stain in the shape of her lips.

My mom circles the counter to hug me, and it's like looking into a mirror thirty-five years in the future, only her own dark curls have been flat-ironed into submission and shaped into a shoulder-length cut.

"Hi baby. Glad you're finally here," she says, pulling me in for a hug.

"'Finally' seems a bit aggressive," I counter. "I'm only five minutes late."

She tilts her head to one side as she scans my empty hands. "Did you forget the wine?"

Shit.

She gives a tiny smile. "Don't worry. I keep an extra bottle on hand just in case." *Just in case you forgot* is what she really means, though she kindly omits that part. And true to form, I am living up to her expectations. Perfect.

I know my family loves me, but sometimes it feels like they'll seize any opportunity to remind me that I'm the messy one, the flighty youngest child who can never truly be counted on. In their defense, I've never done much to negate it. There's something strangely comforting about leaning into your preset family role. But I'm older now, back from the Big City, and about to embark on a new phase of my life. And I'm ready to change the way they see me.

I shrug it off as I grab an egg roll off a silver-trimmed platter, delighted that my mom's gone with an Asian-themed menu this evening.

My favorite. I dip the roll in the orange sauce in the coordinating dish and chew thoughtfully.

"Remind me to send you my recipe for spicy duck sauce," I tell my mom. "The addition of chili flakes adds so much to the flavor profile."

"Ooh, yes please," she replies.

There are so many beautiful rituals tied to Shabbat, but our family has never been particularly religious. When it comes to our Friday night dinners, and every Jewish holiday for that matter, the Rubin family is all about The Food. It's really no wonder that I've pursued careers in cooking and entertaining.

I grab a knife and cutting board before heading over to the fridge. I extract a handful of green onions, giving them a quick mince before sprinkling them over the egg rolls. My mom smiles appreciatively. Food is one of our mutual passions. And when it comes to presentation, it's all in the details.

A few minutes later, my mom shoos everyone into the dining room, and I take my usual seat at the table between Olive and Emme. Jackson trails into the living room last, eyes glued to the phone he's holding inches from his face. Sarah clears her throat. He smiles sheepishly before shoving the phone in his back pocket and taking a seat next to his mom.

"How's it going on the apps?" I ask him. "Swipe right on any matches who've recently gotten their braces removed?"

He smirks. "Have *you*?"

"Tragically, most of my matches have graduated to Invisalign."

My sister presses her manicured fingertips into her forehead and groans.

"Anyway, I don't need dating apps," Jackson declares, with the unearned bravado of a thirteen-year-old whose voice shifted an octave over the summer. "I've got rizz on the Roblox chat."

"I thought I told you to disable that," Sarah whisper-hisses to her husband, Jordan. He freezes, water glass hovering halfway to his mouth. There is truly no one on earth more surprised than a man whose wife is saying something for the second time.

My mom is wide-eyed as she glances between us, clearly desperate to rein the conversation back in. With all the grace and subtlety of a linebacker on ice skates, she interrupts loudly, “Let’s do Roses, Buds, and Thorns!” effectively drowning out Jordan’s half-hearted attempt at an apology.

“Oooh, I’ll start.” Sarah takes the bait as she accepts the basket of challah my mom is passing around the table. “Let’s see. My rose is that I got two new clients this week and a brand sponsorship with an up-and-coming, nontoxic countertop cleaner. My thorn is . . . hmm.” She furrows her brow. “I actually don’t think anything bad happened this week.”

“Of course it didn’t,” I mumble. I tear a slice of challah in half, spraying crumbs across my dinner plate before shoving it into my mouth.

“And my bud is that tomorrow is exactly two months until Jackson’s Bar Mitzvah!” she finishes, turning to beam at her son.

The table cheers, and Jackson gives a little fist pump.

“Okay, my turn,” my mom says. “My rose is that I’m getting to celebrate Shabbat with my beautiful family.” She glances around the table at each of us, her cheeks pink with joy before her lips turn downward. “Sadly, my thorn is that Mr. Steinberg passed away this week.”

We all let out a murmur of sympathy. My mom is the assistant director of a nursing home. For her, death is an unfortunate daily reality, but some passings hit harder than others. Mr. Steinberg was one of her favorite residents, forever charming staff with photos of his grandchildren and repeated attempts to smuggle in his beloved cat, Knish.

“But my *bud*,” she says, her voice taking on a hopeful tone as she winks at me from across the table, "is that Brad Hoffman stopped by the home for funeral preparations, and great news: he is still single!"

"Sorry, who is Brad Hoffman? And why does it matter that he's single?" Jordan looks genuinely perplexed, and Sarah rolls her eyes in exasperation. Her husband grew up in a central Pennsylvania suburb with a much smaller Jewish community, and even though he's been part of our family for years, he still hasn't quite grasped how things work around here.

I grab another slice of challah from the breadbasket and shove it down my gullet before I can make a snarky comment. Luckily, Bubbie can always be counted upon to fill a silence.

"Because!" she crows. "The Hoffman family owns the largest funeral home in the area, and Brad is next in line to inherit it. Imagine marrying into that *mishpacha*! Our little Ali would be set." She puts extra emphasis on the Yiddish word for "family," but it's the last sentence that really stings. I know she means well, but it feels like she's suggesting that I need to marry someone wealthy to be okay. That I can't take care of myself.

"Sounds like a modern-day fairy tale. That is, if you don't mind being married to a literal undertaker who looks like a platypus," I retort.

"I think he's cute," my mom protests somewhat unconvincingly. "And he's rich! Plus, his family has great shul tickets."

"Oh, well, that changes everything."

My mom sighs wearily. "I just think it would be nice for you to settle down and meet someone. You've been single for ages. You deserve a boyfriend."

"I already have a boyfriend." I tip my head toward Benny. He grins at me, the smile extending from his chubby baby cheeks all the way up to his big brown eyes. A dribble of snot escapes his nose, but before it can drip down his chin, his little pink tongue darts out and laps it up.

"His personal hygiene leaves something to be desired, but honestly, I've seen worse."

Mercifully, the conversation moves on. The rest of the family attempts to take turns sharing the highlights of their week, but one person's bud gets spoken over another's, my family's voices quickly devolving into a loud hum of indiscernible chatter, until finally, I'm the last one left.

"Okay, let's wrap this up," I say loudly. "My rose is that Mom made sweet-and-sour chicken tonight, which is my personal favorite. My thorn is that on Tuesday, I spilled iced coffee all over my favorite sweatshirt. You know the one with all of Shawn Mendes's tattoos in their anatomically accurate locations? And my bud . . ."

I pause here for dramatic effect, making sure all eyes are on me. My new promotion is on the tip of my tongue. But suddenly, that's not what flashes through my mind. It's Graham's face. The slight upturn of his mouth as he studied me from across the table. The sparkle in his eye when he spoke about his grandmother. The way my skin heated beneath his gaze.

My stomach flutters at the prospect of seeing him again tomorrow. More than the promotion, more than anything, this is the bud I'm truly hoping will blossom. And truthfully, the one my family would be most excited to hear about. But I want to keep Graham a secret a little bit longer, to savor this feeling of giddy anticipation. To keep it to myself, safe from my family's input and speculation. Plus, if I tell them now, I'll probably return from my date tomorrow to discover a wedding chuppah set up in the backyard. I shake my head to dispel the horrifying thought.

". . . is that my boss just put me on a huge account," I finish. "He says if I nail it, he's going to make me a full-time planner!"

The table dissolves into murmured congratulations. Across the table, my mom beams at me, looking as proud as she did the day I first announced I'd been accepted into culinary school. Even Sarah looks impressed.

"Mazel tov," Bubbie says, wrapping her long, hot pink fingernails around my wrist and squeezing it supportively.

"Which means," I continue, "that I'll finally be earning enough money to move out and buy a place of my own."

At this, the table goes quiet. Bubbie loosens her grip on my wrist. Sarah can't hide her grimace. Even Jordan looks down at his plate, sensing the mood shift. My mom turns pointedly to my dad, clearing her throat gently. He's the first one to break the silence. Predictably.

"Well, maybe let's just see how it goes first," he says quietly. "No need to rush into anything."

I cross my arms, already slipping into sulky defense. "What's that supposed to mean?" The words are spoken purely out of frustration because I know exactly what he's suggesting as well as what he'll say next. And he doesn't disappoint.

"It means that real estate is an investment. One that requires a lot of careful consideration, money, and planning."

Somehow, I manage to suppress an eye roll. My dad is a CPA and when we were growing up, he never missed an opportunity to lecture us about financial security. The words "safe investments are happy investments" are going to be etched on the man's tombstone.

"Yes, Dad, I know. That's why I'm living at home. To save up so that I can afford to make a down payment. I listen when you talk." *Mostly.*

"Sure. Until you decide that you're over this job, and you move on to something else. *Again.*"

My face turns hot. It was only a matter of time before I was called out for being a serial career changer. I had just hoped we'd make it to entrées first.

"I think what your father is trying to say," my mom offers gently, "is that you tend to lose interest in things quickly. I mean, you only lasted a year as a second-grade teacher before deciding to go to culinary school, and then you only worked in that hotel kitchen for a little while before deciding you wanted to be a party planner."

"People in their twenties change careers all the time," I protest. "Sarah did, and I don't see anyone giving her a hard time."

"You know, I think I'll start bringing out the soup," Sarah offers, shooting me a sympathetic glance. Then she turns her attention to her husband. He's refilling his wine glass and seems oblivious to the hole her eyes are burning into the side of his face until she gives him a hard nudge with her elbow.

"Oh, yeah. I'll come help you," he says, shoving back his chair a little too quickly.

"Ali," my mom continues once the two of them have disappeared into the kitchen. "You have always been a free spirit, and we love that about you. It's the Aries in you. You're a true fire sign."

I roll my eyes. My mom is, at her core, a hippie, and she has a penchant for attributing all human behavior to astrology.

Undeterred by my scowl, she continues. "You're passionate and spontaneous, and we love the way you embrace all your different creative passions."

My father grumbles something under his breath about how he's the one funding these creative passions. Mom continues as if she hasn't heard him. Not that she's one to talk about pursuing creative passions. She studied to be a painter but never worked as an artist. Instead, she married my dad, popped out two kids, and got a nine-to-five job in the retirement home. After that, her painting career was relegated to a hobby.

"But you're also spontaneous, a fly-by-the-seat-of-your-pants type of girl. A true bohemian who doesn't like being tied down." Her voice is as sweet and cautious as a kindergarten teacher's—which is somehow worse than the sound of yelling would be. "Buying property is a commitment, and I'd hate to see you dig yourself into a financial hole, only to feel trapped when you're ready to switch things up again in a few years. That's the beauty of renting, right?"

I slump back into my chair. I know how my parents see me. How most people probably see me. I'm extroverted and loud and fun. I'm the friend you want at your birthday party, because I'll be on the dance floor with you all evening and help you shut down the bar at the end of the night. But I'm not someone who's taken seriously. Not the friend you ask to watch your cat, or the daughter you make executor of the will. Those are the sorts of things that are left to Sarah. Perfect, organized, reliable Sarah.

Honestly, I get it. From the outside, it seems like I'm jumping from career to career. But it's not just restlessness. I'm looking for the profession best suited to my creativity, and each job has brought me closer. Teaching taught me about crowd control and juggling multiple demands at once. Restaurant work gave me grit and trained me to stay focused in the throes of chaos. I'll always love cooking, but it was just one piece of the puzzle. This pivot into event planning isn't starting over. It's combining all the things I love doing. And sure, I could rent a place in Baltimore, make sure I'm really in it for the long haul, do the sensible thing. But I rented for years in New York. I'm sick of temporary. What I really want is something I can hold on to. Something that's truly mine.

I sit in silence the rest of the meal, barely tasting the sweet-and-sour chicken. By the time Sarah and her family head home, I've excused myself, claiming to be tired. But I've also made a resolution. I'm going to nail this account, land this promotion, and prove to my family that I'm not a flake. But first, I'm going to meet up with Graham.

4

The Bluebird Cocktail Room is one of my favorite spots in Baltimore, a hidden gem buried in a Hampden side street. When I pass through the wrought iron gate, I spot a figure perched on one of the porch's wooden swings, rocking back and forth gently and staring down 36th Street. Graham. He's early.

"Hey there," I say. He startles at my voice, as if I've awoken him from a daydream. "Sorry, I didn't mean to scare you."

His expression softens into a smile. "Not at all. I was lost in thought, I guess."

"Yeah? What were you thinking about?"

"Nothing, really. Just that I haven't spent much time in this neighborhood. There's something so . . . charming about it."

"There really is." Bluebird is a newer addition to Hampden, one that's undeniably romantic. The exterior brick is covered with moss and twinkling lights. An illuminated sign directs us up the stairs and into the lounge. It casts milky white light across Graham's features, highlighting the angular line of his jawbone. He's wearing a cardigan, just like the night we met. This one's a waffle knit in a midnight blue that matches his eyes. Paired with a white tee, dark khakis, and his rumpled blond hair, he looks like the world's sexiest British Lit professor.

"After you," he says, pulling the door open and gesturing toward the interior.

Inside, I slide into one of the yellow velvet booths against the back wall, and Graham takes a seat in the wooden chair across from me. The interior is just as dreamy as the outside, all dark walls and heavy wood, dimly lit by a handful of crystal chandeliers.

Graham thumbs through the menu, a smile tugging at the corner of his mouth as he studies the illustrated pages. "Oh, wow. It's like a storybook."

"Yup. All the drinks are literary-themed." We place our orders—a Briar Rose for me, and The Three Brothers for him—and get fries for the table. A moment later, the waitress delivers our drinks and I take a small sip. The chef part of my brain instinctively parses out the cocktail's components. Tahini, prickly pear, sesame seeds. An unexpected but delicious combination.

I level my gaze at Graham.

"Alright, enough beating around the bush. The people want to know: what is the status of your tattoo? Is it still there? Did you cover it up with a less spine-chilling design? Or did you have it removed at the earliest possible opportunity?"

Graham's lips curl upward. "What do you think?"

"I'll show you mine if you show me yours."

An endearing pop of color springs to his cheekbones. He leans back in his chair and affords me a shy smile.

"It's still here. A source of great pride and even greater terror."

I laugh softly, surprised by how much this delights me. He hasn't erased this special piece of our shared history. I wonder if he's thought of that evening as often as I have.

"Gotten any more since?"

Graham shakes his head.

"That's disappointing. I half expected your first tattoo would be your gateway ink. Aren't covert tattoos required for moody academic types such as yourself?"

"Alas, this is my one and only. I've always figured, why mess with perfection?"

He gives me a knowing smile as our gazes hold, memories of our shared evening filling the space between us. Now it's my turn to flush. I clear my throat, eager to steer the conversation back to safer ground.

"So. What have you been up to for the past eight years? Are you married? Kids? Do you have a last name?"

Graham barks out a laugh. "Starting off easy, eh?" He takes a sip of his drink. "My last name is Wyler. No wife or kids that I know of. After we met in London, I finished uni, ran the corporate rat race for a bit, then spent a couple of years in New York working on my master's. Now I work a pretty soulless job in finance. Nothing too exciting, but it pays the bills."

My heart skips a beat. Up until this moment, I'd always thought that was a cheesy expression, but suddenly it feels like I've thrown myself into arrhythmia.

"You were in New York?" I ask slowly. "When?"

"For the past two years. I just arrived in Baltimore in the spring."

My mouth falls open in disbelief. "I was there too. What are the odds?"

Truthfully, the odds are high. More than eight million people live in New York City, so it's not surprising our paths never crossed. Still, there's something about the idea of us unknowingly circling each other for the past few years that feels strangely like fate. That is, if I believed in fate. Which, I remind myself sternly, I do not.

Graham rests his elbows on the table and leans toward me. "Tell me about you."

I take a moment to drink him in: the lean muscles of his forearms that press into the wooden tabletop, the disheveled mop of golden hair that's at odds with his otherwise orderly appearance. Behind his glasses, his cerulean eyes are focused solely on my face, instead of darting around the restaurant like most of the guys I've gone out with. Graham is the sort of person who listens with his entire body. And despite myself, I desperately want him to be hanging on to my every word.

"Let's see. After I graduated with a teaching degree, I lasted exactly one year in the classroom. Turns out teaching requires a special kind of patience that I simply do not possess. Then I went to culinary school in New York, spent a couple of years working in a hotel kitchen. Which I loved, but still wasn't a perfect fit. And now I'm back home, Goldilocksing career number three as an event planner. As you can imagine, I'm the jewel in my family's crown."

Graham laughs softly, but his expression is kind. No trace of the condescension I normally sense with that admission. "Well, I think it's brave to pursue your passions, instead of just playing it safe," he says. "You're fearless. I envy it."

"That's one way to look at it. Most people just think I'm impetuous. That's sort of my signature role," I go on. "My sister, Sarah, is the perfect one, the golden child. After they had her, my parents thought they couldn't get pregnant again. They considered adoption, but it never worked out. Then one day, there I was, a seven-and-a-half-pound bundle of joy. Sarah's ten years older than me, so she's also always taken it upon herself to act like my second mom, while I am the eternal baby of the family. No one takes a thing I do seriously. I know they believe party planning is just another phase. Mostly I don't bother fighting it. Everyone thinks I'm the class clown, so I lean in."

Graham twists his lips, mulling this over. "Families are tricky," he says after a minute. "It's very hard to change the way people see you. Especially the ones who have known you your whole life."

"And how does your family see you?"

"Don't hate me, but I think I'm closer to your sister, Sarah," he admits. "Everyone counts on me to be the responsible one."

"Is that why you came here to help your grandmother? Because you're the one she puts her faith into?"

He gives me a small, sad smile that doesn't reach his eyes.

"Something like that."

"Did your grandparents also move here from England?"

He shakes his head. "No, they're Baltimore natives. My mom grew up here. She was backpacking through Europe with friends when she met my dad and ended up following him back to London."

I grin, delighted. "Sounds like the plot of a charming rom-com."

Graham's face darkens. "Trust me, it wasn't. My dad was never faithful to my mom. She did her best to ignore it, to keep the family together for my sake. But he left anyway when I was five. I've only seen him a handful of times since."

My heart sinks at his words. "Oh, Graham, that's terrible. I'm so sorry."

He shrugs but doesn't say anything further. I think back to the way Alfie always described Graham in college. Focused. Serious. Committed to being at the top of his class. He never hung out with us at the bar because he was always studying. And now it makes sense. Graham holds himself to a high standard. He's committed to succeeding because he doesn't want to let anyone down.

I trace the rim of my nearly drained glass.

"Your mom didn't want to move home after that?"

"No. My grandparents begged her to come back, but my mom was too proud. She didn't even tell them about my dad leaving for a while. I guess she was afraid to admit she'd made a mistake following some bloke who wasn't even worth it. But that's the kind of person she is. She leads with her heart. Doesn't let anyone tell her what to do."

One corner of his mouth rises in a half smile as he stares at me from across the table.

“Kind of like someone else I know.”

My heart flutters as his eyes lock on mine again. Then his gaze drops to his half-empty drink.

“She’s tough, though. Really strong. She got a work visa and eventually filed for citizenship. She always had that American spirit about her. Tenacious, determined. Utterly fearless. Threw herself headfirst into everything she did. She was an amazing mom too. I can’t imagine being a single mother who was pretty much on her own, but she always showed up for me.”

He swirls his drink stirrer around the ice cubes at the bottom of the glass. “Anyway, I promised myself at an early age that I’d never be like my dad. I’d never be the kind of guy who would let someone down or walk away from a commitment.” He pauses, the ridges on his forehead smoothing as his expression shifts into bemusement. His eyes flicker playfully.

“Not even a daft agreement to get a tattoo with a complete stranger.”

I stare at Graham, dumbfounded. I’ve been on more dates than I can count with man-children who blamed their personality flaws and poor habits on their parents. But not Graham. Instead, he’s harnessed his childhood hardships as motivation to become a better person. I’m not sure I’ve ever met anyone quite like him. I don’t know how to put all the things I’m thinking into words, so instead I say, “It must be nice to get to spend time with your grandma.”

The smirk melts off Graham’s face, and his eyes go soft.

“It’s the best. When I was a kid, I spent every summer with my grandparents. Once I hit my teenage years, though, my visits became fewer and further between. When my grandfather passed last year, I felt horribly guilty about how much time I let go between visits. In the four years I've lived in New York, I only ventured down to Baltimore a handful of times. Getting to spend so much time with Granny now is a gift."

A tiny smile forms in the corner of his lips. "We used to do jigsaw puzzles together when I was a kid. When I announced that I was planning on spending a few months here, my grandmother bought half a dozen new puzzles. We've just finished the first one." Warmth spreads over me as I picture Graham and his grandmother bent over a pile of cardboard pieces, laughing, and nibbling scones while a fireplace crackles in the background. It's cozy and British and completely congruent with his personality.

He lifts his chin toward me. "And how about you? Are you happy to be back home?"

"I am," I admit. "I was close with my grandma growing up too. We didn't do puzzles, but we'd watch *The Price Is Right* together and fangirl over Bob Barker. Then we'd go to Macy's to see how many coupons we could use at one time." Graham grins and I continue. "My family drives me nuts sometimes, but I missed them when I was living in the city."

It's true. We were so close growing up, and as much as I miss the energy of New York, a piece of me has been restored since coming home.

After settling the bill, Graham turns to me, eyebrows raised in invitation. "Want to take a walk?"

We stroll down 36th Street, our path illuminated by twinkling streetlights as we pass whimsical window displays and soak up the smells that drift through restaurant doorways. When we come to a familiar sign, I grab him by the hand and drag him through the Bookstore Next Door's magenta doorway.

Graham lets out a low whistle as he surveys the floor-to-ceiling display of used books. He makes his way slowly through the front section of the store, pausing to brush his fingertips across the spines of a Dickens collection displayed on a wooden cart.

"One of your contemporaries," I say. Graham's mouth tilts up into a smirk.

As he picks up one of them, gingerly flipping the aged cover open, I slide past him, making my way to the cookbook section. My eyes drift over the books, which are haphazardly stacked in no order, until I'm drawn to one particularly interesting title. I pull the book off the shelf, examining the cover. *Jewish Festival Cooking.* There's blocky handwriting scrawled across the front in several places. "Good chopped liver, page 132," it reads in one corner. "Charoset like ours, page 25," it says on another.

I flip the book open, thumbing through the pages. There are more notes jotted through, along with half a dozen food stains. All evidence of a well-loved cookbook. I find myself trying to visualize the book's original owner, wondering how she used these recipes. Did she host family dinners for the High Holidays? Or were the highlighted recipes simply family favorites that she prepared for Friday night dinners?

"Looks like someone's uncovered a buried treasure."

Behind me, Graham is so close I can feel his breath on the back of my neck, and the hairs on my forearms rise.

I turn to face him and take a steadying breath to quell the butterflies currently performing the Macarena in my belly.

"Used cookbooks are the best," I say. "You get so much more than a recipe. You get a history. What making food meant to someone."

Graham's eyes burn into mine. "I think you and this book belong together. It's fate." There's that word again. *Fate.*

My heart hiccups in my chest. Maybe I'm not such a non-believer after all.

"You might be right," I say, my voice now barely a whisper. "And who am I to argue with fate?"

His face is so close to mine that I appreciate for the first time how long his eyelashes are. So long that they brush against the lenses of his glasses, fanning out like wings. His lips part, and I catch a whiff of lingering gin on his breath. My own breath is coming out in fast spurts now, and I shift one inch closer to him. Graham's gaze drops to my lips. My pulse is hammering so fast against my throat that I wonder if he can see it.

Just then, someone clears their throat loudly. Graham and I whip our heads around at the same moment to see a store employee lingering at the bottom of the two-step staircase.

"Sorry to interrupt," he says. "But it's nearly closing time."

The tension in the air deflates like a popped balloon. Taking a step back, Graham flips his wrist over to glance at his watch. It's an old-fashioned design, with a large face and a black leather strap. On anyone else his age, it would look wildly out of place, but it suits Graham perfectly. It's classic, just like him.

"Oh wow, it's nearly six," he says. "Time really got away from me."

"You know, most guys our age wear Apple watches," I observe wryly. "Do you have to wind that thing?"

"Call me retro, but I hate the idea of carrying a computer on my wrist."

"Cat-eyeglasses are retro," I reply. "You, my friend, are a millennial Mister Rogers."

Graham grins, then tips his chin toward the cookbook in my hands. "So, what's the verdict? Are you going to buy it?"

I flip the front cover again to check the price sticker. My heart sinks a bit at the sight of the thirty-five-dollar price tag. Closing the book, I brush a thumb across the cover reverently before sliding the book back onto the shelf.

"Unfortunately, I've got a pretty tight budget at the moment," I confess. "Being an intern doesn't pay much, and I'm trying to save up so I can move out of my parents' place."

A crease forms between his brows and I can tell he wants to argue the point. But before he can say anything further, I redirect the conversation.

"Anyway, there are a ton of great restaurants in the city. How would you like to grab dinner with a professionally trained chef?" I slide an inviting hand over his, grazing his knuckles with my fingertips. A long, tense beat passes as his body goes rigid. Then Graham takes a step backward, allowing my hand to drop. The store's temperature suddenly cools.

"I, um . . . actually have dinner plans," he says. "In fact, I should probably get going."

"Oh. Sure." Disappointment floods through me, followed quickly by confusion. What just happened? It seemed like things had been going great, but all of a sudden, it's like a switch has been flipped. Was it something I said?

"Let me walk you to your car," Graham says primly. The low, flirtatious tone in his voice has disappeared. "It's getting dark."

I'm still struggling to catch up with the abrupt mood shift, but I mask it with a snort of amusement. "You can always count on the Brits to be chivalrous."

With a grand sweeping motion, he gestures for me to go ahead of him. It's gotten chillier outside, and I pull my jacket tighter around me as I step onto the sidewalk. From the corner of my eye, I see Graham lift his arm, like he's considering putting it around me, but then he drops it limply at his side. The air is thick with sudden tension, though for the life of me, I can't figure out where it came from. Wordlessly, I lead him down the 36th Street sidewalk until we reach my car.

But before I can get inside, Graham shifts his body to stand in front of the door.

"Listen, Ali," he says. "There's something I need to tell you."

He stares at me for a long beat, and I watch as a jumble of emotions play across his handsome features. But the moment his lips finally part, we are deafened by the blare of car horns. A trail of cars careens past us. Their occupants hanging out the window, their faces adorned with purple and white face paint. They whoop loudly as they wave pendants bearing the name of our city's football team before disappearing down the darkened street.

"Tomorrow's the first game of the season," I tell Graham, as I shake my head. "There are no sports fans like Baltimore sports fans. They almost make me want to care about sportsball. Even though I haven't tuned into a Ravens game since the time Taylor Swift was in the stands."

I take a step closer, pausing to appreciate the way his pulse jumps in his throat. "What was it you wanted to tell me?"

Graham opens his mouth again, then abruptly shuts it. He shakes his head.

"It's nothing."

Bending forward, he brushes his lips against my cheek. My skin ignites at the point of contact, sending a burst of heat through my limbs. When he pulls back, his eyes are clouded with an unreadable mix of emotions.

"It was wonderful to see you again," he says, his voice soft. "Get home safely, okay?"

I nod as I slide into my car, shutting the door behind me. After buckling my seat belt, I turn to look back at him through the window, desperate for one last chance to analyze the perplexing look on his face as he kissed me goodnight. But he's already walking away.

5

I've never been a morning person, but by 8 A.M. on Monday, I'm fully showered, caffeinated, and dressed in what Cher Horowitz would describe as "my most capable outfit": an oversized plaid blazer over a crisp white tank top and wide-leg black trousers. After choosing to ignore my mom's helpful suggestion that I pair the look with some nude pumps because "the outfit is threatening to swallow me whole," I've opted instead for my favorite black booties. Despite my petite stature, I've always been morally opposed to wearing heels, and I'm not about to start abandoning my principles today.

I make it into the office fifteen minutes ahead of our nine o'clock meeting with Claire and her fiancé, and by the time I'm settled into my chair in the conference room, I'm radiant with confidence.

"Well, good morning, sunshine," Asha says as she glides through the glass doors, clutching a copper Starbucks thermos. She's looking as chic as ever in a loose camel-colored sweater with the sleeves pushed to her elbows and a pair of flared jeans, her glossy black hair cascading down her back. A pair of gold bangles glisten on her wrists.

"I think this is the first time you've ever beat me into the office. Did you sleep here?"

"No," I retort, lifting my chin. "I'm just . . . prepared. Today is the day I prove to Antoine that I'm ready to become a full-time planner."

"Cheers to that!" Asha replies, lifting her latte in a toast.

Just then, the doors fly open, and an uncharacteristically frazzled Antoine comes storming through.

"The one day I oversleep, the client arrives early," he whisper-hisses. "They're already in the lobby. I haven't even had time to pull out the mood boards."

"I've got them right here," I say, gesturing to the fabric pinboard full of samples we've prepared for this morning's meeting.

"You're a goddess." Antoine breathes a sigh of relief, and I feel a surge of pride. The meeting hasn't even started yet, and I'm already proving myself to be a valuable member of the team.

The glass doors swing open again, and Trudy steps inside, bringing with her a cloud of expensive perfume. Her gray bob is perfectly coiffed, and she's got a Burberry scarf draped around her neck in a way I could never replicate, no matter how many video tutorials I watched. Claire trails in behind her, red hair flying wildly.

"Good morning!" Claire calls, giving us one of her huge, toothy smiles.

"Good morning," Antoine replies briskly. He glances behind them expectantly. "I thought the groom was joining us this morning?"

"Oh yeah, Teddy's just parking the car," Claire says. "I thought parking would be easier here than in New York, but driving in downtown Baltimore is no joke." She pulls out a chair for her future grandmother, then takes a seat next to her. "So, how was everyone's weekend?"

"It was lovely," Asha says. "And yours?"

"Great!" Claire chirps. "Teddy and I had dinner at this amazing place in Canton where we got bangin' crab nachos and drank margaritas out of hubcaps. And yesterday, we did one of those pirate cruises in the Inner Harbor. Pretty cool, except I'm nearly certain that I hit an eel with my oar, which led to some unfortunate dry heaving. Teddy says it's unlikely that an eel escaped from the aquarium and that it was probably just a fish, but I had to abandon ship after that. Despite my passing resemblance to the Little Mermaid, I've never really warmed to creatures of the sea."

I bite back a grin. Claire is really growing on me.

Just then, Antoine straightens in his chair, an expectant smile stretching across his face.

"Ah, here he is."

Trudy lifts her head, her face alight with love and pride at the arrival of her grandson. Claire turns to look over too, but my back is to the door, so I sneak another quick glimpse at the samples, triple-checking that everything is in order before we begin. Asha stands to introduce herself, and I think I'm hearing things when I'm hit with an all-too-familiar British lilt.

"Sorry I'm late. Parking was a proper nightmare."

Time seems to grind to a halt, and an awful, sinking feeling forms in the pit of my stomach. It feels like that moment in a movie right before a car crashes, where everything goes still, and all you can do is stare helplessly, your heart in your mouth, knowing that something terrible and life-altering is about to happen, and there's nothing you can do to stop it.

In slow motion, I rotate my body to see a figure with a mop of thick blond hair filling the doorway. When our eyes meet, the air whooshes out of the room, and everything goes silent. The only sound is the hammering of my own heartbeat against my eardrums.

"Everyone, I'd like to introduce you to my fiancé," Claire says. "This is—"

"Graham," I say on a breath.

Every head in the room swings toward me. Antoine arches one eyebrow, looking as shocked as I feel.

"Sorry, do you two know each other?" he says.

"No, I—" I pause, my brain scrambling to catch up to my mouth as I do my best to process what's happening. There must be some kind of misunderstanding.

"Sorry, Claire," I say at last, latching on to the one thing that still makes sense. "I thought you said your fiancé's name is Teddy?"

"Oh!" she says with a laugh. "Teddy's a nickname. Get it? Like Teddy Graham? Graham pretends to hate it, but we both know he secretly loves it." She tilts her head to the side, curious. "How did you know his name was Graham?"

"Oh, I, um . . ." My brain has gone completely blank as I fumble for a reasonable explanation. Ultimately deciding the best lies are the ones grounded in truth, I quickly say, "I was in line behind him at Spruce the other day. Such a small world, right?"

Asha laughs politely, but I don't miss the curious stare she's giving me. My attention is still focused on Graham, who's staring back at me slack-jawed, the color slowly draining from his face.

"You know what? I'm going to run to the bathroom before we start," I say. I jump to my feet, shoving my chair back so quickly that it scrapes across the linoleum floor with a painfully loud squeak. Antoine looks like he wants to protest, but then, deciding it's probably not a good look to deny the bodily needs of his employees, nods toward the doorway with a strained smile.

I race down the hallway, pausing just outside the bathroom doors. Inhaling deeply, I pace in the tiny corridor, as I attempt to replicate the deep breathing techniques I learned on the Calm app. Which I could probably do with greater success if I didn't dedicate ninety-five percent of my usage to replaying the Harry Styles sleep story.

I hear the soft tread of footsteps approaching, and fully expecting them to belong to Asha, I start mentally preparing how much I'm going to tell her. But when the figure rounds the corner, a pair of ocean-blue eyes hitch onto mine.

"Hey," he says. His voice is cautious, tentative. "I just came to see if you were alright."

I stop pacing then, the anxiety that has been pumping through my veins now replaced with something else. White-hot anger.

"Interesting," I say. I'm sort of impressed by how much rage I've imbued into a single word. "Asking if I'm okay pretty much suggests that you know I wouldn't be. Any reason why that might be? Could it be because the guy I was on a date with two days ago turned out to be the groom in the wedding I'm planning?"

A flush crawls up Graham's neck at the bluntness of my proclamation. His jaw goes tight. "Ali, it isn't like that."

"It isn't like *what*?" I hiss, my fury now dialed all the way up. "Mansplain this to me, please, because I am dying to understand. I can't wait to hear how you justify being a philandering, unfaithful asshole. Does Claire know you cheat on her?"

"I don't cheat on Claire," he says, his voice taking on a hard, indignant edge.

"Oh, really? So, you didn't go on a date with me two nights ago? I just hallucinated that?"

"It wasn't a date! I ran into an old friend, and we had drinks together. Last time I checked, there's no law against that."

My heart deflates at the unbothered way he brushes off the time we spent together this weekend. *Friends.* So that's all this ever meant to him. My brain flashes back to Claire's weekend recap, the way she was so excited to share all the adorable, couple-y things they did together, and a wave of anger washes over me. *How dare he do this to her?*

"And yet, you neglected to mention that your dinner plans were with your *fiancée*."

Graham's shoulders sag with defeat and the lines on his face soften.

"You're right. I should have mentioned Claire, and I didn't. But when I sensed you were interested in rekindling something beyond friendship, I immediately removed myself from the situation."

I blow out an indignant huff.

"Well, aren't you Mr. Perfectly Fine."

My blood curdles with blistering heat as I glare at him. Still, there's a nagging sense that Graham *was* trying to tell me something at the end of the night. There was a moment, just before we were interrupted by the football fan brigade, when he tried to get a word in. But he could have tried harder. He *should* have tried harder.

What stings most of all is that I temporarily abandoned my emotional safeguards and let myself get invested. I let myself wonder, what if? What if Graham was someone important? I hate that he's brought out this side of me. Being carefree and lovably detached is part of my brand. Now suddenly I'm the sort of girl who's smitten after one date? Two thumbs down, honestly. 0/10.

I cross my arms and narrow my eyes. "Fine. You didn't cheat on her. *Technically speaking.* But a lie by omission is still a lie. And why didn't you mention anything about the Black-Eyed Susan?"

Graham crosses his arms. "I never lied to you. I told you I moved to the States to help my grandmother with the family business, and I did."

"You didn't find it was noteworthy that your family business is one of the most renowned hotels in Baltimore? I thought it was something wholesome and adorable, like making homemade jam."

Graham's lips twitch as he attempts to repress a smile. "You thought my family's business was making jam? In Baltimore City?"

Well. He's got me there. It's not his fault that I was too mesmerized by his obnoxiously well-shaped lips to press him for details. I must have been in my follicular phase.

"Don't turn this around on me! You were deliberately misleading. You made it seem like you swooped in like some British superhero to rescue your hapless, elderly grandma from financial ruin. I've met Trudy, and there is nothing hapless about that woman."

Graham pinches the bridge of his nose. "The Black-Eyed Susan has been in our family for four generations. And yes, it was hugely successful for years. But it took a major hit during the pandemic, and it never really bounced back. And then my grandfather passed, and it was too much for my grandmother to manage on her own. I came here to help her try to get the hotel back on its feet, but the books . . . well, they're not great. Things are a lot worse than my grandmother realizes. She's a proud woman who waited too long to ask for help. I don't think she was ready to admit how bad things had gotten."

He takes a breath, as if he's reluctant to admit the next part out loud. "We just had to let two longtime staff members go. Running the hotel the same way we have in the past is no longer sustainable. We need to do something big, something that will remind people how grand the Black-Eyed Susan once was. So, when my grandmother suggested that Claire and I drum up publicity by hosting our wedding at the hotel, it seemed like an easy way to kill two birds with one stone."

"How romantic," I deadpan. "Make sure to include that in your vows."

Graham continues, ignoring the jab. "We've hosted a few events here and there—corporate events and the occasional quinceañera—but it's been a while since we've held an event as large as a wedding. The free publicity could really help us turn things around, especially with the aid of social media, which my grandparents never used. It will remind people that the Black-Eyed Susan is just as relevant today as it was fifty years ago. That it's an irreplaceable part of Baltimore's landscape. That's the kind of exposure that money can't buy."

"Uh-huh. Plus, I'm sure there's the emotional component of wanting to tie the knot there."

Graham's face is blank, uncomprehending. "What do you mean?"

"I mean, of course you want to marry the love of your life at a place that means so much to you and your family."

Graham blinks rapidly, clearing away the look of confusion. "Oh, yes. Of course."

I shake my head. This dude is even more dense than I'd realized. To be honest, I'm having a difficult time reconciling the Graham I know with the guy standing in front of me. The memory of our shared history sparks another thought.

"Does she know?" I ask. "About the tattoo?"

Graham's cheeks go pink. "I mean . . . she's seen it. Obviously." I kick myself mentally for asking such a stupid question. Of course Claire knows about the tattoo. They're *engaged.* I'm sure there's not one inch of each other's bodies that's gone unexplored. The thought sends my stomach roiling.

Thinking about Graham and Claire being intimate cues an unwelcome memory. Graham and I fumbling in the darkness of his tiny London bedroom, the shape of our silhouettes outlined by moonlight. Graham, stripped to the waist as he unhooked my bra. The sensation of cold air tickling my exposed chest before he captured one nipple between his lips to warm it. Judging by the pops of color staining his cheekbones, odds are favorable that he's currently haunted by a similar thought. He pushes his glasses up his nose, a nervous habit I'm growing increasingly familiar with.

"She knows I got it while I was at university. I just . . . haven't shared too many of the other details."

I cross my arms and give Graham my most withering look. "Wow, you're really starting your marriage off on the right foot. They do say secrets are the cornerstone to any healthy relationship."

Graham's eyes narrow, his expression mirroring my own. I take a fortifying breath before asking the question that's truly been eating at me. Because Graham can insist Saturday night wasn't a date all he wants, but it doesn't change the fact that it sure felt like one. There's an undeniable chemistry between us, and I know he felt it too.

"Just tell me one thing: if it wasn't a date, then why didn't you tell me the truth?"

Graham opens and closes his mouth a few times, but no words come out. Which makes sense since there's no way he can rationalize his way out of this one. The fight seems to leave his body as his shoulders deflate.

"Look, what's done is done," he says finally. "We're going to be working together, so let's move forward and make the best of this." Blowing out a sigh, he glances over his shoulder. "I should get back in there. See you inside."

I watch wordlessly as he turns and walks back toward the conference room. The moment he disappears around the corner, I let out a shaky breath, my bravado instantly evaporating. The initial flare of anger has faded, leaving me with the unpleasant sensation of being gut punched. I can't believe that after every crappy dating experience I've had, I let myself consider the possibility that Graham could be different. The feeling is followed by a pang of hurt. It's true that I hardly know the guy, but there was something about Graham that put me at ease, that made me feel like I could let my guard down. I told him things about myself that I'd never normally share on a first date. And what did he do with that trust? Stomped all over it without a second thought.

I rock back on my heels and weigh my options. My first instinct is to march back in there and tell everyone exactly what kind of guy Graham really is. But then rational thought prevails, reminding me that doing so will put the kibosh on this wedding. And that hurts *me* because I need this event to be a success. Antoine made it clear that this wedding was my golden ticket to a future with the company, and consequently my future as a homeowner. Unleashing drama would not only burn that opportunity, but also destroy my credibility. I hate that Graham is getting away with this, but for the sake of my own self-preservation, he's left me with no choice.

With a growl, I dig my nails into my palms, gather my resolve, and head back into the meeting.

"Sorry about that," I say, as I take my seat at the conference table. "I've never learned my lesson about iced coffee. Stuff goes right through me."

The corners of Trudy's lips pucker like she's just bitten into a lemon. Even Asha lets out a barely audible sigh. Fortunately, Claire comes to my rescue, barking out an easy laugh.

"Girl, *same.* Although it can come in handy when you're, you know . . ." She presses a hand against the side of her lips and whispers behind it, "Backed up."

Trudy clears her throat pointedly, as if to signal that she is very much ready to move on from this topic.

"Asha," she says. "You were about to show us the samples."

"Yes," she replies, looking equally relieved by the shift in conversation. "Since you are giving us free rein with the design of your special day, we thought it might be nice to choose a style that highlights the hotel's grandeur and old-world opulence. We envision a day that's suited to its venue: classic and timeless, elegant, but with a vintage touch."

She pulls out a fabric-covered pinboard, which showcases a sample invitation in the center. It's a crisp ivory with handwritten calligraphy and a dusty pink, satin ribbon tied around its center. A cluster of vintage stamps dress up the corner of the accompanying envelope, and a handful of flowers in matching shades are pinned alongside it.

"Wow, this is beautiful," Claire breathes, running her fingertips along the petals. "What type of flowers are these?"

"English roses," I say quietly. They're my favorite flowers and one of my few contributions to the vision board. Of course, I didn't realize at the time how on the nose they'd be. You could choke to death on the irony. I sneak a furtive glance at Graham to see if he's thinking the same thing, but he's making a point of looking everywhere in the room but at me.

"In terms of color scheme, we think white, ivory, and dusty pink, with a few pops of blue mixed in, will highlight some of the hotel's most striking features, such as the pink marble columns in the ballroom, the ornate chandeliers, and of course, the magnificent, gilded staircase," Asha continues.

Trudy beams. "You know, the Black-Eyed Susan is registered as a historic landmark. When it was built in the late 1920s, it was one of the last high-rise buildings developed with classical ornamentation." A pang of sadness strikes me as I remember what Graham said to me earlier. As much as I loathe him at this moment, the prospect of his family's hotel closing is heartbreaking. The Black-Eyed Susan is iconic. It's hard to imagine the city without it.

"Very impressive. I love the vision," Trudy continues approvingly. Antoine looks so relieved I think he might pass out.

"Once you've got the guest list together, we can start organizing the save the dates," Antoine says. "I think this will truly be an affair to remember."

Well, he's got that right.

For the first time since the meeting began, Graham steals a glance at me. Maybe I'm imagining it, but it seems like there's sadness behind his eyes. About the Black-Eyed Susan, or our earlier conversation, where I accused him of being a cheater. Or maybe it's something else entirely. But before I can attempt to parse out the emotion on his face, he tears his eyes away.

Antoine, who fortunately seems not to have noticed the awkward glances we've exchanged, shuffles the papers in front of him.

"Should we go ahead and schedule our next meeting?"

6

After Claire, Graham, and Trudy depart, Antoine holds a brief meeting to sketch out a timeline for the next four months. I try my best to focus, but this morning's brain-melting turn of events make it a near-impossible task. Antoine's words roll past me in an indiscernible jumble, drowned out by the roar of my own panicky thoughts.

When the meeting ends, Asha offers to take me out for a celebratory lunch, her excitement for my big opportunity evident. In a panic, I make a vague gesture toward my stomach and ask for a rain check. Her expression is clouded with a mixture of disappointment and confusion as I bolt through the conference room doors, yelling over my shoulder that I'll be back in thirty minutes to no one in particular.

I feel terrible shutting Asha out, especially since part of me is desperate to confess everything over a bottle of sauvignon blanc. She's always been a big-sister figure, and right now, I am in desperate need of big-sister advice. Besides, how the hell am I going to make it through the next four months if I don't tell someone the truth?

At the same time, Asha risked her own reputation when she convinced Antoine to bring me on as an intern. Even though she's always been there for me, I want her to start thinking of me as a colleague, not just her best friend's impetuous little sister. Clueing her in on this mess won't help with that situation one bit. Plus, if I tell her the truth, I don't just run the risk of her judgment; my future at the company is also on the line. I've sacrificed so much to start over as an event planner, and a conflict of interest as big as this could ruin everything. The last thing I need is to let some guy torpedo everything I've worked for.

Because at the end of the day, that's all Graham is. Just a random guy I spent one night with eight years ago. It's not like we have a whole history together beyond that. He means nothing to me.

Except.

I bite down on my bottom lip, forcing myself to mentally omit the shared tattoo. I really need to stop romanticizing that night in London. Our matching tattoos are the result of a drunken dare, not some forged, unbreakable bond. The sooner I can drill that into my brain, the better off I'll be.

Still, a situation of this magnitude requires immediate backup. The minute I step out onto the street, I whip out my phone and fire off a text to my two best friends.

9–1–1. Need to schedule a FaceTime circa right the fuck now.

I've barely hit "send" before the phone starts vibrating. It's Chloe. Her best and worst trait is that her cell phone is always in her hands. At least in this instance, it's working in my favor. I answer immediately.

"Hey," she says. "I texted Lexi too. Hopefully she's around." She squints at the screen, and I can tell I've interrupted something.

"What are you working on?" I ask, as I head toward my car. I don't have a destination in mind, but this is not a conversation I'm comfortable having in public. Especially not in the city I grew up in, where someone always seems to be listening.

"Just trying to blur out the details of some dude's watch with a photo editing app. It's got a distinctive face, which obviously detracts from his anonymity."

In addition to her day job as a publicist, Chloe's recently picked up a side gig of soft-launching relationships on social media. This basically entails posting photos on her client's Instagram stories that reveal a sliver of the person they're dating without showing their face. It's hugely helpful for celebrity clients who want to acknowledge their partner on social media without forsaking their privacy. She also works with a fair number of non-celebrities, mostly women in their twenties who want to appease their anxious, grandchild-thirsty parents without forking over too many details on the family group chat.

My mind drifts to the distinctive look of Graham's watch. It's the type of personal detail Chloe would have to blur if he were a client. It looked like an antique, the face yellowing and the leather scuffed, and I wonder fleetingly if it belonged to his grandfather. Maybe he wears the family heirloom to feel closer to him. Graham seems like the type to do something like that.

FFS. Why am I romanticizing this man? I need to shut down this line of thinking immediately.

A moment later, Lexi's face fills the screen, and I spot her fiancé, Jake, in the background, slurping from what appears to be a bowl of matzah ball soup. So many people envy Lexi for scoring a handsome rock star like Jake, but Jake knows he's the lucky one locking down my ridiculously talented best friend.

"Hey, Al," Lexi says. "Is it okay that Jake is here?"

"Of course," I say. I know she'd tell him to get lost if I asked her to, but I'm also pretty sure these two would die if they spent more than ten minutes away from each other, and I've got enough problems already. The last thing I need is lovebird blood on my hands.

I've reached my car now. Having determined that I'm too rattled to drive anywhere, I slip into the front seat and slam the door behind me.

"Okay, what's up?" Chloe says. Lexi nods to confirm I've also got their full attention.

"So, remember I told you about that time I got matching tattoos with a British guy I met during my study abroad semester?"

"Legend of the Tattoo Twin? Of course we remember," Chloe says. "You tell this story every time you exceed your tequila safe zone."

I sigh. The best thing about close friends is that they know all your secrets. But the worst thing about close friends is that they know all your secrets.

"Well, last Friday, I ran into him at the coffee shop by my office."

Lexi lets out a little squeal.

"Ohmigod!" she gushes. "Graham, right? What was that like? Did he remember you? Is he still hot?"

"He's definitely still hot," I confirm. "And still grumpy, but like in a sexy way?"

"Like Heath Ledger's character in *10 Things I Hate About You*," Jake offers brightly.

I roll my eyes. Just when you think Jake can't be more likable, he'll remind you that he's also a closet rom-com connoisseur.

"Did he remember you?" Chloe asks.

"Oh, he remembered me," I grumbled. "We went out for drinks, and walked around the city, and made googly eyes at each other in a charming bookshop. It was basically a fucking Hallmark movie."

Lexi squeals again. Even Chloe is smiling, seemingly oblivious to my sardonic tone.

"Oh, I'm not done," I say, holding up a hand. "We got a new client a few weeks ago, and this morning, we had our first meeting with the groom. Who turned out to be tall, handsome, and *British*."

"Wow, what a coincidence!" Lexi says. "Two Brits in one week. What are the odds of that? You don't meet too many English people in Baltimore."

I level my gaze at her meaningfully, as if to say, get there faster. She goes still as the realization hits her and her mouth drops open.

"No *fucking* way," she breathes.

I yank open my glove box, extracting the emergency bag of Doritos I keep inside.

"That's right," I confirm as I shovel a handful of Cool Ranch into my face. "Of all the offices in all the towns in all the world, Graham Wyler walks into mine. And now I'm going to have to plan his wedding, while pretending we're complete strangers who don't have matching tattoos and have never seen each other's genitals. Oh, and I forgot to mention: my entire career at the company hinges on how this event goes. My boss told me if it goes well, he'll promote me to assistant planner. Which was basically my entire reason for moving home to begin with."

My friends go silent as the weight of the stakes settle in.

"I'll get the wine," Jake says after a moment, before disappearing off screen.

"But . . . if Graham's engaged," Lexi says slowly. "Why would he go on a date with you?"

"That's the million-dollar question," I grumble. "He claims it wasn't a date. Just two acquaintances catching up. Which is complete BS. Sparks were flying. *And* he almost kissed me."

But even as I say the words, I'm second-guessing myself. Was there really chemistry between us, or was it just wishful thinking? Am I just projecting my own lingering feelings onto someone who doesn't share them?

"Wait, back up for a second," Chloe continues. "You ran into this guy three days ago? Why are we just now hearing about it?"

I bite my bottom lip, contemplating what to say next. Chloe is right; it *is* weird that something this major happened in my life, and I didn't immediately tell the two of them.

The truth is, after running into Graham, I was afraid to voice my excitement to the two people who know me best. Because if it didn't work out, their shared disappointment would be reverberated right back at me. And now, that's exactly what's happened.

Things were different a year ago, when the three of us were single in the city together, swapping bad-date war stories over happy hour margaritas. But the two of them have both found love and satisfying careers, while I'm still the messy single friend, once again starting over and struggling to find herself. Part of me is mortified to admit that after all the shitty relationships they supported me through, this thing with Graham was just another nonstarter. I feel an unspoken pressure to find happiness like they have, and now I've let all of us down. Again.

"You guys have been busy," I say finally. "You both have a lot going on and I didn't want to bug you."

"Ali," Lexi says softly. "How could you say that? We are never, ever too busy for you."

Warmth spreads across my chest. Deep down, I know how much these two women care about me. I never should have let my insecurities talk me into shutting them out.

"Well, that's good to hear, because right now, I'm teetering on the edge of a panic attack."

"Okay, take a breath," Chloe says in that even, soothing voice that's probably incredibly effective with clients. Based on the way my pulse starts to regulate, it's safe to say that it works on me too.

"Everything will be okay, Ali. Let's talk this out."

I sigh. "Why can't things ever be easy? It's my first major gig and I'm already being sabotaged. Is it such an ask for things to go according to plan?"

"*I never planned on someone like you!*" Jake's voice rings out in the background.

Chloe shakes her head. "Guess you've been forcing Jake to watch *Newsies*."

"'Forced' is not the word I'd use," Lexi protests. "He loves it! And like, how amazing would it be if he played Jack Kelly in his next limited Broadway run?"

"You couldn't handle it," I say. "Your vagina would literally explode."

Jake's ridiculously handsome face fills the screen again, and he flashes his signature dimple. If I hadn't gotten to know him so well over the past year, I think my own vag would be in danger of spontaneous combustion.

"May I offer a suggestion?" he asks. Under normal circumstances, the thought of unsolicited male input would push me over the edge right now. But it's impossible to be annoyed with Jake, especially when he turns on that charming Southern drawl.

"What if you just told the bride the truth?" he continues. "Maybe then you'd mutually agree to put someone else on the account?"

"Oh, Jake. You sweet, naïve buttercup," I sigh. "What am I supposed to say? 'Hey Claire, funny story. Turns out we're actually *shlong* sisters! That's right . . . I banged your fiancé, right after we got matching tattoos! What a wild night that was. Anyway, have you guys settled on a honeymoon destination yet?'"

Jake's mouth falls open, but before he can say anything, Lexi shoves him out of the screen. She stares at me wide-eyed. "I'm sorry, you *slept* with this guy!"

I suppress an eye roll. Lexi's dating experience before she met Jake was virtually nonexistent and the bar for shocking her is embarrassingly low.

"It was my semester abroad. Shagging London locals was part of the curriculum," I explain. "Besides, everyone knows that if you're going to do something as romantic as getting matching tattoos with a stranger, ending the night with sex is obligatory. And it wasn't like I was ever going to see him again. What are the odds that eight years later, I'd be planning his wedding?"

Chloe is chewing on her bottom lip. "What's the bride like?" she asks.

"Claire? She's basically the coolest girl alive. Gorgeous, down to earth, killer sense of humor. In another life, we'd totally be friends."

Even though we hardly know each other, Claire and I clicked immediately, and I can't stomach the idea of dropping this bomb on her. And while I may be impulsive, I'm not the kind of person who would deliberately hurt someone. The mere thought of it sends my heart lurching.

Lexi slips a thumbnail past her lips, which she only does when she's majorly stressed. I'm temporarily blinded by the luster of her oval-cut diamond ring.

"What are you going to do?" she asks quietly.

I blow out a sigh. "I don't know. I could step back from this account, and hope that Antoine considers giving me another chance down the line. It'll mean a few more months of living with my two boomer roommates and their fridge full of expired condiments, but I can't see any other way out."

My heart turns heavy at the thought. Not just because turning down this opportunity means putting my goals on the back burner, but also because it would disappoint Antoine. I hate the idea of letting him down. The man's kind of my hero.

Chloe's mouth sets in a hard line. "No," she says simply.

I raise my eyebrows. "No?"

"No," she says again, more definitively this time. "You love event planning. And the Ali I know would never give up on her dreams. Especially not over some *guy*. So, this is what you're going to do: you're going to put on your big girl panties and forget last weekend with Graham ever happened. And then you're going to land this promotion."

I nod, a renewed sense of confidence filling my chest. I let out a long breath.

"You guys are right," I say. "This will be fine. It was a one-time issue that won't affect my ability to do my job. I'm going to be a professional."

"That's right! You've got this," Lexi agrees. Then her face falls a bit. "I'm sorry about the way things worked out with Graham. It sucks when the good guys turn out to be shady."

I nod, but something about this whole mess isn't sitting right. It's hard to rectify the Graham I hung out with on Saturday night with the soon-to-be groom I met this morning. Especially given the way that Graham looked when I accused him of being unfaithful. As if the label stung him to his core.

Which makes sense if I think about it. The comment draws an unflattering parallel to his father. Given how adamant he was about being a better man and not following in his dad's footsteps, it is sort of surprising that he's gone down the very same road. It just doesn't line up with everything else I know about him.

I shake the thought away. Because if there's one thing I've learned about people over the years, it's that they can always find shitty new ways to surprise you.

Except for men holding fish in their dating profile pics. Those guys are exactly who you think they are.

My sour mood builds for the rest of the week, and by the time I'm at lunch with my mom, Sarah, and Bubbie on Sunday afternoon, per our weekly tradition, it's reached full crescendo. We've barely settled into our table at Goldberg's Bagels when my mom brings up her favorite topic.

"You'll never guess who I ran into at the Giant this morning," she says, in that practiced casual way, as she looks at me expectantly.

"Let me see. Theodosia Burr-Alston, Aaron Burr's long-lost daughter?"

My mother clucks her tongue. "*No.* Sharon Hoffman. Brad's mom. She was so excited when I told her you're back in town! She asked if you were dating anyone, and I said you weren't, and she said Brad wasn't either, and—"

"Alright, I'll go out with him," I mutter. Everyone goes silent as they swing their heads toward me, shock evident on their faces. I take an enormous bite of my everything bagel with cream cheese before I have the chance to take it back. Nothing beats New York bagels, but Baltimore bagels are a close second.

My mom's jaw literally drops. Clearly this wasn't the answer she was expecting. To be honest, it also wasn't the answer I was expecting to give.

"Oh! Well, great," she says, once she's recovered herself. "I invited Sharon to join our mah-jongg game tomorrow night. I can give her your phone number then!"

Bubbie nods her head approvingly. "One more *shidduch* and you're set," she announces through a mouthful of tuna. My mom looks pleased at this. There's an idea in Judaism that if you make three successful *shidduchim,* three romantic matches that lead to marriage, you automatically go to heaven. And since my mom introduced my second cousin Arielle to her now-husband, Noah, she's already a third of the way there.

"There you go." I raise my bagel like I'm giving a toast. "I'm sure that'll cancel out the crab cake you had at Pappas last weekend."

"Shh!" my mom hisses. She presses a finger to her lips, her eyes wide with panic as she glances nervously around the room. "Do not mention the consumption of shellfish here. They'll kick us out."

I shrug, and slump back in my chair. Sarah is still staring at me, confusion etched across her face. Part of me is dying to clear it up by telling my big sister exactly what went down with Graham. At the same time, the last thing I'm interested in right now is telling my sister that I've managed to screw up, *again.* Besides, it's official. The perfect man does not exist, so why not throw in the towel and give Brad a chance? After all, how bad can a date with him really be?

7

It's official. This is the worst date of my life.

It's Saturday night, nearly a week after I agreed to be set up with Brad Hoffman, and it turns out that there is not enough red wine in the world to make this evening palatable. Even though Brad's taken me to RA, my favorite sushi spot in the city, I've been counting down the minutes until I can politely call it a night since the moment we arrived.

"We actually just installed lights like these in the funeral home," he says, gesturing toward the installations above our heads. These are the first words we've exchanged in over five painful minutes.

I glance upward and do my best to feign interest. "Bar lights?"

"No, red lights. They're super flattering. Lighting in a funeral home is so important."

"How so?"

"Think about it. Why do they keep places like this so dim? It's because everybody looks better in the dark. Including the dead. Everyone wants to see their loved ones looking their best when they're saying their goodbyes. And funeral cosmetology can only take you so far."

I raise one eyebrow. "Funeral cosmetology? Like, makeup?"

"Of course. But it's more than just makeup," he says, the volume of his voice rising to match his growing enthusiasm. "I wash and condition their hair, trim their nose hairs, shave off any unwanted mustaches. It's like the best spa day they've ever had. Only they don't fully appreciate it because, you know. They're dead."

I envy the dead at this moment. They may have left this world before their dreams were fully realized, but at least they no longer go on first dates.

"Wow. I didn't realize being a mortician was so . . . hands-on. I imagined you just handled the business side of things. Managing the accounts and shaking hands and whatnot."

Brad's wide mouth stretches into a smile, his beady eyes illuminating. He really does look like a platypus.

"Nope, we do it all. Being a funeral director is a lot like being a wedding planner, actually."

I blink at him. "How do you figure?"

"You're in charge of one of the most important days in a person's life. You oversee the entire production from start to finish, and it's up to you to make sure everything goes perfectly."

Brad reaches an arm across the table to take my hand in his. The dark hair extending from his shirt sleeve extends all the way to his knuckles. I do my best to contain a shudder while he speaks. "I think you and I have a lot in common."

I offer him a limp smile as I extract myself from his grip. My eyes drift around the room, conducting a quick scan of the restaurant in an attempt to locate all the emergency exits. Just then, a rush of cool, outside air draws my attention to the front of the restaurant, where a familiar figure in khaki chinos and a green Barbour jacket stands in the doorway. Panic wells up in my chest.

No, it can't be. Baltimore is full of restaurants. It's not possible that of all the places to eat around here, Graham would walk into this one.

But then a woman with a crop of bright hair trails in behind him, and my worst suspicions are confirmed. Claire and Graham approach the maître d', who frowns as he thumbs through his iPad. Despite the warning bells going off in my head, I can't quite manage to tear my eyes away from Graham. My eyes drift over the square line of his jaw as he leans over to say something to the maître d'. I'm turning away, not allowing myself to continue staring at him when Claire catches my eye.

"Oh, hey!" she calls with a wave. "Teddy, look! It's Ali, our wedding planner." Graham's body goes rigid as he whips his head toward me. Fortunately, Claire doesn't seem to notice as she grabs his hand and begins leading him toward our table.

"Hi," she says brightly, extending her hand to Brad. "I'm Claire, one of Ali's bridal clients."

"What a pleasure," Brad replies, pumping it with vigorous enthusiasm, and I do my best not to think about where those hands have recently been. "I'm Brad, her date."

Claire's eyes light up. "A date, huh?" She grins conspiratorially at me. "I do love the idea of love's engineers finding happily-ever-afters themselves."

"Uh," I sputter. "We aren't actually—"

"Do you mind if we sit with you for a few minutes?" she asks, gesturing to the two empty chairs at our four top. "I could have sworn I made a reservation online, but the guy up front is insisting he doesn't see my name on the list, and every other table is taken. I'm sure something will open in a bit."

The horror on Graham's face mirrors my own, and I can practically hear the words running through his head. *Please God, no.*

"Actually," I say, as I start to rise, "we were just about to leave. You guys can have our table."

Brad drapes an arm around my shoulder. "Want to head back to my place? I'm dying to show you my collection of antique surgical sets. I just scored an amputation kit on eBay that dates back to the Civil War era. It's got a tourniquet, a couple of hooks that were used to pull arteries from limb stumps, and these long Liston knives that—"

"You know, on second thought," I say, sinking back into my seat. "What's the rush? One drink with friends can't hurt."

I gesture for the waitress and tap the empty wine bottle on the table, signaling for a refill. Screw my mom's free pass to heaven. There's no way I'm about to go home with a man who has the capacity to Joe Goldberg me.

"This is such a fun surprise," Claire says. She wiggles out of her jacket and drapes it on the back of the chair before sliding into the seat next to me. Graham stiffly mimics the gesture, although his discomfort seems to go unnoticed by everyone else. Underneath his jacket, he's wearing a thick, forest green sweater that brings out the gold highlights in his hair. It's repulsive.

Gingerly, he sits down across from Claire. Beneath the table, his leg grazes mine, causing a flush of color to spring from his collar. Truthfully, I'm not faring much better. My treacherous body is crackling with electricity, goosebumps rising on my shin at the point of contact. I absolutely hate that he still has this effect on me.

Brad looks over at Graham. "Sorry, I didn't catch your name."

"It's Graham," he replies bluntly.

Brad tilts his head, looking positively delighted.

"Oh, wow. You're British!" he says.

Graham's eyes narrow. "How terribly observant."

"So, Brad," Claire says. "What do you do for work?"

Brad's chest puffs out with pride. "I'm a mortician. My family has owned the largest Jewish funeral home in the area for four generations."

Claire leans forward, captivated. "A mortician? That's *such* a cool job! Tell me everything. Like, what's the grossest thing you've ever had to deal with?"

Brad purses his lips, showcasing the purple wine stains in the corner of his mouth as he considers the question. "Probably maggots. We typically don't have much of a problem with them, but if a body isn't handled properly, they'll descend quickly. Blowflies can smell a dead body from ten miles away, and a single fly can lay up to three hundred maggot eggs."

Not a moment too soon, our server returns to the table with the second bottle of wine.

"Here you go!" she says brightly, holding out a bottle of Merlot. She flashes us an enormous grin that takes up half her face, and Claire beams back at her, matching her enthusiasm.

"Excellent." I grab the bottle, refilling my glass practically to the brim, and then chugging half of it in one long gulp.

"Damn," Claire says, eyeing my glass. "For a person of your stature, you sure can hold your booze."

"You have no idea," Graham murmurs. I shoot him a glare as Claire raises a questioning eyebrow.

"About how little body size has to do with alcohol tolerance," he amends quickly.

"Speaking of liquids, I'd better take a trip to the little boys' room," Brad says. He stands up and, toes pointed outward, waddles off to the bathroom.

When Claire returns her attention to me, her expression is positively jubilant. "A mortician? Girl, *respect.* This is probably the coolest date ever!"

"Wanna bet?" I mutter.

"I wouldn't advise betting against you," Graham says. My head snaps toward him again, and my eyes fill with warning as they sear into his. Then his expression shifts into a look of concern.

"Are you okay? With this guy?" he says quietly. My eyes swing to Claire, worried she's clocked his too-familiar tone, but she's busy filling her wine glass just as high as mine.

Turning back to Graham, I shrug. "Sure. I mean, yes, I'm on a date with a man who knows exactly how to dispose of a body. But I'm sure my mom could recover my remains and avenge my death. She watches a lot of Lifetime movies."

Claire snorts into her wine glass, but Graham's frown deepens.

"Well, he seems really into you. Even if it is only for the purposes of necrophilia," Claire says. She beams at me, and it's impossible to deny how likable she is. No wonder Graham fell for a girl like her. Even if he is completely devoid of a sense of humor.

I nod my head slowly, suddenly aware of how quickly the wine I've guzzled went to my head. "You'd be surprised, Claire. I've thought guys were into me plenty of times before, and have been so very, very wrong. Just last week, I went on a date with a guy who turned out to be engaged."

"No!" Claire's red lips shift into a little O. She looks at Graham and then turns back to me. "Please say you're joking." Graham's face turns bright red as he fidgets with a straw wrapper, folding and unfolding it like an accordion.

"'Fraid not. It's rough out there for a single girl," I tell her, ignoring the slur in my words as I refill my wine glass for the third time. Or is it the fourth?

"You should consider expanding your preferences. I started dating both men and women in college and I was shocked by the difference. Women talk things out instead of playing mind games with you. Once you realize you can have your orgasms with a side of emotional maturity and the potential to share clothes, men become a hard sell." She laughs, then stops abruptly before throwing an arm around Graham's shoulders. "Except for this dime piece of course! He's perfect, obviously."

Mercifully, our server returns, effectively putting an end to this line of conversation.

"Can I get you anything else?" she asks, just as Brad is sliding back into his seat. He's grinning at me from across the table like a wolf who's just realized he's about to drive a plump little piggy home in his Tesla. I realize with chagrin that even though I'm dying to get away from Graham, leaving here with Brad is an even less appealing option.

"How about a round of sake bombs?" Claire asks. I take a moment to consider the idea. On the one hand, I'm already toeing the line between pleasantly buzzed and performing sorority recruitment songs intoxicated. One more drink is likely all it will take to nudge me over the threshold. On the other hand, a one-woman performance might stand to improve the evening. Especially considering the Motown-themed set list is a goddamn delight.

I tip my head in confirmation. "Let's do it."

"Oooh, this is going to be so much fun!" Claire squeals, clapping her hands together gleefully.

She turns back to the server. "Can we get a round for the table?" she asks.

The woman beams at her. "You've got it. And how about some food?"

Claire picks up the menu and gives it a quick scan. "I'll do a Crazy Monkey roll, and two orders of the tuna roll. Plus, an order of pineapple cheese wontons for the table. And"—she tosses a playful look in Graham's direction—"a steak teriyaki bowl for this one."

The server gives her an appraising once-over. "I like a woman who takes charge. Do you always order for your man?"

Claire grins back at her. "Graham always orders the same thing at sushi restaurants. I try to get him to branch out and be more adventurous, but he's not exactly known for his spontaneity."

Graham shrugs but doesn't deny it. Strange how I seem to be the only person who can draw it out of him. It's probably for the best that things never worked out between us. I would torpedo his tidy little life.

Once the server departs, Claire returns her attention to me.

"I'm *so* glad you're on the planning team. I was worried the wedding might be a bit dry, given the host." She pauses, shooting an apologetic look at Graham, who shrugs but doesn't look particularly offended. There's something slightly off about the way she refers to it as "the wedding" as opposed to "our wedding," but the alcohol I've consumed has left my brain feeling entirely too fuzzy to parse it out.

"It's a reasonable concern," Graham admits. "My grandmother is definitely . . . on the formal side."

"There's the understatement of the century," Claire smirks. "I adore the woman, but she makes the Dowager Countess of Grantham look casual."

She turns back to me with a grin. "But we're in good hands with Ali. You're fun, I can tell."

"That's me, the good-time gal," I mumble against the brim of my wine glass.

I steal a glance at Graham, who's staring at me intently, a small wrinkle forming between his brows. I roll my eyes and turn away. How dare he look at me like that, as if he feels bad for me. As if he knows me.

Our server returns with a tray of drinks.

"Cheers to a spontaneous evening!" she says, as she sets a glass out in front of each of us. "Are y'all doing anything fun after this?"

"Who knows where the evening will take us?" Claire laughs. She presses her elbows into the table and leans toward the other woman.

"What time do you get off? You should join us."

"I'm off at ten," the server replies. "Think you guys will still be here?"

"Only one way to find out," Claire says with a wink.

Something nags at the corner of my brain, but before I have a chance to think much into it, Graham lifts his glass, eyes narrowing as he stares at me over the brim, and I'm hit with a tsunami wave of déjà vu. Just like that, we're back in London, embattled in the drinking game that will forever link us.

"Er, I'm not sure sake bombs are a great idea," Brad says. Whoops, I'd totally forgotten he was here.

"Sundays are our busiest day, since we have all the funerals for people who died over Shabbat. In fact, we should probably be heading out. It's getting late."

"One round," Graham says, and I don't mistake the challenge in his voice. He has that same determined look in his eyes that he did eight years ago, and I feel my own competitive urges rise. Every head at the table swivels in his direction; even Claire looks shocked.

"Damn, Teddy. I'm not sure what's gotten into you, but I like it," Claire grins. "Also, is it me, or is our server a dead ringer for Zendaya?"

Predictably, one round turns into three, with only Graham tapping out early, and by the time we finish, the déjà vu of my last time recreationally drinking with him has come full circle. Only this time, it's Brad who's looking green around the gills.

"I'm not feeling so hot," he announces to no one in particular. "I don't think I should drive. Let's settle the bill and call an Uber."

"Lemme just use the bathroom," I say. But when I stand up, the ground shifts beneath me, and I grab onto the edge of the table to regain my balance. Graham's arm shoots out, and his fingers wrap themselves around my wrist.

"Are you okay?" he asks, his voice a low scrape. Behind his glasses, his eyes are filled with concern. I wrestle my arm free and turn away.

"I'm fine," I mumble. The last thing I need is his faux sympathy.

He may have fooled me once, but there's no way I'm falling for his "I'm such a good guy" act again.

Still, the walk to the bathroom forces the realization that I'm a lot drunker than I'd previously thought. Reluctant as I am to admit it, my tolerance isn't nearly as high as it was in my early twenties. I splash a bit of cold water on my face, then stare down my reflection in the bathroom mirror.

"Get it together," I say pointedly to my reflection. "You are a strong, independent woman, and you are not going to let some dude get in your head, no matter how sexy his voiceover would sound in a nature documentary."

"Amen, sister." Behind me, a toilet flushes and a woman with flawlessly shaped eyebrows steps up to the sink beside me. "Unless it's a British accent, of course. Then I'm toast."

"This pep talk isn't having the effect you probably intended," I tell her. "But I appreciate the effort."

By the time I return to the table, all the dishes have been cleared and Brad is shrugging into his coat, looking eager to leave.

"You ready?" he asks me. "I just called an Uber. We can pick up my car tomorrow."

"She's not going home with you, mate," Graham says through gritted teeth, and there's something about the way he's standing, chest puffed out, his fists closed tightly at his sides, that looks positively primal. Angry heat flashes through my body. Is he serious right now? I don't need to be saved, least of all by *him*.

Claire looks at Graham, then back at me, clearly confused by whatever unspoken thing is happening here. But then one corner of her mouth rises as if something has just dawned on her.

"Oh, that's right," she says. "I completely forgot! Ali is running a wedding errand with us tonight!"

Brad's brow furrows. "Tonight? After we've all been drinking?"

"Yup. We are, uh . . . going wine tasting! To pick wines for the reception. I mean, what's a few more drinks at this point, right?" Claire lets out what is probably intended as a giggle, but after three sake bombs sounds more like a passing garbage truck.

Brad looks perplexed but also entirely too nauseated to argue the point.

"Oh, right," he says. "I guess that makes sense."

"Don't worry, we'll make sure she gets home safely," Claire reassures him, and Brad's shoulders sag with relief.

"Okay," he says, resolved. "Well, my ride's here. I'll call you tomorrow, okay?"

"Definitely," I reply, already mentally changing his contact info in my phone to "You'll Never Be This Desperate."

Brad reaches out a hand to Graham, who shakes it reluctantly but is still shooting daggers at Brad with his eyes.

When he departs, Claire turns to me, grinning devilishly.

"Eek! Sorry that was such a bad date," she says. "But glad we were able to stage a rescue. Sorry it took me a minute to recognize Graham's strategy for extraction. He's a doll that way, isn't he? Always trying to do the noble thing."

"Oh yeah, he's a real stand-up guy," I say through gritted teeth.

She throws an arm around my shoulders, and I can smell the sake on her breath. "We can walk back to our place. It's only a few blocks away, and then Graham can drive you home. He only had that one drink."

"No!" Graham and I both say at the same time. Claire's mouth drops open as she looks back and forth between us.

"I mean, I couldn't ask you guys to do that," I say, careful to use the words "you guys" in the lingering hope that I won't be spending any part of this evening alone with Graham. "I mean, it would be completely out of your way to drive to the suburbs and then back again."

Claire shrugs. "It's no big deal. Besides, a car service would cost a fortune."

She's not wrong. Still, I'm desperate to find a way out of this, because as unenthused as I am about spending thirty minutes in an overpriced, overheated Uber, I'm even less excited by the prospect of spending that time alone with Graham. I turn to him and raise a skeptical eyebrow. "Do you even have an American driver's license?"

Claire chortles. "*He* does. I'm the one who doesn't. Never thought there was much of a point."

I shift my skepticism in her direction. "Why is that?"

"I never had a need for one growing up in Vancouver or when I studied in New York. And since we're only here for a few months, I didn't see the point in getting one now," she explains.

"What do you mean, 'only here for a few months'?" I ask slowly, because somehow, I'm still not understanding what she's getting at. She blinks at me, like it's perfectly obvious.

"We'll be moving back to New York after the wedding," she says after a beat. "For my job. Doesn't really make sense to commute. Graham's company is based there too. And once he gets the hotel back on its feet, he can help his grandmother remotely."

Oh. I don't know why, but the idea that Graham will be moving back to New York after the wedding had never occurred to me. It makes perfect sense—of course he plans to live in the same city as his wife. Yet somehow, I hadn't considered his impermanence in Baltimore. Especially after the way he spoke about his grandmother over drinks. It was clear that he really cares about her, that he seemed thrilled to finally be living in the same city as her. I flick my gaze over to him, but he's staring at the ground. I blow out an exhale.

"Well, the least I can do is buy you a coffee for the road."

8

After stopping to get an espresso for Graham and dropping Claire off, Graham and I head to the parking garage, where we slide inside a silver BMW. I don't know much about cars, but the leather interior is worn, and the electronics are dated. Probably a hand-me-down from his grandfather.

A yellowed photograph on the dash catches my eye. From the passenger seat, I can just make out the image of an older man sitting beside a towheaded tot. Graham and his grandfather, most likely. Driving his car must make Graham feel connected to the grandparent he lost. The thought of it tempers my anger. Slightly.

But the moment he pulls out onto the street, my rage is resurrected. I swivel in my seat to glare at him.

"What the fuck was that all about?"

Graham's brow lowers, but he keeps his eyes forward.

"What do you mean?"

"That whole possessive caveman act?" I put on my best British accent, which, admittedly sounds more like Russell Brand than Graham. "*She's not going home with you, mate.*"

Graham scoffs. "Trust me, I did you a favor. There was something off with that wanker."

I throw my hands up in the air.

"Do you think you have some kind of claim on me? Because news flash, we went on one date, and you have a *fiancée*."

Graham clenches his jaw but doesn't say anything. Of course he doesn't. His behavior is indefensible.

"You are my client," I continue quietly. "You and I have a professional relationship and nothing more. So start acting like it."

He nods briskly. "Noted."

Rolling my eyes, I fold my arms across my chest. We merge onto I-83 and I make a silent vow to ignore him for the rest of the drive.

By exit 10, I crack. Predictably.

"So," I say. "You're moving back to New York."

Graham's hands tighten on the steering wheel as he bites down on his lower lip. The sight of his teeth pressed against the pillowy pink flesh sends a rippling sensation through my stomach. I tear my gaze away, staring instead out the window.

"Yeah," he says after a minute.

I nod slowly, still not looking at him. "That's interesting. Because when we were on our Not-a-Date the other night, you made it sound like you were planning on staying here long-term."

Graham clears his throat, and when he speaks again, it sounds rehearsed. "I should be able to get the hotel back on track within the next few months. It's possible that I'm more concerned about the books than needed. Once it's all sorted, I'll join Claire in the city."

"And what about *your* career?" I ask, and I'm surprised at the hard edge to my words. I like Claire a lot, but something about him putting himself last in this equation is rubbing me the wrong way.

Graham lifts one shoulder in a shrug. "My job as a financial analyst is completely remote, so I can live anywhere."

"And you've been able to keep up with work while helping out at the hotel?"

Graham's perfect posture goes even more rigid. He lifts his chin and I detect a hint of pride. "I've had to work a bit at night and on the weekends, but I've managed it so far."

Well. Must be nice to have an answer for everything.

"Sounds like you've got it all figured out," I mutter.

Annoyed for reasons I can't quite put my finger on, I slouch against the headrest, only then noticing how far back the seat is. The last passenger in this car must have been a lot taller than me. Not that this is a particularly challenging feat.

Reaching below the seat, I fumble for a handle to pull the seat forward, and my fingertips brush against something hard and rectangular. Without thinking, I grab on and drag it out. It's a book, and the moment I register what's written on the cover, my mouth goes dry.

Jewish Festival Cooking. My heart skips an entire beat.

"Why do you have this?" I whisper. Even in the darkness, I can see the color draining from Graham's face.

He's quiet for a long beat. When he finally replies, the words are so soft I barely hear them.

"I went back and bought it."

"You went back and bought this . . . for me?"

His nod is barely perceptible. "Yes."

A million conflicting emotions battle for my attention, but anger forces its way to the front of the line.

"What the *fuck*?" I say, my voice heated. "Like, *why*? What was your plan, exactly? Were you going to go out with me again? Lead me on forever?"

Graham's controlled demeanor finally breaks.

"No, of course not!" he snaps back, his voice louder than I've ever heard it. He's gripping the steering wheel so tightly that his knuckles are turning white. Then he blows out a shaky breath, and his posture deflates a bit.

"I don't know what I was going to do. I didn't have a plan, Ali. I wasn't thinking at all."

The silence stretches taut between us, and a few tense minutes pass before he speaks again.

"Look," he says quietly. "I know I've completely lost the plot here. I never should have gone out with you the other night. I can see now that it was a poor idea, and I'm sorry. The last thing I meant to do was hurt you."

Emotion wells up in my throat, and I bite the inside of my cheek, forcing it back down. *God, what is it about this guy that gets under my skin?*

"Then why did you?" I mutter. "Why did you go?" The silence stretches for so long that I'm positive he isn't going to answer at all. But then I hear his voice, so soft that I have to strain to hear it.

"Because I wanted to see you again."

The air between us crackles as his confession hangs in the air. A mix of conflicting feelings washes over me: on the one hand, I don't appreciate mind games, and the swing of Graham's emotional pendulum is starting to give me whiplash. On the other hand, I feel validated that he's admitting our plans weren't as "friendly" as he'd previously suggested. But before I can make up my mind, he starts talking again.

"I don't know what it is about you," he says tightly. "Under normal circumstances, I am a rational, levelheaded person. Someone who never does anything reckless or without careful consideration. But every time I'm around you, I turn into someone completely different."

Memories wash over me: Graham wincing as the needle pierced his skin, laughing as we compared our matching tattoos, sighing as he ran a hand down my bare back. But resentment fills my heart as the weight of his words settle over me, and the images fade away as quickly as they arrived. Of course he sees me as the problem. So, if he wants me to stay out of his way, then that's exactly what I'm going to do.

"Let's just get through this wedding planning process and avoid each other as much as possible," I say through gritted teeth. "Then you can be off to New York and never have to spend another minute worrying about my bad influence rubbing off on you."

Graham throws his head back against the seat rest.

"Ali, that's not what I meant," he says softly. "You just . . ." His brow furrows and then he closes his mouth again. *That's what I thought.* I cross my arms sullenly and turn to stare out the window.

A few minutes of silence pass between us. Just when I'm certain the conversation is over, I hear Graham's voice again, quiet and strained.

"Why did you leave?"

I whip my head around to study him in the darkness.

"What?"

"The morning after, in London," he says. "I woke up, and you were gone. You didn't leave a phone number or anything. I had no way of finding you."

A memory flickers across my mind. A sliver of early dawn winking through cheap, vinyl blinds. The wooden corner of a bed frame. Tiptoeing toward the door, shoes in hand. And then, a quick glimpse back at Graham, his pale limbs and golden hair draped across his twin mattress. I feel a sudden heaviness in my stomach. I've had more one-night stands than I care to remember, and I've never thought twice about leaving without saying goodbye. But there had been something that night with Graham that felt different, my early morning departure tinged with regret and thoughts of what might have been.

It's a memory I had pushed so far to the corner of my mind that I'd forgotten all about it until Graham shook it loose. I feel a momentary twinge of pleasure knowing that I hadn't imagined our connection, that the evening had been more to Graham than just a meaningless hookup. I don't normally linger after sex. I'm not the girl who makes a guy morning-after pancakes. I'm the one who leaves before he wakes up and hopes she hasn't left a thong behind on a flammable surface. Still, if Graham wanted to find me, he could have tried harder. He lived with Alfie, after all. He could have gotten my contact information if he wanted it that badly. Then I remember he's engaged to someone else, someone whose wedding I'm orchestrating, and my heart hardens. I need to stop giving this man credit he doesn't deserve. This situation right here is *exactly* why I normally keep my guard up.

"What did you think was going to happen?" I say through gritted teeth. "I was going back to the States, and you were staying in London. It wasn't like we were ever going to see each other again."

"You didn't even let it be an option," he says quietly. He blows out a long exhale. "I just . . . I guess I didn't realize that night meant nothing to you. Because it sure meant something to me."

I open my mouth, then shut it again. There are a million things I want to say, starting with how that night meant more to me than I've ever cared to admit, even to myself. Would things have been different if we'd shared our Baltimore connection then? But none of the words jumbling around in my brain feel right. Besides, what good could possibly come of revisiting this now? The last thing I need to do is make things more complicated than they already are.

I press my lips together as we drive the rest of the way in silence.

9

"Thanks for meeting with us again. We want to be as considerate of your time as possible, but given the tight schedule, we have a lot to cover."

I've managed to avoid Graham for the past two weeks, but our first catering meeting with our clients has thrust us back into each other's company.

Asha glances up at Claire, Graham, and Trudy, who are sitting across from us at a table in the Black-Eyed Susan's restaurant. Then she looks back down at her iPad.

"We've already decided to go with an open bar, attendant-passed drinks and hors d'oeuvres, and a three-course dinner," she says, as she drags her pen down a checklist. "All we need to do is choose what you'll be serving for each." She turns to me and smiles encouragingly.

"Food is Ali's area of specialty. She's a formally trained chef and has experience working in hotel restaurants, which is why we're thrilled that she could work so closely with the head of your kitchen to prepare today's sample menus. Ali, the floor is yours."

I clear my throat and plaster on my most confident smile. Food is where I shine, and this is my opportunity to show off my skills. Plus, working on these menus over the past two weeks with José, the Black-Eyed Susan's chef, has been one of the most enjoyable highlights of my job so far, as well as a major confidence boost. Budget cuts meant that Trudy had to let some of the kitchen staff go, so I got the sense that José was more than happy to have an extra set of hands. And given the hit that Graham has taken on my normally unflappable self-esteem over the past few days, I'm glad to take it.

"Right," I say. "After some planning with your executive chef, I'm proposing two sample menus. You're going to be tasting from each, and then you can decide what you like best."

I'm very excited about the food we've prepared for this morning's meeting. A pair of servers begin setting out plates with small bites from our first, Asian-inspired menu: seared ahi tuna with wasabi and crispy wontons, Peking duck potstickers with plum sauce, sticky glazed chicken, and miso-glazed sea bass.

I watch with a familiar tinge of pride as everyone tucks in and murmurs their appreciation. Even though I didn't cook this food, there's still a secondhand sense of satisfaction in knowing that you've contributed to a meal that brings pleasure to others. But as much as I enjoy José's cooking, I've saved the best for last.

"While I'm confident that your guests would enjoy this menu, we can also go in a different direction, with cuisine that is more locally inspired. Comfort food but elevated, with an emphasis on the flavors that define Baltimore. It's a bit of an unexpected choice for a formal affair, but at the same time, it's classic. Most importantly, it will remind people what makes the Black-Eyed Susan special." My eyes flick to Graham after the last sentence. He might be a jerk, but he was right about one thing. If there's any hope of saving the hotel, people need to be reminded that it's a historic institution, deeply ingrained in the fabric of the city.

I nod to José, who wheels out a cart containing tiny portions from the sample menu that he and I planned together. Tiny spanakopitas are a nod to Greektown and gnocchi cacio e pepe is reminiscent of Little Italy. There are fried chicken wings and wedge fries evocative of Baltimore's legendary chicken boxes, and for the main course, jumbo lump crab cakes with spicy remoulade sauce.

Trudy purses her lips as she considers the spread in front of her.

"I'm not sure," she says slowly. "It all feels a bit . . . heavy for a wedding."

But then to my surprise, Graham shakes his head.

"No, I think it's exactly right," he says. "It's a perfect representation of the city, and I think it will do wonders for reminding people what makes our hotel special." Graham turns to me, his mouth curving into a gracious smile, and I know he's understood my intentions. His gaze lingers on mine for a beat too long and my cheeks heat.

Trudy turns to beam at Graham. "We are so lucky to have you back home and helping us. In fact"—she pauses to flick an invisible piece of lint off her pant leg—"I think the two of you are more than equipped to handle the planning from here on out."

Graham and Claire open their mouths to protest, but Trudy holds up a hand to silence them. "I never intended to micromanage. This is your day after all. And it seems like you two have found your footing. To be honest, this is the perfect time for me to step back. I have a few trips coming up anyway."

Under normal circumstances, I'm thrilled when extended family decline to involve themselves in wedding planning. The phrase "too many chefs in the kitchen" isn't exclusive to restaurant work; overly involved families often means tears, drama, and general chaos. The worst is when different sides of the family battle for control, making calls without consulting one another and leaving vendors with dizzying, conflicting directives. But something about the idea of losing Trudy fills me with panic. Maybe it's because I've come to think of her as a shield. Her departure feels like stripping away the tough peel of an orange, exposing the tender, vulnerable flesh inside.

Claire shakes me out of my quiet panic.

"You deserve to relax," she says to Trudy. "We've got it under control here."

Trudy gives her a grateful smile. "Thank you, dear. You've always taken wonderful care of my grandson."

Claire gives Graham's forearm a squeeze and my eyes bore into the place where their skin touches. Heat rushes up my neck. I need some air.

I stand up too quickly, shoving my chair back with more force than I intended.

"You know what?" I say, as a thought mercifully dawns on me. "José mentioned that your pastry chef prepared a tray of gelato samplers as an alternate dessert option. Let me grab it so you can choose your flavors."

I'm aware of Graham's eyes on me as I head toward the kitchen, but don't dare to look back until I reach the metal doors.

Relief washes over me the minute I step into the gleaming, chrome kitchen. It may seem counterintuitive, but I always feel my calmest within the chaos of a bustling kitchen. The more energy that buzzes around me, the more energized I feel. Lexi used to call me an emotional vampire, but the truth is I'm just an extroverted extrovert. An ESFP personality, specifically, according to an online quiz I once took during a particularly long subway delay. A noisy kitchen will be especially helpful for drowning out my thoughts, which have been consumed of late by a certain British voice.

Alas, the kitchen is relatively quiet. The restaurant isn't open for dinner yet, so the reduced staff are at their individual stations, preparing their mise. José, who's standing by the staff exit dressed in his winter coat, looks up at me.

"Miss Rubin," he says, smiling warmly. "Is everything okay? Your face is all flushed." Even though we only met this month, we clicked instantly. Maybe it's because I become the best version of myself when I'm in the kitchen.

I return his smile. "Chef, please. Call me Ali," I remind him. "And everything is great. I was just wondering if I could grab the gelato samples?"

"Of course." He raises the pack of cigarettes in his hand and inclines his head toward the door. "I was just about to step out. Are you okay to grab them from the downstairs walk-in?"

"Definitely!" I reply. Honestly, I'm down for anything that will delay going back into the dining room and facing Graham.

The staircase leading to the kitchen's basement is ancient and narrow, the wooden stairs groaning beneath my weight. The walk-in freezer fills up most of the dimly lit space, and I take a deep breath when I step inside of it. A blast of cold air is exactly what I need to clear my head and shake off the prickly heat that seems to seep into my skin whenever I'm in the same room as Graham. A circumstance that fills me with self-loathing. I'm supposed to be a professional, for God's sake, not a tween girl with a crush. Then again, it would be a lot easier if he'd quit looking at me in that penetrating way, like he can see right into my soul.

After a quick scan, I locate the aluminum tray of gelato samples on the bottom right shelf. Lifting the lid, I inspect the neatly labeled samples before zeroing in on my favorite, the perfect love-match that is chocolate and hazelnut: gianduia. My favorite.

Carefully, I secure the lid and head back to the freezer door. But when I pull on the handle, it doesn't budge.

"What the . . . ," I mutter to myself. Setting the tray down, I grab the handle with both hands and pull harder. Nothing.

A cold trickle of sweat forms on my lower back. *Shit.* This can't be happening. My gaze drifts to the floor, where it locks on a small wooden wedge propped against the wall. A doorstop. The staff must realize the door sticks and use this to keep it from closing behind them. Information that would have been *significantly more helpful* before I got myself locked in here.

Darkness creeps into the edges of my vision as my heartbeat hammers in my ears. *Deep breaths, Ali.* This isn't the time to panic. There are half a dozen people upstairs, all of whom will notice I'm missing imminently. I'm not going to be stuck here forever.

As if my thoughts were audible, I hear the low echo of footsteps descending the stairs. Salvation!

I bang on the door with both fists. "Help! I'm stuck in here!"

A second later, the door cracks open and the cerulean eyes of my rescuer settle on me. *Of fucking course.*

"Nope," I say. "I've changed my mind. Leave me to perish."

Graham opens the door wider and takes a step toward me. I take one step back, maintaining the distance between us. He winces.

"You didn't come back. When I went into the kitchen to see what was going on, one of the chefs said you were down here."

"Yep. I was just testing out your freezer's potential for cryopreservation. Happy to report that conditions are optimal. Kindly resurrect me when we have a female president."

Graham bites down on his stupid, pillowy lip. *Fuck. Me.*

"Sorry to disappoint, but we're fresh out of liquid-nitrogen tanks. Sort of essential for preserving the body."

I groan. "Why is every man I meet so knowledgeable about corpses?"

Graham lifts his chin, his eyes pinning me in place. "What were you really doing down here?"

My palms turn damp under the intensity of his gaze. *Definitely not hiding from you,* my brain answers.

"I came to grab the desserts and the door locked behind me. But now that you've staged your heroic rescue, I'll just be on my way—"

"What do you mean? These freezers don't lock from the inside. Watch." He releases the door handle.

"No!" I shriek, lunging forward to grab it before it shuts. Too late. The door slams shut behind him, its taunting echo ringing in my ears.

I grab onto the handle and shove my body against it, twisting with my last ounce of strength. In a shocking turn of events, it doesn't budge. Dread pools in my belly.

"Huh? That's impossible." Graham's brows knit together. "There is no locking mechanism on the inner door actuator. I remember that from tagging along with the kitchen staff during their safety training when I was a kid."

"Oh, well, thank goodness. Did you hear that, Door? A man just said it isn't possible that you're locked! You may now release us." I give the handle another useless jiggle. "Wow, I'm stunned that didn't work. Maybe it only responds to masculine voices? Try commanding it in your soothing British baritone."

Graham squats, running a fingertip across the edges of the door before letting out a low growl. "Damn it. There's a bloody ice buildup around the frame." Rising back to standing, he drags a hand through his hair and lets out a weary sigh.

"This is exactly the kind of thing I was worried about," he mutters.

"What kind of thing was that, exactly? Getting the full Jack Dawson experience in your family's walk-in?"

Graham shakes his head glumly. "Things like this slipping through the cracks. These freezers require annual maintenance checks. My grandfather used to stay on top of all that stuff. But now that he's gone . . ." He trails off without finishing, looking so much like a forlorn little boy that I almost feel a pang of sympathy for him. Almost.

"Do you have your phone?" I ask. "I left mine in my purse."

Graham reaches into the back pocket of his jeans and extracts his cell phone with a look of triumph. But when he clicks on the screen, the corners of his mouth drop.

"No signal," he says.

"No service in our aluminum tomb? Classic." I can hear the hysteria starting to rise in my voice, and I take a deep breath, attempting to steady myself. "So, now what?"

Graham shrugs. "We wait. Someone will come find us eventually. I found you."

It's the word "eventually" that finally ignites the kindle of panic. The bottom of my stomach hollows out and a hot ripple snakes through my rib cage. Sucking in a cold breath, I begin pacing back and forth in the tiny space. Graham eyes me warily.

"Are you okay?" he asks.

"Peachy keen," I say a little too loudly. I swipe away the beads of sweat that are already starting to form on my upper lip. "Never been better."

Graham frowns. "You've worked in restaurants. Haven't you spent time in one of these freezers before?"

"It's not that," I grumble. "I just . . . don't like small spaces." There's more to the story, obviously, but it's not something I'm interested in unpacking with him of all people. But then Graham narrows his eyes and studies me with that penetrating gaze of his, and I know I'm not getting off that easily.

"Tell me," he says softly.

I quit my pacing and let out a resigned sigh. "Okay, fine. When I was a kid, I went to sleepaway camp every summer. There was a bus that took a group of us from Baltimore to the Poconos. One summer, I bet a few of my friends that I could fit inside the overhead compartment."

Graham shakes his head. "What is it with you and bets?"

I roll my eyes. "It seemed like no big deal at the time. An easy win. I was always the smallest kid in the grade, and my friend Olivia said I could keep her iPod Touch for the entire first week if I did it."

I pause for a beat before continuing. "Anyway, I fit in there easily. But then when I tried to get out, the sliding door got stuck. I was probably only in there for ten minutes before a counselor helped me out, but it felt like hours. Ever since then, I get claustrophobic in small, locked spaces."

I can still remember that moment so clearly. The way my chest tightened as I tugged fruitlessly at the handle before pounding my fists against the door. I could hear my friends laughing outside and realized they thought I was faking it as a joke. I was shaking and breathless by the time my counselor got the door unstuck, even though I forced out a laugh, pretending to have found the whole thing amusing. But the fear has stuck with me ever since.

I've been avoiding eye contact with Graham while recounting the story, but I finally allow myself a peek at his face. I almost expect him to be laughing, but his features have melted into an expression of sympathy. Which is worse, somehow.

"I'm so sorry," he says. "This must be really scary for you." But when I take a second to check in with myself, I realize the opposite is true. Talking about this with Graham seems to have melted all the tension from my body, and I no longer feel afraid. For some unfathomable reason, being with him makes me feel safe. And that might be the scariest thing of all.

"I'm okay," I say. But the last word comes out in a stutter, as my teeth begin to chatter. I rub my hands up and down my arms. "Emotionally, at least. Turns out freezers are pretty cold."

Graham's jaw ticks. Gaze still locked on mine, he grabs the hem of his sweater, pulling it over his head. The T-shirt he's wearing underneath rises, revealing a sliver of toned abdomen. My mouth goes dry as I catch a glimpse of the top of our mutual tattoo. He catches me staring and his cheeks go pink before he tugs the tee back over his exposed skin.

"Here. Take my jumper," he says gruffly, handing me the balled-up fabric.

I raise a disbelieving eyebrow. "Won't you be cold?"

Graham shakes his head. "I'll be fine."

I mutter a thanks and slip the fabric over my head. Graham's musky citrus scent fills my nostrils, and it takes a level of restraint I didn't know I possessed not to press my nostrils into the cotton. *Why does he have to smell this good?*

My pulse is racing and I'm no longer certain if it's solely due to panic. Suddenly desperate to put space between us, I begin pacing from one edge of the freezer to the other. I do my best to avoid eye contact with Graham, but I can feel his eyes tracing my movement.

"It's good that you're moving," he says, as he bounces up and down on his heels. "Maintaining your internal body temperature is crucial. And the best way to do that is keeping your heart rate up."

I shoot him my patented 360-degree eye roll. I don't need him to explain first aid; I was a certified lifeguard for two years of summer camp, thank you very much. Still, the way he's tightening his arms around himself highlights the lean muscles of his arms, and I find myself unable to tear my eyes away from the newly exposed skin.

I bite the inside of my cheek. I can think of plenty of ways I'd enjoy keeping my heart rate up with Graham right now, none of which are remotely appropriate.

My gaze slides up to Graham's face. Judging by how his own cheeks are flushed with color, it's clear he's thinking the same thing I am. Terrific. We're going to die in this walk-in and our final thoughts will be sinful fantasies involving each other's naked bodies while his unsuspecting fiancée waits upstairs. We are monsters.

I shiver again and Graham takes a step toward me.

"Is it okay if I put my arms around you?" he asks softly. "There isn't anything in here we can use for blankets, and you're obviously freezing."

I glare at him. "I'll pass, thanks."

Graham raises a brow. "You'd literally rather freeze to death than let me touch you."

"Correct."

He shakes his head. "It's going to be rather awkward when they discover our frozen corpses and realize we elected to freeze to death in solitude rather than seize our last chance for survival by preserving body heat."

I huff out a laugh. "Not as awkward as it's going to be when the coroner examines our corpses and realizes we have matching tattoos. Can you imagine the conspiracy videos that will flood the internet? It'll probably be the most popular episode of *60 Minutes* ever and I won't even get to see it. Now *that* is a tragedy."

A muffled sound escapes Graham's lips, and I notice he's trying to suppress a smile.

"Sorry, are you *laughing* right now?"

My words shake the rest of his grin loose.

"I can't help it. You're funny," he admits.

I shrug. "My lot in life. It's a blessing and a curse."

Graham takes a step toward me. "Please, Ali. Accept my platonic, exclusively-for-the-means-of-survival hug. For my grandmother's sake. Imagine how terrible the press coverage will be if I let you freeze to death on her property."

I purse my lips, considering. "Trudy is innocent in all of this."

Graham nods as he advances another step. "I'm sure it will only be a few more minutes until someone finds us, anyway. Just let me get you warm and then you can go back to your regularly scheduled loathing." He takes one more step forward and now he's standing directly in front of me.

My eyes trace a path up his neck, pausing to admire the sharp line of his jaw and his full, moody lips, before finally settling on those incredible blue eyes. He's scrutinizing me behind his glasses, and from this close up, I notice the little flecks of green encircling his pupils.

Graham takes a fortifying breath before wrapping one arm around me and then the other, pulling me tight against him until our chests are touching. Heat radiates from his body, warming me instantly, and I note the juxtaposition of the hard planes of his abdomen through the soft fabric of his sweater.

I swallow when he hooks his index finger under my chin and lifts my face upward. His breath skates over my lips.

"You're going to be okay," he says softly. "We're going to get out of here, and you're going to be okay."

I stare up at him, willing myself to summon hatred for this man. But the feeling never surfaces. Instead, my heart tugs against my sternum as a sense of comfort envelops me, warm and reassuring. Then again, one of the earliest signs of hypothermia is confusion and a lessened ability to think rationally. Check and check.

I know I should step back, put some much-needed space between us. But my body refuses to cooperate with my brain. Instead, it feels like we're being drawn closer to each other by some sort of magnetic force. His arms tighten around my waist, pulling me flush against him.

Without thinking, I slide my hands underneath the fabric of his shirt. Graham's breath hitches when I skate my fingertips against his back. Goosebumps rise on his skin at every point of contact.

He lowers his head and I feel myself rise onto my tiptoes, my body now moving of its own accord. The next stage of hypothermia must be starting to kick in, because my breath is coming out in sharp, labored bursts. Yet despite the many symptoms of impending death, I no longer feel cold at all. This is absolutely the end.

His lips are a fraction of an inch from my own now, our noses brushing against each other. My heart is slamming wildly against my rib cage.

"Ali," he says on an exhale. His eyes flutter shut for a moment. When he opens them again, there's a heat behind them that thaws every bit of lingering chill in my body and melts away every rational thought that tells me kissing him right now would be a terrible idea.

Just then, the freezer door flies open. Graham and I whip our heads around to see José standing in the doorway. His eyebrows shoot up to his hairline at the sight of us.

"Am I interrupting something?" he asks tentatively. His gaze drops to the place where my hands are still buried beneath Graham's shirt, and I yank them out as we simultaneously jump apart. I bite down on my lip as Graham surreptitiously adjusts his pants.

"Your freezer door sticks," I say at the exact same moment that Graham announces, "I need to call the freezer maintenance company." José's face falls.

"Shoot. We're all so used to it that I forgot to warn you."

"Don't worry about it, José," Graham says, his voice strained. "I'll take care of this immediately." Then he slips past him, hurrying up the cellar stairs.

José turns back to me, and I give him a small smile before stepping out of the freezer and into the blissfully warm basement. On the way back to the dining room, I slip the gianduia sample out of the tray and onto the prep counter for later. After the morning I've had, I deserve a treat.

It isn't until I step into the kitchen that I realize I'm still wearing Graham's sweater.

10

"I think you're really going to like The Natty Beaus." It's the second Sunday in October, and I've invited Claire and Graham to stop by the tail end of another client's reception to hear their band and see if they would be interested in hiring them. With such a short planning timeline, it's a simpler strategy than meeting with multiple performers. Plus, I'm excited to show off the affair we've planned for Miguel and Jeremiah, two English teachers who met in their Teach for America cohort. The Peabody Library is the perfect venue for a pair of book lovers. And of course, it's undeniably romantic.

Claire's bobbing her head to a Dua Lipa cover when her cell phone vibrates in her pocket. She frowns at it. "Hang on, I need to take this." She slips past us, disappearing through the doorway. Since Asha is otherwise engaged, making sure that departing guests receive their favors, that leaves me and Graham. Alone.

Graham jams his hands in his pockets and rocks back on his heels.

"I, um, wanted to thank you for what you did with the wedding menu. The way you came up with something that would foster our rebranding without explicitly letting on that you knew about it. That was kind of you."

I shrug. "Always receptive to feedback on my general awesomeness, but I'm just doing my job." I shift my weight between my feet. "Also, I left your sweater at the hotel's front desk."

I neglect to mention that I slept with it for three consecutive nights, pressing my nose against the soft fabric until I could no longer detect his citrus scent. That is classified information, known only by me and God.

"Oh. Thanks," Graham says. "I had completely forgotten about it." But he's staring at the ground when he says it, and my gut tells me he's lying.

The awkward tension in the air thankfully dissipates as Claire skips back over to us, her cheeks pink with excitement.

"Okay, that was one of the producers for Cash Castillo, and get this," she says, her words pouring out in a rush. "They want a writer with improv experience to perform in a couple of sketches with Cash, and they asked *me*. I need to get back to New York ASAP to start writing and filming a few pre-recorded segments for the upcoming season."

She pauses, biting down on her bottom lip before confessing the next part. "Since it will mean putting extra hours on top of my regular day job, I'm going to have to stay in New York for the next few weekends."

Graham's brow furrows, but he doesn't say anything. True to form, I jump to fill in the silence.

"I mean, wow. That's amazing, but . . . what about planning? Your wedding is only twelve weeks away," I protest.

"I know it's not ideal," Claire says. "But this is an incredible opportunity. Besides, you guys will be *fine*. I mean, you were such a dynamic duo during the tasting the other day. You've got things under control here."

Realization finally dawns on me, turning my blood cold. With Claire gone, Graham and I will be planning this wedding alone. No, not alone. *Alone together.* This can't be happening.

"How many weekends are we talking?" Graham finally asks, and I'm not sure which of us is more afraid to hear the answer. My brain is already spiraling. But I mean, how long can filming a few skits take? A weekend? Two, tops? We've already scheduled most of our appointments on Saturdays and Sundays to accommodate her time in New York. I'm sure we can push back a couple of our upcoming meetings until she returns. It won't be ideal with such a short timeline, but we can make it work.

Claire grimaces again. "Four."

No. Absolutely not. There is no way I am going to spend the next month alone with Graham. Well, not completely alone, I guess. Thank goodness for Asha.

Graham pales. He seems as disconcerted as I am to lose the buffer Claire has unwittingly provided during our previous meetings. Or maybe he's just upset to be apart from his fiancée. Four weeks is a long time to be apart from the love of your life. Plus, Claire is cool as hell; I wouldn't want to spend time away from her either. At the same time, I can see that he's reluctant to discourage her from an opportunity she's clearly thrilled about.

Still, he manages a weak smile that doesn't reach his eyes. "Congratulations," he says finally. "This is going to be great."

"Thanks, Teddy." A wide grin stretches across her face as she throws her arms around him.

I turn away to give the two of them privacy, my chest tightening at the memory of Graham holding me like that in the freezer. Pulling out my phone as a distraction, I see there's a new message in my group chat with Lexi and Chloe. Chloe's sent us a link to an article about a new reality dating show called *Ready to Mingle* that features a gaggle of D-list celebrities. I grin when I see her least favorite client's handsome face at the top of the page.

Chloe: Over/under odds that Chad is the first to be voted out?

Lexi: Depends on how soon he whips out his scrotum piercing

Chloe: Thanks for unearthing that repressed memory

Lexi: 👿 🤮

Lexi: Or maybe he'll find true love at last, like an Ashley on Bachelor in Paradise.

Chloe: . . .

Chloe: I could work with that.

Ali: Please don't ask me to plan the wedding.

I grin as I drop my phone back into my purse. I can't help but love Chad, a former *Bachelorette* contestant and the bane of Chloe's existence. There's so much vacant space in the man's brain I'm surprised a Spirit Halloween hasn't moved in. His heart's always in the right place, though.

I turn back to my clients and notice Graham is standing there alone, staring intently at his phone.

"Where's Claire?" I ask.

Graham glances up and looks around, brow furrowed as though he's just noticed she's no longer beside him.

"Oh, uh. She headed out so she could start packing." The air feels tense, and I can't decide if it's because he's upset with Claire for taking so little interest in their wedding, or he's worried about the extra solo time he'll now spend with me.

I clear my throat. "Will this be okay? Working together without her?"

"Of course." Graham nods quickly but doesn't meet my eye. "Besides, we still have Asha." He drops his eyes back to his phone screen. "Listen, I've got a client call soon, so I've got to run. Shoot me a text to let me know when our next meeting is?" And with that, he departs, leaving me alone at the edge of the dance floor.

"Now remember this order: sweet, sour, seal, and sticker."

Two nights later, my mom, grandma, and I are gathered around the navy-blue island in my sister's immaculate transitional-style kitchen, candy and packing supplies arranged in tidy piles in front of us. Sarah summoned us here to stuff favor bags for Jackson's Bar Mitzvah, and true to character, she has plotted out the task with military precision.

"Back up: what comes after sour again?" I ask.

My mother tsks. "Ali, leave your sister alone."

"No can do," I shrug. "As the youngest child, it's my duty to be as annoying as possible at all times."

I attempt to shoot a good-natured grin at Sarah, but she's bent over the countertop, brow furrowed as she surveys the rainbow-hued stash. My sister can normally handle anything without breaking a sweat, but tonight, her shoulders seem uncharacteristically tense.

"You know, you could have hired a party planner to do this. Saved yourself some trouble." I put a hard emphasis on the words "party planner," since I'm still annoyed that she declined to hire Antoine Williams Events, or anyone for that matter. My big sister thinks she can do everything herself, and normally she can. But she's only one person, and she already has a lot on her plate. I sometimes worry that she's going to crack under all the self-imposed pressure. Besides, I *want* to help her. It would be nice if for once, she wanted my support, instead of the other way around.

"Give me one more second to set up. I want to film this for TikTok," she murmurs. She reaches up to fiddle with the ring light on her tripod, then swings her full attention back to us.

"Okay, I'm going to model this one more time." She holds up one of the game controller–shaped treat boxes like she's a flight attendant performing a safety demonstration.

"First, sweet." She dumps a spoonful of jelly beans into the box. "Then sour." She adds a scoop of sour gummy candy. "Then seal and sticker." She folds the box closed, tucking the lid into the base, and sealing it with the sticker that reads "I Leveled Up at Jackson's Bar Mitzvah."

"There you go. Easy peasy."

"Sour, seal, sticker, sweet. Got it," I say.

My mom shoots me a warning look as she picks up a box.

"Are you sure it doesn't make sense to work as an assembly line?" she asks my sister.

Sarah shakes her head. "I think it will look better on camera to have our hands crisscrossing. Intergenerational activities are very trendy right now. Besides, everyone works at their own pace, and I'm sure I'll pack faster than the rest of you. This is the most efficient way."

She twists the camera in our direction, positioning the screen over the countertop.

"Okay, you guys can start. Make sure your hands look enthusiastic," she directs.

My mom opens her mouth. Then, thinking the better of it, snaps it shut again. With a resigned sigh, she starts filling her box with a spoonful of jelly beans.

"So, Ali," she says, turning her attention to me. "You never told us how your date with Brad went the other night. Are you going to be seeing each other again?"

I swap the sour and sweet piles, then tug a sticker off the sheet and adhere it to the center of my forehead.

"Sadly, that relationship bit the dust," I say. "Gone and buried. A total dead end." My sister groans, then switches the piles back without skipping a beat.

"It never gets easier," Bubbie laments. "I had a date with a fellow last week, and he stood me up!"

My mom looks aghast. "You didn't tell me that."

Bubbie shrugs. "I was mad at first. But he turned out to have a good excuse. Poor schmuck dropped dead."

"Mom!" My mother looks horrified. "That's awful!"

Bubbie shrugs. "Eh, we're old. It happens."

I give Bubbie's shoulder a conciliatory rub. "Men. Just when you thought you'd heard all the excuses."

Bubbie nods in agreement. "It's his loss. Now he's going to miss my big birthday blowout."

Bubbie is celebrating her ninetieth birthday in March, and unlike some people (*cough* Sarah), she asked me to plan the event for her. The details are still hazy since my mom nixed Bubbie's suggestion of having the party at a casino. But I'm excited to start planning as soon as I put Graham and Claire's wedding behind me.

I switch the sticker and jelly bean piles before beginning another box.

Sarah steps behind her phone to replay what she's filmed and lets out a disgruntled sound.

"Mom, you have to stop moving at glacial speed," she laments. "Ali, take that sticker off your forehead. And Bubbie, quit eating the inventory."

Bubbie shrugs as she pops another jelly bean into her mouth. "I'm starving. There's nothing to eat around here."

"I assembled a vegan charcuterie board," Sarah protests, gesturing toward the untouched platter of olive tapenade and gluten-free crackers.

Bubbie glances dubiously at the spread. "Like I said."

"Oh shit," I say. "Turns out I've been doing sour before sweet this entire time. I'm going to have to start all over."

Sarah presses her fingertips to her temple. "You guys are the worst."

I peel another sticker off the sheet.

"You know what they say," I tell her as I stick it to the front of her shirt. "You get what you pay for."

11

I manage to avoid Graham for the rest of the month, but since our tight planning schedule requires an expedited timeline, we're due to meet at Sugar Babies Bakery the first Monday in November for a cake tasting. Even though Claire said she was happy to let us take creative direction for most of the wedding planning, I firmly believe that choosing cake is a very personal decision, so there was no way I could sign off on just picking one for them.

I've just parallel parked—expertly, I might add—when my phone buzzes with an incoming text. Glancing down at the screen, I see Asha's name. Dread pools in my belly as I read her message.

> Was up all night with Ravi, who was puking his guts out. No way I'll make it to the cake tasting. Sorry to leave you flying solo, but you'll be fine! Food is your thing!

I feel like I might hurl myself. The thought of being alone with Graham turns my palms slick. Especially after his guest-starring appearance in last night's R-rated dream. We were back in the basement freezer, lips molded together, his fingers knotted through my hair. His tongue urgently explored my mouth as we stumbled backward into shelves, sending cans of food rolling onto the floor. He dragged his lips down the column of my throat, teeth grazing the tender skin. I could still feel the phantom heat of his breath on my skin when I woke up this morning. I have a sudden urge to pull out of the parking spot, leave the state, burn off my fingerprints, and start a new life.

Pull yourself together, I tell myself. *You are a strong, capable woman. Your sexual attraction to this man is not going to get in the way of your promotion. You can do this.*

But can I? Can I sit here and casually watch him lick frosting off his plump, porn star lips like I'm not a person who hasn't had sex in three months? It's possible that my vagina has hermetically sealed from lack of usage. And what if this is just the first of several wedding errands we have to run together? I mean, how long does the stomach bug last? And what on earth am I supposed to do in the meantime?

Closing my eyes, I try to imagine what Chloe would say if she was here. Most likely, she'd start by leveling me with one of her trademark, no-nonsense expressions. Then she'd tell me to take a deep breath, pull it together, and go eat some dessert in an unerotic fashion. And as usual, she'd be right.

Resolved, I nod to myself, take a deep, steadying breath, and exit the car.

When I step into the bakery, I'm greeted with the inviting aroma of vanilla and freshly risen dough. It's a scent combination I normally find comforting, but today, it does nothing to soothe my jitters.

I sense Graham before I see him, goosebumps sprouting on my forearms, and a second later I spot him sitting at one of the small round tables, looking ridiculously attractive in a crisp navy suit over an ice-blue button-down. The first thought my treacherous brain emits is that there's no way we'll ever find a cake topper that adequately captures his hotness. *Fuck my life.*

Graham is restlessly drumming his fingertips on the tabletop, his eyes darting around the bakery. When they land on me, he draws his hand quickly into his lap and straightens.

"Good morning," I say. I put on my most professional voice and hope it masks the butterflies in my stomach. "Thanks for meeting me here. Hope you're ready to taste some cake!" I cringe internally. I sound like I'm reading cue cards.

"Morning." Graham's eyes dart around the mostly empty space. "Uh . . . shouldn't we wait for Asha?" he asks.

I exhale slowly, forcing a pleasant smile on my face.

"Asha isn't coming. Her kid has a stomach bug. And based on what I know about how stomach bugs travel through my sister's house, it could be days before we see her again."

"So, it's just us?" he asks. Graham's brows knit together, which has the unpleasant effect of making him even more attractive. Everything he does has the unpleasant effect of making him more attractive.

"Just us," I confirm.

Graham clears his throat and a long beat of silence passes.

"Oh, I have something for you," he says, reaching into his jacket pocket and extracting an envelope. He hands it to me.

"What is it?"

"Our next payment for your services."

Studying the envelope, I raise an eyebrow.

"Did you address this with a typewriter?"

"Gran keeps one in her office. What can I say? I love old-fashioned things."

"Listen, I appreciate your grandmother's Emily Gilmore energy. I fully expect all her correspondence to be elegantly hand-lettered, with ink sourced from the estate sale of a founding father. But I regret to inform you that the only people who address letters with a typewriter are the ones mailing anthrax."

Graham presses his lips together tightly but doesn't respond.

"Thank goodness you included your return address," I continue. "Otherwise, I might have suspected the sender was Alfred Hitchcock, or perhaps the teenage girls who revealed Deep Throat's identity."

"Are you finished?" he asks.

"Nearly," I say. "Just one final question. Why bother with a typewriter at all? Were you unable to send a telegram on such short notice?"

Graham closes his eyes and draws his fingertips across his forehead, like he's trying to ward off a headache. "Do you maintain this level of professionalism with all your clients?"

I shake my head. "Definitely not. You're getting the VIP treatment. Keep an eye on the mail for your free tote bag."

Graham glares at me across the table. Thankfully, the tension is dispelled when the door to the kitchen swings open and a bakery employee makes his way over to us. He places two aluminum trays on the table, one containing small squares of cake and the other tiny plastic bowls full of icing. Each component is neatly labeled.

The bakery employee, who can't be a day older than eighteen, pushes a lock of curly brown hair out of his eyes and grins at us. "Who's ready for cake?" he asks.

"Oh shoot, they've neglected to include a rum pudding flavor," I lament. "Now what will you choose?"

Graham smirks at me. "I've never tried rum pudding, believe it or not."

"Scandalous! Did the Windsor family ban it from the royal residence or something?"

"You guys are adorable," the employee says, his grin widening. "Congrats on your wedding!"

"No, we're not—" I protest at the exact same time that Graham says, "She isn't—" But the employee is already headed back into the kitchen.

Awesome.

I pick up a fork as I survey the options, and Graham raises an eyebrow. "I didn't realize you were also tasting."

"The audacity of that suggestion," I say. "You think I'm just going to sit here and watch you enjoy delicious cake?"

"That's fair," he concedes, as he picks up his own fork. In perfect synchronicity, we both reach for the crimson cake at the center of the tray.

"I didn't take you for a red velvet person," I say, impressed.

Graham smirks. "Well, you know what they say about making assumptions."

He dips his fork into the sample, and I watch as it disappears behind his lips, my eyes glued to the pulse of his throat. He lets out a low hum of pleasure as he swallows, and I have a sudden, overwhelming urge to lean forward and trace the curve of his Adam's apple with my tongue.

Clearing my throat, I make a desperate attempt to change the subject.

"So, how's it going at the hotel? Do you feel like you've been able to help?"

Graham brightens. "I do, actually. My first job out of uni was with a firm that specialized in marketing and rebranding, so I've been able to use the skills I developed there. There are so many small things that can make a big difference: modernizing our advertising, redistributing the budget, tapping into community resources. I've always enjoyed helping failing businesses turn things around, so this has been a real passion project. I know the Black-Eyed Susan can be as great as it once was. All it needs is a bit of love and a fresh pair of eyes."

The glow that's spread across his features as he speaks makes him look a decade younger, and I catch a momentary glimpse of the boy I met playing Kings in a London bar. Then a thought occurs to me.

"You said before that you do most of your consulting work remotely. Why do you have to be in Baltimore to help with the hotel?"

Graham scrubs an uneasy hand across the back of his neck, and I can tell I've struck a nerve.

"I suppose I don't *technically* have to be here. Although I do think there's something to be said for hands-on work."

I raise an eyebrow, and a small, shy smile forms in the corners of his mouth.

"Okay, fine. The truth is, I spent most of my summers here as a kid but haven't been back much since. By the time I was a teenager, I mostly wanted to spend term breaks with my friends. My mom has never been keen on visiting, so she didn't push it. But I've missed this place. Baltimore has always felt like a home away from home. So, when I saw an opportunity to make myself useful here, I ran with it."

"Hmm." I reach for the chocolate with raspberry jam, my fork clanking against Graham's as he aims for the same piece.

"You're doing this on purpose!" I protest.

"I swear I'm not," he laughs. Our eyes lock, and a pleasant shiver runs down my spine. Graham, ever the gentleman, gestures for me to take the first bite of cake, and I scoop it into my mouth, savoring the perfectly complementary flavors. If this was my wedding, this is the combination I'd choose.

"Besides," Graham continues, dipping his own fork into the cake. "My grandparents did so much for me growing up. My mom was so reluctant to ask for support, but I know they helped her out anyway, especially with my schooling. I want to repay them, and this feels like the right way to do it." There's a tiny smudge of frosting in the corner of his mouth, and I instinctively reach forward to brush it away with my thumb. Graham freezes and I feel my cheeks turn hot. I start to pull my hand away, but Graham wraps his fingers around my wrist, holding it in place. We stare at each other for a beat before he murmurs something inaudible and releases me. The heat from my face spreads down my neck and across my chest.

I pull away, leaning back against my chair and sucking in a huge gulp of air in an attempt to clear the shrouding fog of lust.

"So. Have you made a decision?" I manage. Graham's eyes are wild and questioning when they connect with mine.

"About the cake," I clarify. "Or did you want to check in with Claire?"

An odd look crosses Graham's face at the mention of his fiancée, as if he'd completely forgotten about her.

"Oh, Claire. Right. She doesn't like cake. So, it's up to me."

"She doesn't like cake?" I faux gasp. "Just when I thought the woman had no flaws."

Graham doesn't offer the smile I'd be hoping for.

"No one's perfect," he says quietly, holding my gaze. Then he blinks rapidly, dispelling the tension.

"Let's go with the chocolate-raspberry. It seems like it would be a crowd-pleaser," he says.

I nod, slipping back into business mode and forcing myself not to swoon at the way he pronounces the word "chocolate."

"Definitely. I'll get that order in for you."

I glance out the window. "I should be getting back to the office. I have some things to wrap up and it's calling for bad weather tonight."

"That's wild. It was in the sixties yesterday," Graham says.

"Yeah, well, welcome to Baltimore in November. I know you've mostly been here in the warmer months, but the change-of-season weather will give you whiplash." I offer him a polite smile as I gather my things.

"I'll check in later about our upcoming appointment. Hopefully Asha will be back by then."

Graham nods, his expression revealing nothing. "Take care, Ali."

12

It takes longer than I anticipated to wrap things up at the office, and by the time I head out at seven, the snow is falling rapidly. There's already an inch coating the ground, and the temperature has plummeted since I was last outside a few hours ago. A gust of cold air slashes my skin, and I thrust my hands into my pockets, digging for gloves, before realizing that, naturally, I'd forgotten them on my desk. My fingers are red and stiff when I reach my car, and it takes me a few extra seconds to fumble with the lock.

My cell phone starts vibrating the second I close the door behind me. *Babs Cell.* She's already called twice in the past hour, and I'm struggling to keep the impatience out of my voice when I pick up.

"I'm on my way now," I say without preamble. Even before she responds, I can sense my mom's anxiety over the line.

"I-83 will be a mess," she says after a beat. "The forecast keeps getting worse and I doubt they've salted the roads. Drive safely."

"I will. See you soon." I drop the phone onto the seat. But a sense of foreboding has already crept in, and by the time I reach the entrance to the highway ramp, my worst fears are realized. There's a stretch of stopped cars as far ahead as I can see, the trail of red taillights indicating that traffic has come to a standstill. Somewhere ahead, a driver is leaning against their car horn, as though honking will magically fix everything.

I let out a groan of frustration. Why is this city so ill-equipped to handle bad weather? Two years ago, it snowed fourteen inches in New York, and everyone simply carried on, conducting business as usual. Here, all it takes is a dusting of snow to completely shut down the city.

Thirty minutes later, I'm still crawling up the highway, having only advanced two exits. My stomach lets out a low rumble of complaint. I wasn't hungry after the cake tasting so I skipped dinner, but suddenly I'm famished. I'm about to reach across the seat to dig inside my purse for a granola bar when a beeping sound draws my attention to the dashboard. Glancing over, I notice the gas light is illuminated. *Shit.* I had meant to stop for gas before heading home tonight, but in my hurry to beat the snowstorm, I'd completely forgotten.

Grimacing, I plug my parents' address into my GPS. According to Maps, I'm a little over eight miles away from their house. I should be able to make it there, though. Right?

But when I've barely moved an inch after another fifteen minutes have passed, I'm low-key panicking. There's no way I'm going to make it home if I don't stop for gas, and at least once I'm off the highway, I can take back roads home. It isn't ideal in this weather, but it will have to do.

Somehow, I manage to switch over to the right lane and onto the exit ramp. According to my GPS, there's a gas station half a mile away. But I've only made it about a minute down the road when I hear a sputtering from the engine. Miraculously, I make it to the side of the road before the car dies completely.

"*Fuck,*" I exhale, smacking the steering wheel with my palm. Closing my eyes, I lean back against the headrest as I mentally scroll through my options. I could try for an Uber but who knows how long it would take to reach me in this weather? It makes a lot more sense to call someone who is already nearby.

I reach for my phone, ready to text Asha, before remembering her family is quarantined with a stomach bug. *Double fuck.* Who else lives around here? So many of my friends lived downtown when I was in my early twenties, but now most of them have moved to the suburbs. For the first time, it occurs to me how lonely I am in a city that's been home for most of my life.

My gut turns over as I realize there's one person I can call. And despite how much I really, really don't want to call him, I can't help but remember the way he talked me off the edge during the freezer incident. Something about his presence eradicated the panic that normally accompanies claustrophobia. And right now, I'm desperate to feel that relief again.

No, what am I thinking? I am not some sort of damsel who needs to be rescued by a knight in shining armor, no matter how piercingly blue said knight's eyes might be. I am a strong, independent woman who has been taking care of herself for years. I've never relied on a man before and I'm sure as hell not about to start now.

I've just resolved to get out and walk to the gas station when someone knocks on my window. The unexpected sound makes me jump, and when I look through the glass, three guys are peering back at me. No, peering isn't the right word. Leering feels a lot more accurate.

One of them takes a swig from a bottle in a brown paper bag. Another guy in a knit cap takes a step closer to the car and bends to meet my eyes.

"Car trouble?" he smirks, and I immediately feel a prickle of fear. But if there's anything I've learned from living in New York City, the one best way to ward off scary people is by making yourself even scarier.

"'Tis winter solstice, and I am preparing my cone of power to praise the gods. Spirits of air, earth, water, and fire, we thank thee! In this hour of greatest darkness, the light shall be reborn!" Then I bang on my dashboard and chant loudly, "The light shall be reborn! The light shall be reborn!"

The smirk melts off the guy's face and he murmurs something to his friends, who back away slowly and then scramble off so quickly that one of them slips and falls on the ice-covered street.

With a resigned sigh, I call Graham. He picks up on the second ring.

"Hey," he says, sounding a bit confused. "Did I forget we had an evening appointment?"

"Um, no. It's nothing like that," I say. "I just . . . wanted to see what you were up to?"

Graham is quiet for a moment. "What's going on?" he asks, his voice low and laced with concern. "Is everything okay?"

"Everything's great!" I say, attempting to ignore the way my voice cracks a bit on the last word. "It's just, um . . . well. I'm still downtown. Traffic was bad so I pulled off the highway and then I . . . sort of ran out of gas." I squeeze my eyes closed tightly as the embarrassing confession rolls off my tongue. Graham is silent for a minute, and I wait for him to start laughing. I mean, I would if I were him. I'm his wedding planner; I should be one of the most organized people in his life right now, not some walking disaster who can't even manage to keep her gas tank filled. But the laughter doesn't come. Instead, his tone is gruff.

"Where are you?"

"A few feet off the Cold Spring Lane exit."

Graham exhales and relief floods his voice. "Okay, you're not far from me. I'm house-sitting my grandmother's place in Roland Park while she's visiting a friend in Arizona. Drop me a pin and I'll come pick you up."

By the time Graham arrives fifteen minutes later, I'm visibly shivering, since no gas also means no heat.

Graham seems to have anticipated this. He appears with a plaid blanket in hand and wraps it around me as soon as I step out of the car. The plush fabric carries a hint of his now-familiar scent—a mix of warm spices and citrus—and I somehow resist the urge to bury my face in it.

"Thanks," I mumble instead. I feel my face heat with mortification, both for the embarrassment of my current circumstances and gratitude for his kindness, despite the way I treated him this afternoon.

"Should we, um—go to the gas station and fill up one of those plastic buckets of gas? I've never actually had to do this before."

Graham shakes his head. "You're freezing, and there's no way traffic on the highway is clearing up anytime soon. Let's go back to the house for a bit, and once the snow stops, we'll get everything sorted."

There's something about his presence, steady and calm and capable, that puts me at ease, and I feel the tension drain from my limbs. I nod and allow Graham to lead me to his car.

"Thank you," I say quietly once we've clipped our seat belts. "This is so kind of you . . . especially after the way I acted today." And then, to my complete and absolute horror, I feel a single, hot tear trickle down the side of my face.

Graham plucks a tissue from a travel holder in his door and hands it to me wordlessly. The kindness of the gesture pushes me over the edge, and I dissolve into loud, deeply unsexy sobs.

"Oh, God," I choke out. "Could this be any more embarrassing?"

Graham places one hand over mine, and my skin tingles at the point of contact.

"Hey, don't be so hard on yourself. These things happen," he says softly.

My head drops back against the seat rest and I close my eyes. But embarrassment has loosened every insecurity I've kept buried and suddenly I'm helpless to stop it from spilling out of me.

"I can't believe I thought leaving the restaurant world for event planning was a good idea. My family was right—I'm too fickle, too impulsive, to ever be successful in this field. I'm not even organized enough to keep a full tank of gas in my car."

Graham is quiet for a moment, and when he speaks again, his voice is strained. "They said that?"

"Not in so many words, but that was the gist."

Graham cuts me a sidelong glance and I notice he's clutching the steering wheel so hard that his knuckles have gone white.

"They're wrong," he says tightly. "You're incredible at what you do. You have an instinct for the way all the pieces fit together. The way you came up with a menu that would both satisfy guests and highlight the hotel? That takes talent. Not only that, but despite how uncomfortable you are working with me, you keep showing up every day. And I respect the hell out of you for it."

His words knock the wind right out of me, the compliments seeping through my veins like honey.

"Thanks," I say quietly. The mention of my parents reminds me that I need to call my mother. I fire off a quick text to her, letting her know that traffic is terrible, so I'm spending the night downtown with a friend. Her reply comes through almost instantly.

LOVE YOU. Be safe. See you in the morning.

I feel a pang of guilt knowing that she's been sitting with her phone in her hand, waiting to hear from me. But at least she'll be able to sleep tonight. It will probably be late when I get home, but with luck, I should be able to slip in without bothering her.

As for staying safe? Given the way his Graham-specific scent is filling the car, I'm increasingly less confident in my capacity for self-preservation.

A moment later, the car slows, and the hulking silhouette of Trudy's house comes into view.

"Um, wow?" I say as we pull into the driveway. I anticipated that Trudy would have a lovely home—after all, the Black-Eyed Susan was wildly profitable in its heyday—but the house before me exceeds all expectations. The Colonial-style estate is as classic and elegant as its mistress, an enormous, redbrick affair trimmed with stately white columns. Black shutters frame the windows like eyelashes. Graham turns off the ignition and turns to face me.

"Before we go in, I should warn you about Genevieve."

Fully warmed now, I release my grip on the blanket, allowing it to puddle around me.

"And Genevieve is . . . your grandmother's stern and intensely loyal housekeeper who fertilizes the grass with the bodies of guests who didn't appreciate her freshly squeezed lemonade?"

Graham's lips twitch. "Not quite. She's my grandmother's King Charles spaniel. The breed is supposed to be sweet and lovable, but as far as I can tell, she hates all living creatures except Granny. I spend most of my time here avoiding her wrath."

"Well, no worries. I love dogs."

Graham grimaces. "Genevieve isn't a dog. She's a hell-beast who escaped the underworld." Nevertheless, he opens the door and I follow him across the well-manicured path to the front porch.

The house is dark and silent when we step inside. But a moment later, I hear a low snarl echoing through the hallway. Graham flicks on the lights to reveal a fluffy white canine with caramel spots standing in the middle of the wooden floor. She looks like a stuffed animal, apart from the narrowed eyes and bared fangs.

"Avoid eye contact and mind your ankles." Graham's voice has dropped to a conspiratorial whisper. "She seems to have developed an affinity for the taste of blood."

Ignoring him, I walk toward Genevieve and crouch down in front of her.

"Hey, pretty lady," I say softly. "Do you want some pets?"

Genevieve glares at me for a minute. But then she trots over slowly and rests her chin on my knee. I rub a hand over the top of her head, then drag it down the soft fur of her back. When I glance over my shoulder, Graham's mouth is hanging ajar.

"Have I gone mad?" he asks incredulously. "She won't even let me feed her. I have to put the food in her dish and then flee the room before she attacks."

I shrug. "What can I say? I'm universally beloved."

"So it seems." An amused smile plays on his lips. "Well, now that you've bypassed Satan's lap dog, let's get you sorted. I can put on some tea."

"No tea for me, thanks. I've never warmed to the taste of dirty water."

Graham shakes his head ruefully.

"Right, then. I think I can rustle up some coffee." He glances out the window. "It's still coming down pretty hard. Looks like we might be stuck here for a while. We could . . . watch a film?"

"Sure," I say, though the word is nearly drowned out by the low growl of my stomach.

"Sorry," I apologize. "I never had dinner."

Graham's forehead creases with concern.

"You haven't eaten?" he confirms. I shake my head.

"We'll need to rectify that immediately." He yanks open the refrigerator, then glances back at me apologetically.

"Granny left the fridge stocked, but I'm not much of a cook. We've got plenty of eggs. Can I offer you a cheese omelet?"

I grin at him. "Lucky for you, I'm a classically trained chef. Mind if I look around?"

Graham steps aside and I peer inside the fridge. Then I move through the kitchen, examining the contents of the fridge and pulling open kitchen cabinets to see what's inside.

"Wow," I say, as I survey the contents of the spice drawer. "Is there anything left in the Whole Foods spice department?"

Graham smiles. "My grandmother is an enthusiastic purveyor of seasoning."

I extract a glass jar container of ground, green leaves. "*Za'atar*? Okay, Trudy." I turn and fix my gaze on Graham. "Serious question: do I have your permission to take over this kitchen?"

"I would be honored," he says sincerely.

"Excellent. You are in for a treat," I say, as I begin pulling ingredients out from the cabinet.

Fifteen minutes later, my creation is sizzling on the stove. Graham pads back into the kitchen. He attempted to take Genevieve out for a walk, but after taking one look at the slush-covered lawn outside, she declined to leave the house and opted for pee pads in the laundry room instead.

After washing his hands in the sink, Graham takes a gratuitous inhale. "Wow, that smells incredible," he says. "What are you making?"

He's only a few feet away, and when I turn to look up at his face, I'm once again confronted with the dazzling blue of his eyes. My heart presses itself tightly against my sternum. *Careful, Ali.* I clear my throat, collecting myself.

"Shakshuka. It's essentially eggs baked in a tomato and bell pepper sauce, with all kinds of seasoning. Traditionally served as breakfast, but like most breakfast foods, it's even better at night." I hold up the spice jar. "And a dusting of za'atar is the secret ingredient."

"Happy we could oblige."

I wipe my hands on a dish towel. "This needs to simmer for another few minutes and the garlic bread is still in the oven. Want to pick out something on Netflix while we wait?"

Graham jams his hands into his pockets and rocks back on his heels. "Yeah, my grandmother doesn't subscribe to any streaming services. She's committed to watching films the old-fashioned way."

"Seems on brand," I agree.

I follow him into the living room, and he opens the cabinet under the television to reveal a meticulously organized collection of DVDs and VHS tapes. I lean closer, brushing my fingertips against the spines and pausing when I get to some familiar titles. *Beauty and the Beast. Aladdin. The Little Mermaid.*

"Were your grandparents big fans of the Disney Renaissance?" I ask. Color floods Graham's cheeks and he shoves his glasses up his nose. "Those are mine. From my summers here when I was a kid."

"That's so cute! Which is your favorite? Your favorite Disney movie says a lot about a person, so I really want you to think carefully before answering."

Graham skims the titles and then pulls a particularly battered-looking case off the shelf. He holds it out to me.

"*The Fox and the Hound*?" I gasp. "You're lying. No one's favorite movie is *The Fox and the Hound.* It is objectively Disney's most boring film."

"How dare you. It's a touching story of friendship between two creatures who are pressured by society into being adversaries."

"I'm forced to note the irony that your favorite movie is a snoozefest about dogs, yet you don't seem to care much for Genevieve."

"Again, Genevieve is not a dog. And I must insist you show some respect when discussing one of Disney's greatest cinematic achievements."

I shake my head. "If you say so. I've never managed to stay awake through the whole thing, Benedict, but maybe you'll be able to change my mind."

Graham's eyes twinkle with amusement. "So, we're back to Benedict, then?"

"Your movie selection speaks volumes," I reply. "Though it is, admittedly, in character." Just then, the kitchen timer dings. "Why don't you turn it on while I plate dinner? At least the spices will be stimulating."

A few minutes later, we're sitting side by side on the tartan sofa, scooping up bites of shakshuka with garlic bread.

"Wow," Graham says. "This is incredible."

"Why, thank you," I say. "It's the perfect weather for it too." We both glance out the window. Outside, the mixture of snow and ice is falling heavier than ever. Neither one of us says it, but it's looking less likely that I'll be leaving here any time soon.

Thirty minutes into the film, I am forced to admit that I am hooked by the story. When the hound's owner is hit by a train, I slap a hand across my mouth, though I'm surprised by the sound of a muffled whimper. It's upsetting of course, but I didn't think I was crying. That's when I realize the sound isn't coming from me. Turning my head, I see Graham's face is streaked with tears.

"Oh my God, are you *weeping*?" I ask incredulously. "Aren't you supposed to be British? Is this even allowed?"

Graham chokes out a wet sound. "Chief was chasing Tod," he protests. "The fox and the hound's friendship is now in total disarray." His face is inches from mine, his damp eyes so breathtakingly blue behind the frames of his glasses. The sight of it sends me hurling back in time, the memory of him looking at me the same way all those years ago now imprinted upon the present. And with a flicker of horror, I realize that I am overwhelmed with renewed affection for this man. We're sitting so close to each other that when he shifts, his denim-clad thigh brushes against mine, sending a spark of electricity up my leg.

His gaze snags on mine, and the air whooshes from my chest. My body pulls toward him like it's being drawn by magnetic force. His gaze drops to my mouth. And the world comes to a standstill.

I'm not sure which of us moves first. But a moment later, I'm clutching the nape of his neck, and his hands are at my waist. And like a collision you see coming but are powerless to stop, our lips crash into each other.

13

For a moment, we are completely still, mouths locked together, as my brain struggles to catch up. But then our lips come alive, and my body ignites like a gas stovetop. His hands reach forward, catching my face between his palms, and when his tongue parts my lips, I let out an involuntary groan. Graham's hands drop to my waist, and he drags me into his lap. I wrap my legs around his hips to straddle him and rock myself hard against him, savoring the delicious friction of his jeans. His body responds immediately, his excitement evident through the hard length of him straining against the denim as he pulls me flush against him. I rake my hands through his hair as his fingertips sweep up my back, leaving behind hot sparks in every place he's touched me.

Then without warning, Graham pulls away so suddenly that I fall backward against the sofa cushions. He stares at me wild-eyed, his pupils blown out so far that his blue eyes look nearly black. His chest rises and falls unsteadily as breath escapes his bruised lips in ragged, shallow bursts.

"I'm sorry. I'm so sorry," he rasps hoarsely. "I don't know what came over me."

I stare back at him, my own breathing equally erratic. And even though I know that he's right, that I really, really need to stop kissing him, the sight of him, all mussed hair and swollen lips, makes me want to abandon every one of my morals and resume jumping his bones.

"This was a mistake. We can't do this." His words are a splash of cold water, extinguishing the flames of my arousal instantly. Then, just as quickly, my lust is replaced by a slow swell of anger.

"It's fine," I say tightly, sliding to the other end of the sofa. The frown on Graham's face deepens as he watches me move away. As if he wasn't the one who just shoved my body off his like I was going to infect him with the plague.

"People kiss all the time," I continue. "It didn't mean anything."

Deep down, I know that what we just did was wrong and totally inappropriate. But despite my words, I can't quite convince myself that what just happened was completely meaningless. My chest aches at the idea that what just happened meant nothing to him.

A ridge forms between Graham's brow and I can see in his face that he's at war with himself, wrestling between two conflicting urges.

"Right," he says after a beat. He drags a hand through his already tousled hair as painful silence stretches between us, the only sound the low hum of the television.

He glances at the clock. "Shit, it's nearly 1 A.M. I know I said I'd get you back to your car, but I really don't like the idea of you going home so late."

I blow out an indignant huff. "I assure you, I'm perfectly capable of managing."

Graham's shoulders deflate. "I didn't mean to suggest . . . I just meant, you're welcome to spend the night here. Not with me, of course. I meant . . . my grandmother has a second guest room. I stay in the primary guest room but it's a separate room than yours and . . ."

He trails off, looking like he wants to crawl into a hole and die, and his obvious mortification is a balm to my own bruised ego. On the one hand, I want to put as much distance between myself and Graham as possible. On the other hand, I *do* hate driving in bad weather. A quick glimpse out the window confirms that the snow and sleet have stopped but the dark roads will still be a mess.

"Fine," I concede. "But you'll take me to the gas station first thing in the morning?"

Graham nods, and relief floods his features. I'm not sure if it's due to my decision to stay over or the fact that I'm not making a bigger deal out of the kiss, but I opt not to question it. I feign a yawn, even though I'm not the least bit tired.

"I think I'll turn in. Where am I headed?"

I follow Graham up the staircase. At the top, he pushes open a door to reveal a guest room. The double bed inside is, predictably, covered in a tartan quilt. I swear, this whole house is straight out of an L.L.Bean catalog. The only thing that's missing is a golden retriever.

Graham ducks into his own bathroom, returning a moment later with one of his T-shirts and a pair of flannel pajama bottoms in hand.

"You can change into this. To sleep in," he says gruffly. He shoves his glasses up his nose and I feel a twinge of satisfaction over his tell of discomfort. A small part of me hopes that he's imagining me undressing just a few feet away from him.

"I'm just next door, if you need anything."

I level my gaze at him, a challenge in my eyes.

"What exactly do you think I'll need?" There's a throbbing between my legs that's signaling exactly which of my needs are currently going unmet. Graham's eyes are burning into mine, his dilated pupils like two smoldering coals. His lips part and I can tell by the flutter visible in his throat that his own heart rate is accelerated, that he wants me just as much as I want him. Pressure builds between us as our gazes hold, my blood humming in my veins.

But then the light behind his eyes extinguishes, and he breaks eye contact.

"We should get some sleep," he says softly. "I'll see you in the morning?"

My mouth has suddenly gone too dry to talk, so I simply nod. Turning, I head into the guest room, shutting the door behind me.

Once inside, I collapse face down onto the bed, groaning into the quilt. *What the hell just happened back there?* Now that we've managed to put some space between us, my arousal has died down (mostly), allowing my frontal lobe to take the stage. Which is unfortunate because logic is the last thing I'm interested in right now.

Because the facts are the facts. Graham is about to be married to someone else. Not only that, but he and Claire are my clients. I'm supposed to be orchestrating his nuptials, for fuck's sake! This morning, we put a deposit down on a cake and now I'm sucking face with the groom? I feel less professional than a bartender on *Vanderpump Rules.* Not only that, but I happen to adore Claire. The last thing I want to do is hurt her.

Asha's face floats to the front of my brain, her features awash with horror. If she thought I was unprofessional during the Shrek wedding, my present behavior might cause her brain to implode. I may only be an intern, but even I know that screwing the groom is against protocol. Besides, the last thing I want to do is create a situation that reflects badly on her. She put her reputation on the line by convincing Antoine to hire me and has since become my unofficial mentor. If Antoine finds out about my history with Graham, Asha's reputation with the company will take a hit too.

I roll over, grabbing a pillow and hugging it to my chest. It's official: moving back to Baltimore is ruining my life. If I was still living in New York, I'd be out in the city right now, crushing dick and enjoying a craft cocktail with my two best friends. The old Ali wouldn't be caught dead wallowing over some guy.

But that's the problem, isn't it? It's getting harder and harder to convince myself that Graham is just *some guy.* Not when my brain keeps replaying that tiny moan of ecstasy when he took a bite of that red velvet sample, or the way I felt when he tucked me against his chest in the basement freezer. As much as I want to deny it, I'm attracted to the man. I have been, ever since that fateful game of darts. Eight years have done nothing to temper that little dip in my stomach every time I'm in his presence.

But I need to get a grip. There's no way I'll ever succeed in this industry if I can't maintain my professionalism around an attractive client. Graham is off limits, and the sooner I get that idea through my head, the better off I'll be.

Sighing, I wiggle beneath the sheets and wrap the quilt around myself. I expect to spend the rest of the night lying awake, but within minutes, I've fallen asleep, dreaming of sky-blue eyes burning into mine.

The smell of brewing coffee rouses me from sleep like I'm in a damn Folgers commercial. When my eyes crack open, slivers of morning light are stretched across the unfamiliar bedspread, and it takes me a moment to remember where I am. But then, memories from last night jolt through me. Graham wrapping me in that warm, plaid blanket. The fragrant spices of shakshuka filling his grandmother's kitchen. The press of Graham's lips against mine and the confusing feeling of rightness that it evoked.

I pick my cell phone off the table to check the time, but the screen is black. Damn it. I completely forgot to borrow a charger last night.

I make a hasty attempt at making the bed and then grab my purse off the floor before heading downstairs. When I reach the kitchen, Graham is pouring coffee into a blue chinoiserie mug. The sight of him conjures a snort of amusement. At the sound of it, he turns to face me, his hair adorably rumpled, and I'm afforded a full view of his getup. He's wearing a navy robe open over a matching pajama set, the bottoms of which are stuffed into a pair of bright red Wellington boots.

"Excuse me, but what in the Paddington Bear are you wearing?"

Graham looks affronted as he runs his hand over the blue striped fabric of his pajama top.

"What? It's an old house, and it gets a bit drafty upstairs. Plus, the lawn was still damp when I let Genevieve out this morning and—" He pauses as he takes in my smirk and a smile twitches in the corner of his mouth.

"And you are taking the piss. Good morning. How do you take your coffee?"

"Cream and sugar, please."

I slide into a seat at the kitchen table as Graham rummages through the fridge. A moment later, he hands me a steaming mug and then slides into a seat across from me.

"The outside temperature has warmed up and the roads look good," he says. "As soon as you're ready, we can head out to get you gas, and then you can be on your way."

"Thank you," I reply, taking a long, grateful sip from my mug.

Graham shifts his weight, his thumb tracing the curve of his own mug handle.

"Ali, about last night," he starts.

"It's fine. We don't need to talk about it," I say quickly, cutting him off.

His eyes are cautious as they trace over my face, as though assessing whether my words match my emotions. I give him nothing, staring down into my coffee. There's not a chance in hell that I'm going to let him know the effect he has on me. That thoughts of our bodies pressed together infiltrated my dreams all night. That despite my best attempts at safeguarding my emotions, he's already wormed his way beneath my shields. Last night was a mistake and the sooner we can forget it happened, the better off we'll be.

He presses his elbows on the tabletop and takes a deep breath.

"The thing is," he says slowly. "Claire is my best friend."

"Graham, we really don't have to—" I start to protest but he lifts a hand, stopping me.

"Please," he says. "Just let me say this."

I press my lips together and nod. Graham clears his throat before continuing.

"I was in a bad place when Claire and I met in New York. It was the first time I'd been in America for an extended period, and I didn't know a soul. She found me in the audience after her stand-up set and insisted we go out for drinks. After that night, we were pretty much inseparable. And for the first time since the semester started, I didn't feel so alone."

I force myself to swallow the boulder-size wedge lodged in my throat. Graham, who seems to have clocked the malaise in my expression, pauses for a beat before continuing.

"When my grandfather died suddenly last year, it almost broke me. Claire and I had just moved in together, and when she found me on the kitchen floor, eight hours after I'd gotten the call from Granny, she completely took over. Packed my suitcase, booked us train tickets to Baltimore, and made sure I was able to say goodbye to my grandfather. I was too overcome by grief to properly look after myself. But she was there for me. She never left my side."

He takes a deep breath, steadying himself.

"Grandpa adored Claire. He only met her twice, but he thought she was good for me. I told my grandparents we were just friends, but he always hoped I'd change my mind. He said I was too serious and needed someone who could make me laugh."

"You, too serious?" I throw him a teasing smirk. Graham's solemn expression slowly cracks into a smile, and I feel a flutter of satisfaction in knowing I'm the one who put it there.

I shake off the feeling quickly. Claire is his fiancée; she's the one who makes him laugh every day, not me. I wonder when their relationship shifted from friendship to something more.

His expression darkens again. "I thought I was okay, but I wasn't. I couldn't function for months after his death. I was sleeping all the time, couldn't keep up with my work. My boss was on the verge of sacking me. But Claire refused to let me drown in my grief. She forced me out of bed and got me into therapy. I wouldn't have my career if it weren't for her. I owe her a debt I can't repay."

Behind his glasses, his blue eyes swell with emotion.

"I can't let her down, Ali. I can't hurt her."

He looks so forlorn that I find myself reaching across the table to lay a hand over his forearm, mentally kicking myself for lusting after this man. I was so quick to pin him as a philandering jerk. In reality, he's just a guy who wants to do right by the people who care about him. To be the type of person his own father never was.

"Listen, I get it," I tell him. "Claire is cool as hell, and I'm committed to protecting her at all costs. What happened last night didn't mean anything. We just . . . let our past attraction get the best of us. It was a one-off and now that we've gotten it out of our systems, we can move forward. Maybe even try to be friends."

"Friends?" Graham raises his eyebrows. In fairness, I can understand his skepticism. Especially considering the way our bodies have begun unconsciously leaning toward each other during this conversation. "Friends" don't experience this ever-present sense of hunger, this pull of unadulterated lust in the presence of a platonic companion. I bite down on my bottom lip as my gaze traces over the curve of his bottom lip, then down the square line of his jawbone.

Then I blink a few times, forcing myself to look away. *God, this would be so much easier if he wasn't an absolute smoke show with a soft spot for Disney classics.*

I clear my throat as I lean back in my chair, recalibrating.

"Yes. But if we're going to be friends, you're going to have to ditch King Charles's jimjams before we hit the road. I can't be seen in public with you dressed like that. I have a reputation to uphold."

Graham huffs out a laugh. "You got it, *friend.* But I'm keeping the wellies. They are the intersection of form and fashion."

The click of tiny toenails in the doorway serves to announce Genevieve's arrival. She passes by Graham with a low growl before hopping up into my lap. I drag my hand across the soft fur of her back as Graham shakes his head.

"What an unholy alliance you two share."

"Your jealousy is unbecoming, Mr. Wyler."

Graham snorts as he stands up to grab his keys from a hook by the doorway. He's still grinning when he turns back to me, and despite myself, I feel a flush of warm pleasure in my chest.

"Ready?"

14

Asha is still out on Tuesday. In a turn of events that's shocking to no one, the stomach bug torpedoing through her house has claimed her as its latest victim.

I'm scheduled to meet Graham at the hotel in the afternoon, and when I enter through the lobby doors, he's standing behind the front desk. I stroll over and rest my elbows on the counter as I stare at him with bemusement.

"Tell me: is this a promotion or a demotion?"

Graham grins. "I'm just filling in today. Both of our usual front desk attendants are out sick with the stomach bug. It must really be going around."

"Yikes. Has it been busy?"

He sighs wearily. "It's fine. I'm just trying to cover a lot of territory. We just had a walk-through with a family who's celebrating a Bar Mitzvah here on Saturday night."

"Members of the tribe? I wonder if I know them. I mean, let's be honest, the chances are high."

"Well, they're still in the ballroom. Maybe you can meet them when they're on their way out?" His eyes lock on mine again, and a flutter runs through my belly. Then his gaze drops to the manila folder in my hand. "What's this?"

"Oh." I had been so busy staring at Graham that I'd completely forgotten my reason for coming by. "I got the contract from the bakery and needed your John Hancock." I frown. "Or I guess your King Henry?"

"Don't these things usually just need electronic signatures?"

"Okay, Captain Physical Check."

A grin sneaks across his face. "I suppose that's merited."

The truth is that the bakery *did* send me a digital contract. But I may have printed it out as an excuse to come over and see Graham. Because that's what friends do. They visit each other. Right?

"I figured you'd prefer to sign off with your signet ring," I say.

"What poor luck. I just returned it to the vault."

We're still grinning at each other when I hear a clack of shoes against the lobby's marble floor. The sound of a familiar voice turns my blood to ice.

"*Bubbeleh!*"

Rotating slowly on my heel, I turn around and there they all are. My mother, sister, and Bubbie. The first two are staring at me wide-eyed. Bubbie, on the other hand, is wearing a look of unbridled glee that's historically been reserved for the black and white cookies I brought home during my visits from New York.

"I see you've met Mr. Wyler. What a *shayne punim*, huh?" She reaches forward to clasp Graham's cheeks, which promptly go pink beneath her grip.

"My grandma thinks you're pretty," I whisper out of the side of my mouth, and his flush deepens.

"This is your family?" he whispers back, like everyone can't hear us. Which of course they can.

My mother raises her eyebrows, and I can see her trying to piece the situation together. "What are you doing here, Al?" she asks.

I clear my throat and do my best to avoid her curious gaze, because if we make eye contact, she's going to see right through me. Mothers have built-in bullshit detectors.

"My company is planning a wedding at the hotel," I say. There, not a lie at all. I have just conveniently omitted the fact that Graham is the groom. "What are you guys doing here?"

"Doing a walk-through for Jackson's Bar Mitzvah," Sarah says. She takes in my blank expression and a look of irritation crosses over her features. "You do remember that it's this weekend?"

Jackson's Bar Mitzvah is going to be *here*? Sarah's been talking about the "historic hotel" she's booked for months, but somehow, I didn't put it all together. I guess I never looked that carefully at the invitation. Since I'm living with my parents, I didn't receive my own copy, and I never dedicated much thought to the logistics.

"Of course," I say brightly.

Bubbie leans forward to wrap her red lacquered nails around my wrist. "You're going to bring a date, aren't you? If you still haven't found someone, Joyce from my mah-jongg league is dying to set up her grandson. He's in medical school. He's going to be a doctor! Technically, he does have a girlfriend, but Joyce thinks things are going to fizzle out soon and wants to get on top of it."

"Actually, I already have a date!" I blurt out, because admitting that I'm going stag to my nephew's Bar Mitzvah, where even my eighty-nine-year-old grandmother has a date, is a cross I simply can't bear.

Bubbie's eyes flit to Graham and I see something flicker behind her eyes as she connects the dots. *Oh no. God, no.*

"*Ohh*," she says. She's grinning conspiratorially as she looks back and forth between us, and I can see the incorrect assumption has already formed. "You're bringing Mr. Wyler?"

I open my mouth to protest, but before I can say anything, Graham wraps an arm around my waist, sending a trail of sparks across the fabric of my shirt.

"Yup. I can hardly wait," he says. I whip my head around to stare at him, flabbergasted. *What on earth is he doing?*

My mother looks stunned. "Oh. I didn't realize you were seeing someone, Ali. You haven't mentioned it before." My sister is the only one who's unconvinced. Her eyes narrow as she studies me suspiciously. She knows something's amiss but can't quite put her finger on it.

"Oh, well. I've been so busy with work," I manage, still scrutinizing Graham, whose own placid expression gives nothing away. *Damn the English and their stoicism.*

"Right," my mom says. "Well, we are headed out. But I guess I'll see you at home?"

"You betcha!" I say with a smile. *You betcha? Jesus, what is happening to me?* I sound like a character from a nineties sitcom.

The minute they disappear through the revolving doors, I whip around to face Graham.

"Why did you just do that?" I ask.

Graham bites his bottom lip. "Would you believe me if I said it was a complimentary service for being a valued patron of the Black-Eyed Susan?"

I raise a skeptical brow and he laughs softly.

"Didn't think so." He uses his pointer finger to adjust his glasses. "It just seemed like you needed a save. I know what happened the last time your family set you up. And I guess I felt like I owed you. After what happened the other night."

He shoves his hands into his pockets. "But I apologize if I overstepped. Don't feel any obligation to take me up on the offer. I just thought it might be fun to go. As friends."

"Oh, you're going," I say. "Forcing you to play a game of Coke and Pepsi is the only adequate punishment for your behavior."

Graham's lips rise in a small smile, and I can't help but return it.

"Have you ever been to a Bar Mitzvah?" I ask.

Graham shakes his head. "This will be my first."

"You're in for a treat." I grab a piece of paper off the desk and scribble down my parents' address.

"Pick me up here. I won't subject you to the morning service at synagogue, but the party starts at 8 P.M. Not having to drive there with my parents will make me feel less like I belong at the kids' table."

Graham tips an invisible hat. "It's a date."

Saturday morning comes too quickly. Despite the occasional cracks in his voice, which he wears like a badge of honor, Jackson reads his Torah portion like a champion. I give my sister's hand a squeeze as I watch her tear up with pride.

I've never given much thought to whether I want kids of my own. The role of Cool Aunt has always fit like a glove and felt like enough for me. But sitting here with my family, watching my nephew achieve an important milestone, I can't help but feel a flicker of longing. And I know that a part of me wants this, wants to start a family of my own.

The kiddush luncheon afterward is predictably mobbed, and I lose track of my family immediately. By the time I get through the buffet line and reach the bagel platter, the only flavors left are salt and oat bran. *Bluch.*

I'm still deliberating which is the best of the worst when I hear a familiar voice.

"How does one choose between such grim options?"

At the sound of it, my head pops up in surprise. Graham is standing right in front of me, chewing on a cream cheese and lox sandwich on everything bagel. It looks positively divine. Also, *what*?

"What are you doing here?" I ask.

He blinks. "What does it look like? I'm enjoying a bagel and shmear."

I shake my head. "No, I mean, what are you doing at synagogue?

I told you that you only needed to come to the party. How did you even know we were at Beth El?"

"It's possible that I was Googling a bit and ran across the Bar Mitzvah announcement." Graham uses his thumb to brush a sesame seed from the corner of his mouth. "Ali, I might not be Jewish, but even I know the Torah reading is the main event." He takes a step closer to me and his voice drops an octave.

"Look, I know your family is important to you. And you . . ." Graham's eyes darken as they burn into mine and a heady pressure builds between us. My breath swells as I wait for him to finish that thought. But then he drops his gaze to the floor and the tension that's filled the air between us deflates like a popped balloon.

"I couldn't attend your nephew's party but skip his service. Wouldn't be proper."

My mouth is hanging open, but no words are coming. Truth be told, I have no idea what to make of this conversation. Luckily, Graham lets me off the hook, offering me the second half of his sandwich.

"Please accept this pity bagel? Unless, of course, you were angling for the oat bran."

"I would, but alas, I am not a horse."

Graham breathes out a tiny laugh as he gingerly scoops the uneaten half of his bagel onto my plate, along with some fruit salad. Then he walks his empty plate to the end of the table, depositing it into a trash can. His gaze slices mine as he turns back to look at me over his shoulder. The expression on his face is unreadable.

"I'll see you tonight," he says softly. And with that, he disappears through the doorway.

15

I'm still attempting to shove my feet into the heels my mother lent me when the doorbell rings.

"Coming!" I call. I limp down the hallway and try to ignore the stinging pain that's already forming around my toes. High heels are a sadistic invention. I don't care how great they make my butt look.

When I pull the door open, Graham is standing there in a dark suit, clutching a bouquet of roses like the world's most attractive prom date. His mouth drops open as he stares at me, his gaze running down the length of my pink cocktail dress.

"Wow," he says hoarsely. "You look . . ."

"I know, these shoes are ridiculous," I say. "It's like walking on stilts. I tried to put on flats, but my mom told me I looked like Strega Nona."

"You look perfect," he finishes softly. A ripple of pleasure shoots through me as our eyes meet. He's staring at me with an unwavering intensity that hurts my chest. I'm struggling to breathe as it is, given how ridiculously handsome he looks. The golden strands of his hair have been carefully styled with product, and the sharp cut of his suit hugs him in all the right places, highlighting his broad shoulders and slim waist. The man should wear formalwear daily, as a gift to humanity.

I break our gaze, training my attention on the bouquet in his hands.

"You brought me flowers," I say lamely. Graham's gaze drops to the bouquet in his hands, which he's gripping tightly enough to crumple the paper, as if just noticing it for the first time. His cheeks go crimson.

"Oh, yes. I didn't know what people bring to Bar Mitzvahs. I just didn't want to show up empty-handed."

"No, it's sweet," I reassure him, taking the bouquet from his hands. "Let me just put them in water." I hurry into the kitchen, and when I return a minute later, he's still standing in the threshold, looking more nervous than my actual prom date did.

"Well, we'd better get going before we miss appetizers," I say. "You can normally count on a good cocktail wiener at these things, but knowing my sister, there's going to be a disproportionate number of gluten-free options. We'll want to get there before there's nothing left but spinach and kale bites."

Graham's face breaks into a relieved smile, the tightness of his features loosening. "I'm sure José is delighted. He's always looking for opportunities to eliminate taste from food."

He glances over my shoulder. "Your parents already left?"

"Oh, yeah. They were needed early for photos." What I don't mention is that my mother was only too eager to leave ahead of me to give me "alone time" (her exact words, accompanied by an eyebrow wiggle) with my "date." If the woman only knew.

"Shall we?" I ask. We head toward the car, and I shake my head when he opens the passenger door for me.

"You don't have to do all this," I protest with a laugh. "It isn't a real date." I pause, considering my statement. "On the other hand, I guess this tracks. I never get the five-star treatment from men who are available. Trust me, I've done the legwork."

Graham's smile falters a bit, but then he doesn't say anything as he moves to the driver's side. When he flips on the ignition, a Beach Boys song drifts through the speakers.

"Seriously?" I raise my eyebrows. "Tell me the truth: how old *are* you? Because if you're a 150-year-old teenager who was saved by a benevolent vampire during the Spanish Influenza, I can keep a secret."

"As if I'd confess such a thing to a woman who's clearly Team Jacob."

I snort as Graham shifts the car into reverse. We settle into a comfortable silence and my eyes drift back to the faded photograph on the dashboard.

"May I?" I ask, gesturing to it. Graham nods as he hands the picture to me. I wipe off a thin layer of dust to better examine it. In the photo, Graham, who looks like he's about six or seven. There's an adorably oversized pair of green glasses on his face, and he's dressed in a pair of shorts and a black Orioles T-shirt. He's sitting next to his grandfather on a bench and clutching a Styrofoam cup in one hand. Upon closer inspection, I recognize the small wooden hut in the background.

"Oh, I know this place! This is the snowball stand on York Road."

Graham grins. "Yup. My grandparents used to take me there all the time."

Snowballs are a summer staple in Baltimore. They're a ball of shaved ice that's covered with flavored syrup. The texture is harder than Italian ice, so you have to chip away at them with a spoon. It wasn't until I went to college that I found out they're a local dish most people have never heard of.

"What's your flavor pick?"

Graham scoffs. "Is that even a question? Skylite, obviously."

"Obviously."

It's not clear exactly what flavor Skylite is. Some people have tried to parse out the ingredients in the sugary sweet taste, but really the best way to describe it is blue.

Graham spares me a sidelong glance. "And yours?"

"Chocolate," I reply. "With marshmallow sauce."

Graham purses his lips, nodding in approval. "A respectable choice. If the stand was out of Skylite, of course."

I breathe out a laugh, then return my attention to the photo. My heart twists as I notice the way that Graham's grandfather is looking down at Graham with a look of pure adoration.

"You must really miss him," I murmur, as I brush my fingertips over the image.

Graham blows out a long exhale. "Every day. He was always my north star, a voice of reason. Lately, I've found myself wishing desperately that I could talk to him." He spares me a long glance before shifting his attention back to the road, and my cheeks prickle with heat.

"My mother always said their expectations of her were suffocating. They wanted her to take over the hotel when they retired, and she was not interested. She wanted to live out her own dream, not someone else's. It's why she rarely came back to see them. She was so certain that they disapproved of her choices, so she believed she was doing the right thing for everyone by staying away. But I think deep down, she was afraid that she had disappointed them.

"When she came for my grandfather's funeral, it was the first time she'd been back here in ten years. The regret was written all over her face. And I just . . . I don't want to repeat her mistakes. I don't want to let down the people who matter to me."

I study him thoughtfully. It's the second time he's mentioned not wanting to repeat the mistakes of his parents, of striving to show up for the people he loves, and I can't help feeling like there's a larger issue playing beneath the surface.

"Well, she'll be back here for the wedding," I say helpfully. "Maybe that will be a good time for her and your grandmother to reconnect?"

Graham's grip tightens on the steering wheel. "She won't be in attendance," he replies gruffly.

My mouth drops open. "Your mother isn't coming to your *wedding*? Why not?"

Graham keeps his gaze firmly on the road. "Trust me, she has her reasons."

I shake my head slowly.

"Did you guys have a fight? Or is this about Trudy? I know things between them aren't great." Graham's hinted that the relationship between his mom and grandmother is strained, but surely the two of them would be willing to put aside their differences for something as important as Graham's wedding day.

I watch as a muscle ticks in the square line of his jaw. "It's not that. It's . . . complicated. Just leave it, okay?"

A rebuttal is on the tip of my tongue, but something about the look on Graham's face forces the protest back down my throat. I hand the photograph to Graham, and he slides it back into its place.

His words from an earlier conversation make their way to the front of my mind. I remember the feeling of isolation that Graham described when he first moved to New York. For the first time, it occurs to me that with Claire gone, Graham has hardly anyone here. He must feel incredibly lonely.

"Listen," I offer. "If you need additional family presence at your wedding, my Bubbie would be happy to step in. She'll do whatever you need: walk you down the aisle, safeguard your rings, throw rice, smear lipstick all over your face. I can't promise she won't also hit on you, but she's loyal as hell, and she'll never miss an event that offers cake. I'll be there with you too, and not just because you're paying me."

Graham turns to smile at me, but it's a smile I haven't seen from him before. There's a sadness beneath it, mixed with something else that I could swear looks like longing.

"That means more to me than you know," he says, his voice a low scrape. We lock eyes for a long moment, and my skin prickles beneath his gaze. Then the light changes and he looks away. We drive the rest of the way in silence, the car filled with the weight of unspoken longing and the Beach Boys.

Cocktail hour is in full swing by the time we arrive. Graham's eyes widen as we step into the Black-Eyed Susan's ballroom. The entire surface of the ceiling is covered in primary color balloons, and oversized cubes in matching shades trim the stage, where a DJ is blasting Billboard Top 100 hits. A sign-in board by the ballroom doors spells out Jackson's name with letters shaped like video game controllers. The black tabletops are surrounded by cherry red chairs, and flower arrangements erupting from the heads of blocky video game characters serve as centerpieces. In one corner, a cluster of preteen boys are poking holes in the bottoms of plastic cups in an admirable attempt to shotgun Shirley Temples.

"Is it me, or is this a Roblox Bar Mitzvah?" Graham asks, lifting one eyebrow.

I shake my head. "There's no accounting for the taste of thirteen-year-old boys."

Graham purses his lips as he glances around the room. "You do have to appreciate the impressive dedication to the theme. Did you plan this?"

I shake my head. "I would have loved to. Family events are my favorite kind to plan. But my sister was insistent that she could do it all herself." Without quite meaning to, I add more bite to the last word than I intended. I'm well-aware of Sarah's hyper competence. She's been that way her whole life. It's not that I think she *needed* my help planning Jackson's Bar Mitzvah. I just wish she'd been willing to accept it. To let me step outside my role as her little sister and be her friend and partner.

Graham casts me a sidelong glance, his brows pinched thoughtfully.

"But you're great at what you do," he says, as though befuddled by the idea that anyone wouldn't agree. "Don't they see that?"

"No need to bullshit me, Benedict. You've already hired me." I give him an exasperated eye roll and shove my hands playfully against his chest. But then he catches me by the wrist and the amusement immediately seeps out of me. His gaze is penetrating as his thumb traces circles over the skin of my palm.

"It is getting increasingly difficult to bullshit you," he says, his voice so low it's practically a whisper. I'm not quite sure what he means by that, but my brain has gone so fuzzy that it's impossible to parse out much of anything. My fingers, now moving of their own accord, slide between his, and his gaze drops to the place where our hands are interlocked. A muscle in his jaw ticks.

With what feels like an insurmountable effort, I extract my hand from his. The attraction that pulls me toward him is undeniable, but the reality remains that giving into it is wrong and will only result in disaster.

I take a step back and then toss him what I hope is a passably neutral smile.

"Come on," I say, nodding toward the dance floor. "Let's get you an inflatable saxophone."

The worst part of the entire evening is how seamlessly it's all going. A small, vindictive part of me had hoped that dragging Graham to my nephew's Bar Mitzvah would be an especially creative punishment for him, but two hours in, he's already become part of the fabric of my family. He was especially enthusiastic during the horah, his legs weaving in and out of a box step like he's Tevye the Milkman. And let's face it, my family was thrilled to have a man over five foot eight in attendance to help lift Jackson in a chair. He even gamely insisted on participating in Coke and Pepsi, a party game typically limited to kids, where you're split into two teams, and race to your partner on the other side of the dance floor when your assigned soda is called. Now I'm sitting on a chair at the edge of the dance floor, sipping a glass of white wine as I watch him slow dance with Bubbie to a Stephen Sanchez song.

"Are you having fun?" she asks him.

"I'm having the time of my life. What a *simcha*," he says. He offers her a cheeky smile, clearly delighted by his usage of the Yiddish word. She beams at him.

"Well, if you like parties, you should come to my ninetieth birthday celebration. Ali's planning it, so you know it'll be a hoot."

The two of them turn to look at me, Bubbie's face beaming with adoration. But Graham's expression is laced with admiration, longing, and an indisputable trace of lust. It's all too much, even when accessorized with a glow stick necklace and an airbrushed trucker hat that reads "Mazel Tov Jackson." I bury my face in my wine glass to hide the emotions that are bubbling a bit too close to the surface.

"I wouldn't miss it, Bubbie," Graham says, and she lets out a tiny *hmmph* of satisfaction. Her hands drop to his waist, giving his backside a squeeze. It isn't too much of a stretch since he's so much taller than her that she barely comes up to his shoulders, even with the extra six inches awarded by her overly hairsprayed beehive.

"Oh my gawd, Ali," she exclaims. "The buns on this one! Like two firm deli rolls."

Graham flashes one of his devastating half smiles. "Bubbie, behave yourself," he chides. She giggles again.

"You know," she rasps. "I've always had a thing for accents. There was an Englishman who used to come in all the time when I worked in the candy department at Hutzler's department store. I used to slip him free chocolates whenever he stopped by my counter. Of course, it wasn't all I'd like to have slipped him."

"Bubbie!" I chide. "What about Zayde?"

"What about him?" Bubbie scowls. "Can't a girl keep her options open? Besides, it was the seventies. Everyone was swinging back then."

I shake my head. "I could have lived the rest of my life without that information."

Graham snorts out a laugh and we exchange a grin.

Bubbie winks at him through her non-fogged lens. "I'm joking. I never took another key out of the key bowl. That man was my *besheret*, my soulmate. Just look at the beautiful family we created together."

Graham's eyes drift appreciatively around the room. Then he gifts her a thoughtful smile.

"My grandmother says your soulmate is the one person on earth with a key that fits your lock."

A pleasurable warmth swells inside my chest at the sentiment. But then just as quickly, it's replaced by heaviness, and an invisible hand squeezes my heart. Because isn't it just my luck that I've finally found a man who fits so seamlessly into my world and I can't keep him? Because he isn't mine and he never can be.

The knot of emotion in my chest starts to bubble up, forming a lump that I'm struggling to swallow. Heat pricks at my eyes as I leap to my feet. Through the blur of tears, I can see Graham frowning at me, his eyes traveling back and forth across my face as he struggles to read my expression.

Are you okay? he mouths at me, and instead of replying, I just shake my head, because I know that the minute I try to speak, the threatening tears will spill over, and the last thing I need right now is for Graham Wyler to see me cry.

Shoving back my chair, I take off in the direction of the emergency exit, ignoring the sound of Graham calling my name. When I reach the doors, I hurl myself against the metal bar, stumbling out into the cold night air. But before I can make it all the way through, my heel catches on the doorframe. My ankle twists as I fly forward, landing hard on my hands and knees, and it's the metaphorical straw that breaks me. With a loud, guttural sob, I close my eyes and surrender to the onslaught of emotion. My body shudders as tears wrack my body. Somehow, it's perversely pleasant, a sweet release after bottling up my emotions for so long.

Footsteps echo through the hallway and then the door creaks open. I hear a low curse and then he's by my side, lifting me off the pavement and dragging me into his lap. He brushes the hair off my face as he wipes my tears with the pad of his thumb, his expression unspeakably tender. Then his eyes drop as he does a quick perusal of my body, inhaling sharply when his gaze lands on my skinned knees.

"You're bleeding," he says. His voice is low and hoarse, and I groan.

"This is why I don't wear heels," I sniffle. "They never fail to ruin a dramatic exit scene."

Graham doesn't crack a smile. Instead, he stands up, my body still gathered in his arms, and begins carrying me back toward the doors.

"Uh, where are we going?" I ask.

Graham's voice is strained. "I have Band-Aids and antiseptic in my office."

I glower at him. "Isn't this a tad overdramatic? I'm perfectly capable of walking. It's just a scrape."

Graham ignores me, bypassing the ballroom's side entrance and carrying me down the narrow hallway. He takes a left down another carpeted hallway and then he's pushing through an office doorway, clicking on a light.

His office is exactly how I pictured it. Neat and orderly, just this side of sparse, but with a few Graham-specific touches. There's an ivory cardigan hanging on the back of the door, and an abandoned mug of tea resting on a coaster atop the cherrywood desk. The entire room carries traces of his citrusy scent, which is quickly becoming my favorite smell.

Graham deposits me into one of the chairs facing his desk and then begins rummaging through his drawers, returning a moment later with a first aid kit. He sinks to his knees in front of me, his eyes dark and hooded as he gestures to my torn stockings.

"May I?" he asks, his voice a low scrape. I nod, biting down hard on my bottom lip as his hands reach up under my dress. His fingers slip into the waistband of my ruined stockings, and he drags them down slowly, his knuckles skimming my thighs, before tossing them on the floor. My heartbeat is hammering so hard against my chest that I wonder briefly if he can hear it.

He slides a package of Neosporin between his lips, tearing it open with his teeth. Then he pulls it and squeezes a small amount directly onto my knees, his warm fingers tracing circles over my skin. By the time he peels open a Band-Aid, I'm breathless. All he's done is apply basic first aid, and somehow, it's one of the most erotic experiences of my life.

"Graham," I whisper, and he groans at the sound of his name. Rocking back onto his heels, he closes his eyes.

"I've tried so hard," he mutters under his breath.

"It's fine," I say. "I mean, it's not that much blood. But if you're feeling woozy, I can take it from here."

When Graham opens his eyes again, they are burning.

"I've tried so hard to be sensible, to fight the way I feel about you," he says roughly. "But I can't do it anymore. It might kill me."

His words strike with the force of a freight train, knocking the wind out of me. A long silence stretches between us as I struggle to form words.

"What are you talking about?" I finally manage.

Graham drags a hand down his face.

"It was never supposed to be like this," he mutters, but it seems like he's mostly talking to himself. My stomach coils as I brace myself for whatever is about to pass through those gorgeous lips. He releases a slow exhale and then meets my eyes again.

"When I told you that Claire and I are best friends, I meant that literally. She's one of the most important people in my life. I owe her everything." He levels his gaze at me before continuing.

"But we are not a couple. Not romantically. We never have been."

Time stands still as the weight of his words settle over me. My lips part, but I can't seem to formulate a coherent thought.

Graham drags a hand through his hair. "Writing for American television has always been her dream. But her student visa was expiring, and she didn't know how much longer she would get to stay here. One night at the bar, she jokingly asked me to marry her for a green card. She wasn't serious, but I wanted to help her. She saved my career once, and I was more than happy to repay the favor. So, I said yes."

I blink a few times as I try to process what he's telling me. "But . . . you're British," I finally say. "How can you get her a green card?"

It's a ridiculous detail to focus on right now, but everything is spinning around me like a Tilt-A-Whirl and this fact seems like the one thing I can grab onto.

"My mother's American. I have dual citizenship."

I shake my head, my brain struggling to process his words.

"Let me make sure I have this straight. You and Claire are not a couple, and this is a marriage of convenience?"

"Well, it doesn't feel very convenient right now," he grumbles. "But yes."

His eyes are cautious as they search my face, gauging my response.

"I feel terrible that we lied to you about it," he continues. "But what choice did we have? We can't exactly be going around telling people we're faking love for a green card marriage. ICE is no joke."

Something about this still isn't making sense. I feel like I'm scrambling to put the pieces of a puzzle together without looking at the photo on the box.

"But . . . if the marriage isn't real, why bother with a big wedding? Why not just get married at City Hall?"

Graham barks out a soft, humorless laugh. "That was the original plan. I wasn't even going to tell Granny about the marriage. But she overheard me on the phone with my mother, when I asked her to post my birth certificate for the license. I told her we were going to elope, but she insisted that we consider a wedding at the hotel, the same place where she and my grandfather were married. She loved the thought of it becoming a family tradition. And then it occurred to me that it'd be a brilliant opportunity for a publicity boost. A two-birds-one-stone situation that would allow me to help two of the people I care about most."

"Does your grandmother know that this is a sham marriage?"

He shakes his head. "I wanted to tell her. But she was so excited about the engagement. It was the first time I'd really seen her smile since my grandfather died. I couldn't stand to admit the truth and break her heart. And honestly, the fewer people who know, the better."

He pauses, nibbling on his bottom lip.

"My mum knows. It's why she's refusing to come. I couldn't understand her objection when I first told her. It seemed harmless enough. I figured we'd stay married for two years, or however long it took for Claire's employer to get her immigration paperwork sorted. Then we'd file for divorce. It wasn't like I was dating anyone, and even if I was, I had no intention of getting into a serious relationship. It was all meant to be simple, uncomplicated. A favor I was happy to do for a friend. But then you barged back into my life, and—" He takes a deep breath and then exhales slowly. "You barged into my life, and nothing has been simple since."

The air in the room evaporates. I'm conscious of nothing but the rhythmical thumping of my heart against my chest. Graham takes a step closer.

"I'm lying in bed every night, trying to force myself to stop thinking about you, but I can't. There's no escaping it, and honestly, I'm tired of trying. I don't want to fight the way I feel about you anymore."

The lump in my throat swells. "What are you trying to say?" I whisper, because even though I think I know, I'm desperate to hear him say it.

Graham licks his lips, readying himself. Finally, he looks directly into my eyes. "It's you, Ali. I think it always has been."

My bones are on fire. My chest has gone so tight that I no longer remember to breathe. I blame the lack of oxygen circulation to my brain when I lean forward, throwing my arms around his neck and crashing my lips against his.

16

The moment our lips meet, I fully appreciate the scope of my hunger, and realize how starved I've been since I last had a taste of him on his grandmother's sofa. Or maybe even since that night in London.

His fingertips dig into my waist as he pulls me flush against him. I tug the hair at the nape of his neck, drawing him closer to deepen the kiss. Time blurs as we explore each other with breathless urgency, until finally he pulls back, reaching one hand forward to tuck a curl behind my ear.

"Beautiful girl," he says, his voice a hoarse whisper. His gaze is reverent as it caresses my features, drinking me in. His lips are already dark and kiss swollen, and I don't think I've ever wanted someone so badly in my life. I wrap his tie around my fist, yanking him forward and crushing my mouth against his again.

I groan when he pulls his lips from mine a moment later to drag them down my neck. His tongue traces my collarbone, leaving behind a trail of damp heat. With one hand, he slips the strap of my dress off my right shoulder, planting kisses along the newly bared skin, while his other hand settles on my chest. He palms me through the fabric, and I gasp as his thumb circles my nipple, teasing it into a hard peak.

Kneeling, he kisses another trail down the front of my dress.

When he reaches the hem, he lifts the fabric to reveal a sliver of my tattoo peeking through the top of my thong. He looks up at me through hooded lids, silently asking for permission, and I nod.

Pushing the lace aside, he traces his thumb slowly over the design before pressing his lips against it. There's an unfamiliar emotion simmering in my chest, one that clocks the private intimacy that comes with his acknowledgment of the twinned design branded on our skin. I brush the sentiment away quickly. What's happening right now is raw animal attraction, nothing more. And after so many weeks of mounting temptation, there's a delicious satisfaction in finally giving in to it.

"Tell me what you want," he says thickly, and I look down at him, breathless.

"Everything," I whisper.

That one word propels him into action. In a single, swift motion, he lifts me up, slamming me against the back of the door. My thighs circle his waist as I press my body against his, feeling the unmistakable shape of his arousal. His fingers twist through my hair as his bruised lips find mine again, and I kiss him hard, sending off sparks of electricity.

Desperate to relieve the throbbing between my legs, I grab one of his hands and slide it between us. Graham follows my lead dutifully, reaching under the fabric of my dress to stroke me over the thin fabric of my underwear. My breath hitches when his fingers dip below the waistband, and he slips one finger inside me.

"You're already so wet for me," he says hoarsely. The words tear a guttural moan from my throat, and I drop my head back against the door. His thumb traces small circles over my clit as he slides a second finger inside me, his rhythm growing faster as he pumps in and out.

Pleasure builds in my center, and I feel myself climbing faster and faster toward orgasm. When he bends forward to press his mouth to my chest, capturing one nipple between his teeth through the fabric of my dress, I shatter into a million pieces, my body going limp as I sag against him.

The world has gone blurry and dreamlike. Through the haze, I'm aware of the gentle press of Graham's lips against my skin. He kisses my forehead, my cheeks, my nose, and then scoops me up, carrying me over to the sofa on the opposite side of the room and depositing me on the cool, brown leather.

As the room returns to focus, my hunger returns, reminding me how long I've been waiting for him. Waiting for us to shatter this tension between us, waiting to feel his body against mine. And now I'm not willing to wait a moment longer.

Graham is standing over me, his chest rising and falling rapidly. Reaching forward, I grab him by his belt buckle.

"These need to go," I say, fumbling to undo the clasp. "Right now." He hisses as I tug his pants down, and he steps out of them, kicking them to the side. I go for his boxer briefs next, shoving them down his thighs. I pause for a beat as the tattoo comes into view. It's the first time in my life I've ever considered the sight of it a turn-on. He groans when I bend forward to trace it with my tongue.

"Ali, wait," he says, his voice strained and guttural. "I don't have . . ."

"Check my purse."

He walks back over to the desk chair, fumbling inside my clutch for a moment before extracting a condom.

He raises an eyebrow. "Do you always bring condoms to Bar Mitzvahs?"

I shrug. "Only the ones with an open bar."

He shakes his head, smirking as he makes his way back toward me.

"As beautiful as that dress is, I'm going to have to ask you to remove it."

I rise to my feet, slipping a hand behind my back to drag down the zipper. I unhook my bra and pull it all down in one slow movement, until I'm standing in front of him wearing nothing but panties. I straighten as I stare at him, feeling more confident and powerful than I ever have.

A muscle in Graham's jaw ticks as he surveys me. His eyes are stormy with lust, and I feel a surge of pride at knowing I'm the one who is evoking this response.

"Fuck," he says, his voice so low I can barely hear it.

He reaches a hand behind my back, pulling me closer, before dropping his head to nuzzle my neck. He brings his other hand to my chest, rolling my nipple between his thumb and index finger.

I drag a hand up his back as he continues his gentle assault, until I can't take it another moment.

"Please," I beg. "I need more. I need all of you."

Graham lets out a low growl before tearing the packet open and rolling it over his length. When he finishes, he turns to me, his expression once again serious.

"Are you sure?" he asks. When I nod in confirmation, he sits down on the sofa, spreading his legs and reaching for me. I drag my panties down, kicking them to the side of the sofa. Gripping his shoulders, I straddle his lap carefully, mindful of my injured knees. Then I lower myself onto him slowly until he's filled me.

Graham weaves a hand through the back of my hair, drawing me forward to press my forehead against his.

"You don't know how long I've wanted this," he says on a ragged breath. "How long I've wanted you."

"I've wanted you too," I breathe. And God knows I have. Far more than I've cared to admit to myself.

He cups my face, brushing a thumb over my cheekbone before sealing his mouth over mine again. It starts slow and tender before dissolving into a series of short, desperate kisses as I rock my hips against him. We start to move together, finding our rhythm. Our breathing grows ragged as our pace increases, and I bury my face in his shoulder, biting down on his skin as pleasure starts to blur my vision. And then I'm coming, the waves of ecstasy crashing into me with blinding speed.

Graham finishes a few seconds after me. He collapses back against the sofa, pulling me down onto his chest. Our heartbeats slam against each other as we lay there, our bodies tangled, my head resting against the slick skin of his chest. Graham lazily drags his fingertips through my hair. The sensation of it draws goosebumps.

"Damn," I say, once I'm able to speak again. "You've gotten better at this."

Graham huffs out a hoarse laugh. "Glad I've accomplished something in the past decade."

The mention of a milestone sends me careening back to reality.

"Shoot, the Bar Mitzvah wasn't over. My sister is going to kill me. And worse, we missed the Torah cake."

Graham drags a lazy thumb down my spine. "I might regret asking this, but what is a Torah cake?"

"It's exactly what it sounds like. A cake in the shape of a Torah. And Sarah picked white chocolate cake with raspberry filling, aka the ideal flavor combo."

Graham laughs softly, his warm breath tickling the top of my head. "Anything I can do to make it up to you?"

I lift my head, propping my chin on my hands with a grin. "Oh, I think something can be arranged."

I'm unceremoniously roused from sleep by the sound of my dresser drawers opening and closing. Dragging one eye open, I see Liam Payne staring back at me. No wait, not Liam Payne. His life-sized cardboard likeness, in all his sideswept-hair glory. I'm back in my childhood bedroom and I am not alone. The unsubtle shuffling continues.

"What are you doing?" I groan.

"Tidying up," Sarah says. "I've already spruced up the bathroom. You made a real mess in there."

"Tell me you didn't do that thing where you put all the smaller boxes inside one larger box? You know that really creeps me out."

Sarah perches herself on the foot of my bed, and I drag myself up into a sitting position. We are, as always, a study in contrast. She's bright-eyed and bushy-tailed this morning, dressed in a matching lavender Lululemon set and clutching a green juice. I, on the other hand, am a hungover mess, dressed in a faded Camp Ramah T-shirt and—I glance under the sheet to confirm my suspicions—no pants. And I don't need a mirror to know what my hair looks like.

"What time is it?" I groan, blinking at the clock on my bedside table.

"Nine A.M.," she says. "I've already had a full morning. I took a ride on the Peloton, did a load of laundry—"

"And now you're here, mothering me. Shouldn't you be back at home, doing Kegel exercises or finishing the last of Jackson's thank-you notes? The party's been over for a whole ten hours now."

"Obviously Jackson will write his own letters," she replies, before mumbling something under her breath about organizing the gifts and addresses for him in an Excel spreadsheet. I have no doubt that it's color-coded.

I run a tongue over my dry, chapped lips. Sarah hands me a glass of water from the bedside table and I take a long gulp as she gives me a curious once-over.

"I didn't see you after the candle lighting ceremony," she ventures after a beat. "Mom says you left with your date and weren't home when she went to bed."

"Guess it's a good thing she had me microchipped," I deadpan. I bite down on my bottom lip as I realize I missed the end of Jackson's night. "I'm sorry I left early."

Sarah waves a nonchalant hand. "It's fine. The party was basically over anyway." She grins. "Besides, you looked like you were eager for some alone time with your date." *Ah.* So that's why she's here. The status of my love life is always a top-shelf priority for my family.

"You want details," I say, taking another sip of water.

Her smile widens. "Of course I want details. I've been with the same man since high school. Do you know how often you get to have sex when you have four kids? The chances of someone walking in on you in the middle of the night are astronomical. Now, spill. I want to live vicariously."

Scenes from last night flood across my brain. The damp heat of his breath against my neck. The feel of his fingers digging into my bare thighs. The sense of complete ecstasy when he buried himself inside me.

My face heats at the thought of seeing him again. *Because you like him,* my brain whispers. I swat the thought away quickly. I don't have feelings for Graham. What we have is raw sexual chemistry. And last night, we finally gave in to it.

Part of me is desperate to tell Sarah the truth. But as much as she loves me, she also loves Asha, and I can't be certain she wouldn't spill this secret to her best friend, especially since it involves her. Even if she didn't tell, it isn't fair to force her to choose loyalties. The situation is complicated enough; the last thing I need is to bring anyone else into it.

I shove the blankets off me, pushing off the bed, no longer caring that my T-shirt doesn't quite cover my underwear. I need to get out of here before I say something I'll regret.

"I'm going to grab some coffee," I say quickly, as I slide past her. I refuse to make eye contact with Liam on my way out. The last thing I need right now is to be turned on by another member of the United Kingdom.

17

Asha is finally back in the office when Monday morning rolls around. I'd intended to spend the morning sending confirmation emails to vendors for a wedding we're hosting this Friday night, but when Graham texts that he has a 10 A.M. tux fitting, I volunteer to tag along. Wedding planners typically don't come for fittings, but I insist my presence is necessary to "make sure he sticks with the selected color scheme." Asha gave me a strange look when I announced my change in plans, but since her face is still carrying a slightly green tinge, I imagine she doesn't have the strength to protest.

When Graham steps out of the dressing room wearing a fitted black suit with a black bow tie, my mouth drops open.

"Wow," I say. "I didn't realize they were already casting the next James Bond."

Graham grins, a blush creeping along his cheeks.

"I know we're going to do sage accessories, but I thought I'd at least show you the black tie first."

I nod, smoothing one hand over the lapels, aware of Graham's heartbeat drumming beneath my palm. "I can see why you like this, but I think it needs a quick adjustment. Can I get a closer look?" Then I grab him by the tie and drag him into the dressing room, slamming the door shut behind us.

The minute we are alone in the tiny cubicle, Graham takes my face in his hands, lifting me toward him as he crushes his lips to mine. I let out a tiny hum of pleasure as I tug off his jacket, tossing it onto the floor before moving to undo his shirt buttons.

"Who knew you had a cummerbund fetish?" Graham murmurs as he brushes his lips against my throat. His hot breath draws goosebumps as he skims his way down my neck, leaving behind a trail of featherlight kisses.

"I've always had a thing for them. That's the real reason I went into event planning."

Graham walks us backward, pressing my back against the wall. With one knee, he nudges my thighs apart. His hips rock against mine, his erection pressing into me through the fabric of his trousers.

I unzip his pants, slipping one hand inside and wrapping it around him. He sucks in a breath, and I speed up my movements when I feel him start to pulsate in my hand.

"We can't do this here," he says hoarsely. Part of me knows he's right, but another, more dominant part, can't think of anything other than how much I want him.

"Who's going to stop us?" I whisper.

Then, as if I've summoned it, there's a knock on the door.

"Everything okay in there?" a woman's voice asks.

Graham releases a low, frustrated growl from the back of his throat, backing away from me as he frantically buttons his pants. His cheeks are flushed, his golden hair mussed, his glasses slightly askew. He's never looked sexier.

"Everything's fine," I call, then clap a hand over my mouth, immediately realizing my mistake.

"Ma'am, you are not allowed in the dressing room," the woman says, her voice now taking on a hard edge.

"Oh, I didn't realize! So sorry about that. I'll be right out," I reply.

I shoot a grin at Graham, whose face has now gone completely crimson.

Mortifying, he mouths at me, shaking his head, and I bite back a laugh. His face is still flushed, but his eyes are dancing behind his glasses.

"You know, I don't think I've gotten into trouble in my entire life as often as I have with you," he whispers.

I press my mouth to the shell of his ear. "Welcome to the dark side."

He squeezes my waist and I clap a hand over my mouth once more to muffle my squeal before slipping out of the dressing room.

"Tell me the truth: has a woman ever seen your tattoo and changed her mind about sleeping with you?"

The light in Graham's bedroom has dimmed with the setting sun, casting a shadow over his bare torso. I trace over the outline of the design with my finger, drawing goosebumps from his skin. We're laying side by side in his bed, our toes grazing the cool fabric of the bedsheets balled at the foot of the bed. Graham glances at me over his shoulder and one corner of his mouth rises in a lazy grin.

"Never. But a woman did once ask if she could take a photo of it for her friend. Which I declined. How dare she try and objectify my body?"

I breathe out a laugh as he rolls onto his side to face me. Reaching forward, he strokes a thumb against my cheekbone.

"You, on the other hand, are free to objectify my body any time you'd like."

His hand snakes over my hip as he pulls me closer, sending a spark of electricity that reaches all the way to my toes. Grabbing the hair at the nape of his neck, I press my lips against his. I can't seem to get enough of this man; no matter how many times I have him, I'm never quite satisfied. Based on the way I can feel him pulsing between my legs, I suspect he's suffering from the same affliction.

I trace the bottom of his lip with my tongue, drawing a low groan as his fingers twist through my hair. He uses his free hand to cup my breast, his thumb drawing lazy circles over my nipple.

The kiss is interrupted by a low growl in my stomach. I bite down gently on his bottom lip before pulling my face from his, drawing another frustrated groan.

"I'm going to go grab a snack. Are you hungry?"

Graham smirks, his eyes flashing playfully. "I just ate."

I give him a playful swat before sliding out of bed. I pull Graham's sweater over my head, then turn to look at him over my shoulder.

"Well, I'll be in the kitchen if you're ready for dessert."

My initial survey of Graham's pantry is grim. It's clear that he doesn't do much cooking because there isn't much to work with. I've just grabbed the ingredients to make one of my favorite elevated basics when he pads into the kitchen.

"What's on the midnight menu?" he asks as he comes up behind me. He wraps his arms around my waist and nuzzles my neck.

"Fried peanut butter and jelly," I say, angling my head back to give him better access.

"Mmm," he murmurs, as he drags his nose behind my ear. "Sounds divine."

I shrug as I crack an egg into a small bowl and coat the sandwich on both sides. "I did the best I could with the ingredients in Old Mother Hubbard's cupboard."

Graham laughs softly. "I don't have much motivation to grocery shop when Claire is out of town. Most nights I just eat a bowl of cereal or something."

"That is tragic," I say. I slide the sandwich into the buttered pan, and it crackles with a satisfying sizzle. But it's not enough to distract from the mention of Claire, the proverbial elephant in the kitchen. I clear my throat, readying myself to ask the question that's been plaguing me for the past few days.

"Speaking of Claire, what exactly are the terms of your arrangement? I imagine it involves quite a few sacrifices."

Graham picks up the knife I used for the peanut butter and wraps his lips around it. My mouth goes dry as I watch him lick it clean. It should be illegal to do something this erotic with a butter knife.

"Not really. Our lives are pretty much unchanged. All we need to do is provide evidence that the marriage is real. Shared finances, shared address. We're already roommates, so that wasn't a problem. And it was no big deal to open a shared checking account. Honestly, it makes it easier to pay the rent and utility bills that way."

I chew on my bottom lip before asking a follow-up question in the most casual manner I can summon. "And what about dating? Is that off the table?"

Graham shakes his head. "Claire and I agreed that this arrangement shouldn't interfere with our personal lives. A serious relationship with someone else would get tricky, but that's a non-issue for me. Past that, we're free to see whoever we want."

He places his hands on either side of my waist, drawing me closer. His breath is warm as it tickles my ear. "And right now, I'm very interested in seeing you."

His words send a rush of pleasure racing up my spine. Deep down, I know that continuing to sleep with Graham is a recipe for disaster. But I can't quite convince my body to heed that advice.

When the sandwich finishes toasting a few minutes later, I put it on a plate and set it on the counter to cool. Graham reaches an arm across me to pick it up and takes a bite.

"Wow. That's incredible."

I shake my head. "Admit it. You're only sleeping with me for my culinary talents."

Graham grins as he goes in for another taste. "It's an undeniable perk."

I take the sandwich from his hands and bite into it, chewing carefully as I evaluate it. "This is good, but not nearly as good as it would be on challah."

Graham brushes a crumb from the corner of his lip. "I'll make sure to keep some in stock from now on."

From now on. The words send a ripple of excitement through me. But then, just as quickly, the feeling is flattened, as his earlier words echo in my brain.

"Why did you say a serious relationship is a non-issue? Don't you ever want to fall in love? Settle down for real?"

A dark cloud passes over Graham's face.

"Relationships aren't for me," he says quietly. "My mom followed her heart and look where it got her. My dad was a complete tosser who cheated on her every chance he got, and she ended up raising me as a single mum. And her relationship with my grandparents was never the same after she moved to London. I promised myself I'd never be so reckless. Falling in love is like a forest fire. You burn yourself and everyone around you."

His words feel like a stone in the pit of my stomach. It's not that I expected anything to come of this thing with Graham. After all, what could this ever be other than a brief fling? Still, there's something about hearing him say he's not interested in ever falling in love that threatens to crack my heart in two. It must be written all over my face because Graham's forehead creases as his eyes trace cautiously over my face.

"Sorry, did I say something wrong?" he asks.

I quickly school my features into an expression of nonchalance.

"Not at all. Honestly, I agree with your perspective on dating. Casual is the only way to go."

He sighs.

"Ali, I know this is complicated. I know we won't have a lot of time together. But I like you, and I want to keep seeing you for as long as I can."

I lean back against the counter, bracing myself against the granite. "Absolutely. We don't need to make a big thing of this. It's just sex, right? Doesn't have to mean a thing. Besides, we only have a few weeks before you head back to New York."

Graham nods, his expression flat. "Oh. Yes, of course."

He rinses off the plate and puts it into the dishwasher. When he turns back to face me, his expression has softened.

"Stay with me tonight?" he asks.

I nod. It makes sense to stay downtown, since we have an appointment with a florist early tomorrow morning. Truthfully, everything would make more sense if I lived downtown. I spent the past week staring longingly at Zillow listings. I've got my eye on a townhouse in Fells Point that's got a tiny rear garden where I can grow my own herbs. But there won't be any home purchases in my future unless I can keep my eyes on the prize. Which is all the more reason to keep this thing with Graham under control.

Graham tucks a loose curl behind my ear and presses his lips to my forehead.

If only the prize didn't come with such charming distractions.

Even though we take separate cars, Graham and I still walk into Fleur de Lis at the same time the following morning, and I send a quick prayer into the universe that Asha doesn't notice. Luckily, she's clicking away on her cell phone and barely seems to register our entrance when we spot her in the lobby. But my heart leaps into my mouth when I see another figure with fire-engine red hair standing beside her. My mouth drops open, but it's Graham who speaks first.

"Claire." His voice is strained, unnatural.

She flashes him an enormous smile.

"Hi! Thought I'd come down for the afternoon to surprise you. I just got off the train and came straight here." Graham's face is indeed a mask of surprise, but not of the pleasant variety. Asha's brow furrows as her eyes dart back and forth between the two of them. I can tell what she's thinking, that Graham's lack of excitement to see his fiancée seems odd. But, ever the professional, she says nothing.

I clear my throat, doing my best to smooth over what has suddenly become palpable tension.

"Of course," I say. "No bride wants to miss out on choosing florals." I shoot Graham a warning glance, hoping he'll take the hint to rearrange his face, which doesn't look remotely natural right now. Claire is going to know something is up. But somehow, she doesn't seem to notice.

A florist from the shop leads us to a small office in the back, where she shows us the sample bouquets she's assembled. They're stunning, an artful arrangement of dusty roses and ivory peonies tied together with a muted sage ribbon. Claire and Asha *ooh* and *aah* over them for a moment, until the sound of a cell phone pierces the air, and Graham extracts his phone from his pocket.

He glances down at the screen. "It's my grandmother. I should probably take this." He stands and heads off to the front of the shop. Asha places her hand on my wrist.

"While we're waiting, do you mind if I show you some of the ranunculus they've just gotten in? We need an alternative for the Rosenberg-Abdul wedding, since the father of the groom is allergic to lilies."

I blink at her for a second, since we have no client of this name, before realizing it's a decoy.

"Oh, right. Of course," I say. I glance at Claire. "Give us just one sec?"

She nods, already scrolling through her phone.

I follow Asha to a front display, where she makes a show of pointing out several different blooms.

"There's something not right about this wedding," she says, her voice low. I shrug, avoiding her eyes as I finger the petals of an ivory anemone.

"I don't know what you mean."

Asha's frown deepens. "I can't quite put my finger on it. But something is off."

Desperate as I am to admit the truth to Asha, I made a promise to Graham. And at the end of the day, it's not my secret to tell. But the justification does little to quell the guilt pooling in my stomach. I've known Asha for half of my life. Keeping this from her feels treacherous.

"Probably just pre-wedding jitters," I manage. "I'm sure it's not easy for Claire, being in New York while so much of the wedding details are being handled without her."

Asha presses her lips together and nods, but I can tell she's not fully convinced.

"We'd better be getting back before Claire gets uncomfortable," she says after a beat.

When we head back into the office, the florist hands a contract to Asha, who reviews it quickly before passing it to Claire for her signature.

A moment later, Graham returns to the doorway, all the color drained from his face. He slumps into a chair, pinching the bridge of his nose.

"Teddy, what is it?" Claire asks, placing a hand on his arm.

Graham draws in a breath. "José, our head chef, just called out sick. The hotel is meant to be hosting a murder mystery dinner tonight. I thought it would be a great way to showcase some of the unique ways the ballroom can be used as an event space. But now, we have no one to prepare said dinner. The event starts in four hours; there's no way I'll find a substitute chef in time. I'm going to have to cancel."

He looks so crestfallen, like a little boy who just learned the tooth fairy isn't real, that I have to fight back the urge to throw my arms around him.

"What about Ali?"

My head snaps toward Claire, who's looking at me thoughtfully.

"What about Ali . . . for what?" I ask, uncomprehending.

"Aren't you a professionally trained chef? Maybe you could take over dinner service tonight." She bites her lip, glancing between me and Asha. "Sorry, have I overstepped? I know that this isn't part of your responsibility as our wedding planner. Teddy would of course pay you and . . ."

"That's a great idea. She'll do it." I turn to Asha, gaping.

"Are you sure?" I ask, hoping she'll snap out of whatever lapse in brain synapses she seems to be experiencing and realize what an extraordinarily bad idea this is. She may not realize that spending more time with Graham is a recipe for disaster, but she knows this is way out of the bounds of my job description. "I mean, don't you need help this evening with the Mirza account?"

"All caught up," she says. "My schedule is completely clear. In fact, I'm going to my hot yoga class tonight so you're completely off the hook. I know how much you miss working in kitchens. And I don't believe you had other plans, did you?"

Damn this woman.

"Nope," I manage. I turn to Graham. "I'm all yours tonight." The tips of his ears go fuchsia at the unintended subtext. "Er, I mean, I'm happy to help. In the kitchen. At your hotel."

Graham swallows. "Um, great. Thank you. The event starts at seven, and the kitchen staff already have most of the meal prepped. I can take you over to the kitchen and show you what they've set up."

18

"So. A murder mystery dinner at the hotel. You weren't kidding when you said you were trying to drum up reservations with creative means."

When we step through the doorway of the ballroom, the space is clearly in transition. Black tablecloths cover half the dining tables and vases of black plastic flowers serve as centerpieces. There are even a handful of life-sized skeletons seated at the tables. A paper banner spelling out "Who Dun It?" is hanging in the doorway, but the tape has already slid off one side, leaving it hanging from the doorway like a rope.

"This whole idea seemed a lot better in my head," Graham says, rubbing his temples. "I thought it would be a fun way to introduce a younger generation to the hotel. Now we're down a chef and this space is . . . not quite fully realized."

I head over to one of the tables, studying the place settings.

"You're on the right track," I say. "But you aren't taking full advantage of the resources at your disposal."

I pick a fork off the table and hold it up to the light. "For instance, the silver is gorgeous. Looks brand-new."

Graham's shoulders relax a decimal, and I can tell he's pleased I've noticed.

"Yup. A lot of our stuff was really dated. New flatware gives the dining room a face-lift."

"Definitely! But didn't you say this is 1920s-themed? Now is the time to pull out all your antique stuff."

"I hadn't thought about that," he says. "I bet the basement storage room is a treasure trove."

"See what you can grab," I say. "Some old candelabras with half-melted candlesticks and antique serving platters will go a long way in establishing ambiance. And don't bother dusting them off. The more cobwebs, the better."

Graham purses his lips. "I like it. What else?"

"Lighting is key. Keep the lights as dim as possible. If you go too bright, it will destroy the sinister mood."

Graham looks impressed. "Wow. You're a natural at this."

"It's my job! Putting on themed events gives me life," I say. "I worked in a hotel kitchen in New York and my favorite nights were when they hosted parties like this."

"Well, it seems I've lucked into hiring exactly the right person. And speaking of the kitchen, let me take you back there and introduce you to everyone."

Stepping into the Black-Eyed Susan's kitchen feels like coming back home after a long journey. There are a handful of ways to set up a commercial kitchen, but they all have the same familiar characteristics. Gleaming silver appliances, bright overhead lights, white tiled floors. A calm sense of purpose paired with a prickle of excitement washes over me.

There are half a dozen people working diligently at various stations. When we enter, they each pause, regarding me curiously, and I'm reminded that José and I did the wedding's menu planning alone. Graham gives them a little wave.

"Let me introduce you to the staff," he says. He leads me around the kitchen, introducing me to the small group. There's Alicia, the sous chef, Shanelle and Ansel, the line cooks, and Winston, the pastry chef.

"An in-house pastry chef?" I raise my eyes. "Very impressive."

"Just part-time. But not a lot of places still have an in-house pastry chef these days," Winston agrees. "It's part of what makes this hotel so unique."

"It's nice to meet you, Ali," Alicia says kindly. "We're grateful that you can help tonight. The Black-Eyed Susan is special to all of us."

"This is a pretty special place," I reply, and I mean it. Restaurant kitchens are hardly known for their warm and fuzzy atmosphere, but there's something so homey and welcoming about the staff here that I feel like I've always been part of it.

"Let's get you set up," Alicia says. "And then we can go over the menus."

José has done us all a favor by planning a menu that's both delightful and relatively simple to prepare. We've just finished plotting out the timing of each course when Graham swings into the kitchen, carrying an armful of vintage platters.

"Grabbed these from the basement," he says breathlessly. "Where should I put them?"

I gesture toward an unoccupied food prep station. Graham sets them down gingerly, and I step beside him to get a closer look. His spicy citrus scent is tinged with sweat, and it takes every ounce of self-control not to press my nose against the arm of his sweater.

"These are perfect," I say, brushing my fingertips over the tarnished silver of a twin-handled serving tray. I've seen plenty of vintage serving pieces in the shops on 36th Street, but there's something extra special about these. Perhaps it's because I know exactly how they were used and who they belonged to.

I carry one over to the sink, giving it a thorough soap and water scrub, but refrain from cleaning it with silver polish. Then I carry it over to the cold station, where Ansel has been diligently prepping the charcuterie.

I arrange the meat and cheese carefully on the tray, adding in some sapphire grapes for a creepy effect. I grab a block of Brie, and then use a knife to cut it into the shape of a coffin. I add a drizzle of fig jam to the center of a goat cheese log and stab a cheese spreader through it, giving it the effect of a bleeding stab wound. Once I'm satisfied with the final product, I take a step back, admiring my work. Then I glance over at Graham, who is staring at the board wide-eyed, his hands on his hips.

"Wow," he says after a minute. "That looks incredible." There's something about the way he's looking at me with a mix of admiration and affection that makes my limbs go soft. And God help me if I don't find myself wishing he would look at me this way all the time. I blink, shaking the idea loose from my brain. I need to keep my head on straight when it comes to Graham. Falling for him has the potential to ruin everything.

"Putting on events is my favorite thing," I say after a beat. "Especially when I can incorporate food into a theme. But honestly, these platters elevate the entire thing."

Graham grins at me. "I guess we make a pretty good team."

Alicia clears her throat and I turn my attention back to her.

"Right," I say. "We should get back to it. Where are we with the table decor? Were you able to find any candelabras?"

By the time guests start arriving two hours later, the ballroom has been completely transformed from Grandmillennial-chic to gothic elegance. My florist contact was able to pull together some moody centerpieces consisting of burgundy ranunculus and blood-red hanging Amaranthus. The lights are dimmed, leaving the room mainly illuminated by the flicker of black taper candles in vintage candlesticks. The waiters have set out the charcuterie trays on banquet tables lining the ballroom, and the guests, many of whom have arrived in costume, are mingling and nibbling as they gather clues.

I've just come out of the kitchen to check on everything when Graham approaches. He looks breathtakingly handsome in a tuxedo, his blond hair combed into a neat side part and tamed with product to complete the historically accurate look. Jay Gatsby could never.

Graham, who's gamely playing his part, is deep in conversation as he walks alongside a guest. I overhear him saying something about a fictional affair between the household's heiress and a maid. He nods and gives me a polite smile, but as he passes, he brushes his pinkie finger against mine. It's the slightest of touches, completely undetectable to anyone else in the room, but it lights me up inside like a firework, sending a spark through my hand that reaches all the way down to the tips of my toes.

The rest of the evening goes smoothly, and when I come out to check on the food, I notice a familiar face sitting at one of the tables, chatting with Graham. Trudy.

I make my way over, and she smiles.

"Hey there," she says, clasping one of my hands in hers. "Graham was just telling me that you lent a hand in making tonight such a success."

I return her smile. "Happy I was able to help! It felt good to be back in the kitchen."

She gives my hand a squeeze, a gesture that reminds me of my own grandmother, before turning back to her grandson.

"In fact, the night was such a success that I have some exciting news. One of tonight's guests is a real estate developer. Tonight's event did such a great job highlighting the hotel that he made me an offer I can't refuse."

The smile evaporates from Graham's face. "What do you mean an offer you can't refuse?"

Trudy tilts her head, regarding him curiously. "To buy the hotel, darling."

The blood drains from Graham's face. "You . . . you're thinking of selling the hotel?"

Trudy opens her mouth, then pauses for a beat, seeming to register Graham's look of horror. She flicks her cool gaze to me.

"Excuse us, dear. But I'd like to have a word with my grandson. In private."

A full body flush traces up my limbs.

"Oh, of course." Turning on my heel, I hurry toward the kitchen.

As soon as I push through the double doors, I grasp onto the cool metal of the prep table, taking in a deep breath. I need to relax, pull it together. Staying cool under pressure has always been one of my strengths. It's what's made me so good at working in kitchens over the years. But the pained look on Graham's face feels like a loose thread, threatening to unravel me. I close my eyes and inhale deeply.

A warm hand presses lightly into my shoulder. Turning, I see Alicia's concerned face.

"Everything okay?" she asks. I make a hasty attempt to rearrange my features. When I worked in New York kitchens, I was just another member of the line. But tonight, I'm a leader, and I have a responsibility to hold it together and guide the rest of the staff through the evening smoothly.

"Close call with the blood punch fountain," I say, forcing a smile on my face. "I just need to be more careful, or there will be a second murder victim tonight."

Alicia's lips quirk. "Mr. Wyler's bark is worse than his bite. Besides, I expect he'll be trying his hardest to avoid jail time before his wedding."

The smile on my face freezes. The wedding. The hotel. My heart twists with sympathy as I imagine the conversation Graham and Trudy must be having. *Poor Graham.* He's worked so hard to keep everything afloat for the people he loves, and it's all about to come crashing down.

I do my best to hurry through cleanup, but by the time we've finished packing up the kitchen, it's after ten. When I return to the dining room, it's empty, save for a long figure seated at a table in the back. Graham.

He's staring morosely into a glass of dark red wine, as though it holds the answers to the mysteries of the universe. There's an abandoned white boa draped across the table in front of him, and a few rogue feathers scattered on the floor by his feet.

I slide into the chair next to him, brushing aside a few crumbs left behind from the German chocolate cake that was served for dessert.

"Let me guess," I venture. "It was death by bathtub gin, and the killer got away with it?"

One corner of Graham's mouth twitches but he doesn't look up. "It was Velma, the jaded ex-girlfriend, actually."

"Well, you know what they say. Hell hath no fury like a fictional woman scorned."

Graham breathes out a soft laugh, and I put one hand over his. "Talk to me, Graham."

At last, he lifts his gaze to look at me. His eyes are red behind his glasses, and I know it's from more than just exhaustion. The weight of everything he's carrying is etched into his handsome features.

"I had no idea that Granny was considering selling. When I offered to come back here and help get the hotel back on its feet, she agreed to it readily. I thought she had more faith in me. That she believed I could fix things."

"Of course she has faith in you," I reassure him. "She loves you."

Graham's smile is sad. "That's just what she said. That she loves me and that she loved getting to spend extra time with me over the past few months. But she also said one must always have a backup plan. Something to fall back on if business doesn't pick up after the wedding. Apparently she's been interviewing potential buyers for months."

He drags a hand through his hair.

"It's actually a pretty common practice, what this buyer's offering. Purchasing old hotels to repurpose them as condos. Especially in a city with so much need for affordable housing. And he is offering Granny a very generous amount of money. It would allow her to retire comfortably. Most importantly, she can leave on her own terms. 'Preserve the legacy of the hotel,' as she put it."

Graham blows out a frustrated sigh.

"I just wish she saw things the way that I do," he says emphatically. "Our legacy *is* the hotel. How can she just give it all up? What about everything our family built together? I can't imagine that if Grandpa were alive, he would hand over the hotel so readily. Who even knows if this bloke's honest about his intentions? What if he just goes ahead and demolishes it?"

I watch as his shoulders tighten, the tension practically radiating off him as his hands ball into fists. I ache to lean forward and put my hand on his arm, to relieve some of his stress by absorbing it into my own body. But I can't risk it, not when there's still staff cleaning up around us.

I settle for dragging my chair and inch closer to him.

"I know this hurts," I tell him. "But she was always going to retire eventually. At some point, she was going to have to walk away."

Graham nods glumly. "That's exactly what she said. Now that Grandpa has passed, she's ready to move on to the next phase of her life. I understand where she's coming from. The ideal opportunity has just presented itself. She'd be a fool not to take it."

His forehead furrows. "And as she reminded me, she doesn't have anyone to pass the hotel on to. Mum has made it clear that she doesn't plan on returning from London, and as she pointed out, Claire and I will be returning to New York after the wedding."

Fuck the onlookers. I reach forward and give his forearm a squeeze.

"I'm sick to the stomach at the thought of losing the hotel," he continues glumly. "I had a great childhood in London, but I lived for the summers I spent here. My mother did her best, she really did. But she was a single mom, and I was on my own a lot of the time. When I came here for the summers, I was the center of my grandparents' world. We had family dinners and went to the movies and spent weekends collecting seashells at the beach. But I think my favorite days were the ones spent at the hotel. I loved seeing every part of it: how the kitchen worked, the bookings, the events. Even how the maid service cleaned the rooms. The thought of it all disappearing—it would be like a death in the family."

The sorrow in his voice tugs at my chest. I take a fortifying breath before addressing the elephant in the room.

"Have you ever thought of taking it over yourself?"

Graham tips his head back and studies the intricately tiled ceiling.

"Of course I have. I care about this place so much. But passion can only take you so far. At the end of the day, I don't have a clue how to manage a hotel. And if my mismanagement was ultimately what drove it into the ground, I don't know how I'd live with the guilt. I can't bear the thought of destroying everything my family built."

He cast his eyes back down to his lap. "They did so much for me, Ali. They paid for my education. It was because of them that I was able to go to the best secondary schools, to go on to university and pursue a career. And what for? It's all worthless in the end. I couldn't do the same what they did for me. I couldn't pay it forward and save the hotel."

Graham drops his head, burying his face in his hands. I reach forward to stroke his head, brushing my fingers gently through the golden strands of his hair.

"You are allowed to accept love without feeling like it's a debt that needs to be repaid. Your grandparents didn't spend time with you or put you through school because they expected anything in return. They did it because they love you. You need to let go of this guilt. Loving them in return . . . it's enough."

Graham lifts his head to look at me, the wrinkle of tension in his forehead smoothing as he places one hand over mine. "You're quite an expert on love."

"Well, I am in the business of romance. And you know what they say. Those who can't do, teach."

He affords me a tiny smile, and the barriers safeguarding my heart crack open a fraction. I used to be such a romantic. In love with the idea of being in love, undeterred by my plethora of tragic dating experiences. But then I did find love. And it nearly broke me.

I thought Dev was it. He was the classic nice guy: a first-grade teacher who referred to his students as "my kids" and plastered his fridge with their brightly colored artwork. On the weekends, he volunteered at an animal shelter, ultimately adopting a three-legged dog named Trident. To me, he was perfect. But to him, I was absent. He didn't understand the lack of work-life balance chefs face, or why I was never around to go to trivia nights with his work friends. Dev saw me as insufficient, and for the first time in my life, I saw myself the same way. Because if a man who takes his class lizard home every weekend so it won't feel lonely can't love me, who would?

Graham's smile fades a decimal. There's so much more that needs to be said, but tonight is not the night. Not when the prospect of losing such a large part of his childhood has left him looking this dejected.

He's quiet for a long moment as he traces a fingertip around the rim of his wine glass, and an invisible hand squeezes my heart. It's an unfamiliar feeling, to say the least, and one I don't particularly care for. I've never been especially gifted at knowing the right thing to say when people are hurting. But what I do know is how to have fun.

"Well, that's quite enough moping for one night," I say, rising to stand. I lace my fingers through his and drag him upward. "We're going out."

"Out?" Graham raises his eyebrows. "Out where? It's after ten."

"Admittedly our options are somewhat more limited than they would be in New York. Luckily for you, I know just the place."

19

One semi-brief car ride later, we step through the doorway of Mustang Alley's. I haven't been here in years, but it looks unchanged. A mural of the cityscape trims the perimeter. Strips of navy light illuminate shiny wooden lanes, the ends of which are adorned with sports jersey renderings. There's a dining area across from the lanes, where patrons are sipping from frosted glasses and shouting at the overhead televisions.

"Bowling?" Graham looks skeptical as he glances around the room.

"Not just bowling. Bowling, wings, and beer. All the ingredients needed to resurrect a crappy evening."

A trace of the darkness on Graham's face dissipates for the first time since I discovered him sulking in the dining room.

"Well. When you put it in those terms."

We settle into a lane and Graham picks up a ball, palming it thoughtfully like he's seeing it for the very first time.

"You don't have bowling in the UK?" I ask.

Graham shrugs. "Impossible to know. I never once left my flat."

"I'm sure you'll pick it up quickly. It didn't take you long to learn Kings."

"And look how that turned out."

I snort out a laugh. "Do you regret it?"

Graham raises his eyebrows.

"Regret learning a drinking game?"

"I mean, do you regret the entire night? Making a choice that's led to the world's most nightmare-inducing tattoo?"

The moment the words leave my mouth, I realize I'm afraid to hear the answer. I can't help but consider that everything in Graham's life would be easier if we'd never met all those years ago. Planning his fake wedding would be a lot less complicated, for one thing. And let's not discount the fact that he wouldn't be plagued with the world's ugliest tattoo.

But then Graham fixes his gaze on me, his expression turning serious. "Ali," he says softly. "When it comes to you, I'll never regret anything."

My chest pinches. There's a hot, unexpected trickle behind my eyes and I avert my gaze to the end of the lane. If only I could convince myself that the pull I feel toward this man is nothing more than biological chemistry. Magnetism spawned from physical attraction and nothing more. But it's getting harder and harder to lie to myself.

"You ready?" I ask with a labored smile. "No bets this time. I promise."

A grin stretches across Graham's face.

"Let's do it."

One frame of bowling, two Blue Moons, and an order of barbecue wings later, Graham leans back against his swivel chair, his body visibly less tense than it was an hour ago.

"You were right," he says. "I do feel a bit better."

"Of course you do. You're out with me, the High Priestess of Diversion."

Graham's eyes hold mine.

"You are fun," he concedes. "But it's not your defining characteristic. You're so much more than a good time, Ali. Distracting me with a fun night out was just the means. What makes you special is how much you care about people. The way you make everyone feel loved and cared for."

A warm, fluttery sensation fills my chest. The sensation of being seen is equal parts exhilarating and terrifying.

"It's what I love the most about what I do," I admit. "Cooking and putting on events. Making things. It all comes from the same desire. I feel the happiest when I'm making other people happy."

"Trust me, you make everyone around you feel happy," Graham says.

A server arrives at our lane, carrying a tray with the next round of beer we ordered.

Graham hands one bottle to me before tapping the edge of his bottle against mine.

"A toast."

"And what are we toasting to, Mr. Wyler?"

"To this evening's success. I've been so busy wallowing that I've failed to properly thank you for your help. What you pulled off tonight exceeded anything I ever could have imagined."

I shrug, but the compliment wraps itself around me like a warm embrace. "It was a joint effort. You came in strong with all those haunted mansion serving pieces. I imagine Casper's uncles were none too pleased by the disturbance."

Graham grins at me. "We make a good team."

"We do." He holds my gaze for a moment before the corners of his smile falter, and I know what he's thinking. That with the wedding only weeks away, our time together is coming to an end. Not that it should matter. It's not like Graham and I have a future together. We've both acknowledged this can never be more than a fling.

The overhead music switches to a slow song. Graham places the mostly full bottle on the tabletop and rises to standing. Bending forward, he reaches out a hand.

"May I have this dance?"

I glance around me skeptically. "We are in a bowling alley."

Graham shrugs. "I never got to dance with you at the Bar Mitzvah."

I stare at his outstretched palm for a long moment before placing my hand in his and standing.

"This is a bold move for you, Mr. Wyler."

Graham presses a palm into the small of my back, pulling me flush against him. The feeling of his chest against mine steals the air from my lungs. He laughs softly, his warm breath tickling my cheek.

"What can I say? You have a knack for pushing me out of my comfort zone."

We're barely moving, just gently swaying against each other. There's a pleasant tingling in my limbs at every point of contact, and a sense of peace washes over me.

"Who'd have thought that a Baltimore bowling alley would be such a romantic spot," Graham muses.

"It's different to see Baltimore through adult eyes," I concede. "Growing up, I couldn't wait to get out of here. Spending your entire childhood with the same group of people feels like a prison. Everyone has a set idea of who you are and there is no room for change. The reputation you curated in the third grade follows you for the rest of your life. I was thrilled to escape to New York. A place where you're surrounded by people yet have the luxury of complete anonymity. There are endless possibilities for reinvention."

"I guess it depends on whether being anonymous feels like a good thing," Graham says. "Whether it feels lonely."

"New York can be lonely," I concede. "But I don't feel lonely here. I guess that's the thing about coming home. When you're a kid, you look around your hometown and feel like you don't belong. But when you grow up, you realize it's the only place you ever did." I shrug. "These days, I think Baltimore is sort of magical." Graham lifts one hand forward to cup my jaw, his thumb brushing my cheek.

"I think you're magical," he says softly. "A few hours ago, I was devastated, but being around you completely lifted my mood. There's just something about you, Ali. You just make everything better." He tilts my head toward him, cradling my face in his hands. A storm cloud of emotion looms behind his eyes, and I feel a tightness in my chest. It's an emotion I do my best to avoid confronting and it takes a moment to identify it. Fear.

Graham seems to register that something's off.

"What is it?" he asks softly.

"I'm scared," I admit. It's a level of vulnerability I rarely allow myself to expose, but the authenticity feels oddly natural.

Graham raises an eyebrow.

"Of what?" he asks. "You're the most fearless person I've ever met."

"I'm scared of you," I admit quietly. "Of the way that I feel about you."

Graham leans closer until his lips are hovering an inch from my own. "I never expected this," he says softly, his breath warm against my mouth. "I never expected you."

When he kisses me, it feels different than it has before, unflinching and reverent. Our bodies become one unit, merged by feelings that seem too big for words, and with a muted twinge of trepidation, I wonder how I ever let myself believe that this could be a fling.

"My grandmother left for the airport after dinner," he whispers, his voice a low scape against my ear. "I'm meant to be watching Genevieve again through the weekend."

"Well, then we'd better be getting home," I murmur. "For the sake of the dog."

"How many times do I have to tell you that Genevieve is not a dog?"

Graham smirks as he slips his hand through mine, and with that, we're hurrying out the door and back into the darkness.

Graham doesn't bother to flip on the lights when we stumble through the doorway of his grandmother's house. The moment we cross the threshold, he's twisting his fingers through my hair, molding his lips to mine. I'm not sure how much time passes as we stand there, exchanging frantic kisses like desperate, horny teenagers, before he grabs the hem of my dress, lifting it over my head. He tosses it on the floor behind him, and a muscle in his jaw twitches as his gaze caresses my newly exposed skin. Even in the darkness, I can see the fire igniting in his eyes.

A long beat passes as we stare at each other, drinking each other in, before he charges forward. He grabs my face, thumbs tracing over my cheekbones as he roughly captures my lips. Then he walks me backward until I'm flattened against the entryway wall. My hip bone bumps against the edge of a console table, sending the framed photos on top rattling.

He slides a finger through one bra strap and guides it down until it falls off my shoulder. I let out a shuddering breath when he drags his lips from my mouth to brush them across my exposed collarbone.

I slip a hand between us, stroking the bulge in his dress pants. He lets out a low growl as he bites down on the tender skin of my neck. Encouraged, I undo a button, slipping my fingers into the elastic of his boxers. He inhales sharply when my hand encircles him, the hardness of him sending a ripple of excitement through my chest.

Graham reaches behind me to unhook my bra. It drops to the floor, leaving me topless. I swallow a gasp as the cool air brushes over my nipples, but then Graham captures one in the heat of his mouth, closing a hand over the other. I tilt my head back, arching toward him as he continues his gentle assault, his thumb teasing one nipple to a hard peak while he sucks gently on the other before switching sides. Heat builds between my legs, and I let out a ragged exhale.

"Graham," I croak. "I need you. Now."

Wordlessly, Graham scoops me up in his arms, and begins carrying me up the staircase, which is blessedly illuminated by the moonlight pouring in through the windows. He deposits me into the guest room where he sleeps, lowering me down gently on the edge of his mattress.

His gaze locks on mine as he sinks to his knees. My heart pounds against my chest as his mouth traces up my thighs, planting kisses everywhere except where I want him most. When I let out an impatient whine, lifting my hips toward him in a less than subtle gesture, he lets out a low chuckle. Then, mercifully, he strokes his tongue over my panties, licking me straight up my center. I bite down on my lower lip, groaning.

"Graham, *fuck*." I pant. "Please."

His lips curl upward.

"Always so impatient."

He hooks his fingers into the edge of my panties, pulling them down slowly, torturously, before draping a leg over his shoulder. By the time he eases a finger inside of me, I've lost the ability to form a cohesive thought.

He studies me through hooded lids as his fingers stroke over me, like he's mentally cataloging all the ways I want to be touched. A moan escapes my throat when his tongue brushes my most sensitive spot. Pleasure builds in my core as his tongue laps over me, rhythm building. I ball the sheets in my hands as my legs start to tremble. I rock my hips against him, my surroundings start to blur until I'm no longer aware of anything besides the sensation of Graham's mouth and fingers, until it sends me over the edge with an orgasm so strong that the edges of my vision turn white.

I return to my body slowly, as Graham lowers his body onto the mattress beside me, his body flush against mine. He leans forward, cupping my cheeks, and despite the urgency we felt for each other downstairs, the way he's kissing me now is slow and unexpectedly tender. Emotion wells in my chest as I feel his heartbeat against my own chest and a single word echoes inside my head. *Mine, mine, mine.*

"Ali," he breathes, and there is so much emotion infused into that one word that it brings tears to my eyes. There's so much that needs to be said, but I don't want to spoil this perfect moment. So instead, I hook my fingers inside his undone pants, sliding them the rest of the way down his legs.

"I need you," I repeat, vaguely aware that at some point, my ache for this man has stopped being purely physical. Graham climbs off the bed, removing his wallet from his pants and extracting a condom. I watch as he rolls it over his length before lowering himself on top of me.

He lowers his mouth to kiss me again as he pushes himself inside of me, and then we are moving together, slowly finding our rhythm. I dig my nails into his back as he increases the speed of his thrusts, until I'm hurling over the edge of a cliff, this orgasm even stronger than the last, the aftershocks rippling through my core.

I collapse back against the pillow as I slowly come back down to earth. The cool fabric carries his musky scent, and I take a gratuitous inhale. Then Graham drops onto the mattress beside me. He wraps an arm around my waist, tucking my head beneath his chin and pulling me flush against him. My eyes travel over the length of his body, the thin sheen of sweat that coats his chest as it rises and falls with ragged breath. My gaze lowers to the tattoo on his hip bone, and I trail my fingers over it slowly, reverently.

Graham's palm covers mine as I continue tracing my fingers over the familiar pattern.

"Do you ever wonder," I ask, "if the tattoos have some sort of magical properties that propelled us back together?"

"Like two magnetic poles," he says sleepily. "A pair of opposite forces powerless to fight the attraction that draws them together." He's quiet for a moment and then his breath grows slow and steady, and I know he's fallen asleep.

I awaken to a glimmer of sunshine peeking through the blinds and the sound of my phone buzzing on the bedside table. I reach over to grab it, squinting at the name on the screen.

Babs Cell: CALL ME.

"Why do boomers have such an affinity for 'Call Me' texts?" I muse sleepily. "If they're so hell-bent on speaking by phone, why don't they just call us and forgo the theatrics?"

Graham rolls over and plants a kiss on my shoulder. "And miss the opportunity to terrify the recipient? What would be the fun in that?"

"I can assure you there's nothing terrifying about this. Odds are she wants to know which flavor of Mandel bread I want her to make for Passover so she can bake and freeze it four months in advance of the holiday. Which is obviously a trick question, since the answer is no freezer-burnt Mandel bread, thank you very much."

"I don't know what that is, but I suspect I'll live out my days in blissful ignorance."

I grin as I lean back against Graham's warm, bare chest and dial my mom. But the second she picks up the phone and I hear her shaky exhale on the other end of the line, I know I've made a grave misjudgment. Dread pools in my belly.

"What is it? What happened?" I ask before she even says a word. Beneath me, Graham's body stiffens.

"It's Bubbie," my mom replies, and I can tell by the thickness of her voice that she's been crying. I shoot up straight in bed, faintly aware of Graham's intense stare on the back of my head but unable to look back at him.

"She was having chest pains in the middle of the night," my mom continues. "We rushed her to the hospital. The doctors . . . they think it's her heart. Wait, hang on."

I hear my mom's muffled voice speaking to someone in the background and then another voice comes on the line.

"Hey, Al. It's me," Sarah says. A new feeling blooms in my chest, one that's hot and sour. Because of course my mom called Sarah first. Of course I'm the very last call.

Sarah's voice shakes me out of my bitter inner monologue. "We're at Sinai Hospital. How soon can you get here?" I close my eyes and let out a shaky breath. Now is not the time to get emotional about my family dynamics. My grandmother needs me. "I can be there in fifteen minutes. I'm already downtown."

The weight of the bed shifts as Graham stands up. I stare at his bare back as he rummages through a dresser drawer before extracting a navy sweater and pulling it over his head. Part of me deflates, a feeling that's followed by a rush of guilt. I wasn't ready for our time together to come to such an abrupt end. But nothing cools off a steamy evening faster than a family emergency.

I disconnect the call and begin fishing for my own clothes, which are still strewn across the floor. Already, I can feel my heartbeat start to escalate.

"My grandma is in the hospital," I tell Graham, doing my best to keep my voice steady. "I have to go."

"I'll drive you," Graham says as he drags a belt through the loops of his jeans.

"That's sweet, but you don't have to do that," I say. I give him a reassuring smile as I focus on keeping my voice steady. If there's one thing I've learned over the years, it's to not expect men to provide me with anything other than orgasms. Well, that and to reach something on a high shelf.

But then Graham is kneeling beside me, placing a warm hand over mine. It isn't until our skin makes contact that I realize my own hands are shaking. The reassuring pressure of his touch slows my heart rate immediately, and I feel my breathing start to regulate.

"I'll drive you," he says again, softly. "Just tell me where we're going."

20

My mom and Sarah are sitting side by side on plastic chairs in the waiting room. My dad is stretched on a chair across from them, staring intently at his cell phone. When she spots me, my mom leaps from her chair and throws her arms around me. She presses her face into my hair, and I tighten my grip around her. After a minute, she pulls back, and her gaze travels over my shoulder to Graham. Her expression instantly brightens.

"Oh, hello again, Mr. Wyler," she says with barely contained glee. Nothing soothes the ache of a family emergency faster than a vague potential for grandchildren.

"Please, call me Graham," he corrects her politely.

"Graham," she says. "Thank you so much for bringing Ali. What are the odds that you would be available so early in the morning!" She raises her eyebrows meaningfully, and I suppress the urge to roll my eyes. There's no chance I'm indulging her poorly veiled attempts at fishing right now.

Graham leans toward me, the tickle of his breath against my ear sending a pleasurable tingle down my spine. "I'll be back," he whispers. I turn to tell him that he doesn't need to pick me up since I can go home with my family, but he's already disappeared down the corridor. A tight ball forms in the center of my chest as I watch him walk away. Something that feels suspiciously like loss. A ridiculous feeling, really, since Graham is the furthest thing from being mine to lose. I turn back to my mom, who has the audacity to be giving me a shit-eating grin.

"That man is so handsome," she says dreamily. "And the accent!"

"Seriously?" I say. "We're at the hospital. For Bubbie? Have you gotten any updates from the doctors?" My mom's face falls at the reminder.

"Not yet," she says, casting her eyes downward. "They're still running tests, but we came in during the change of shift. We should hear something soon."

My sister rises and places a hand on my mom's elbow. "Do you need anything, Mom? Want me to get you a coffee?"

My mom shakes her head. "No thanks, baby. If I drink any more caffeine right now, I'll jump right out of my skin." She gives me a tiny smile. "Have you eaten? I didn't know if you had time to eat before you left this morning."

"We didn't have time to grab anything, but I'm fine," I say.

Sarah's mouth curls upward at my use of the "we" pronoun, and I know exactly what comment she's repressing. Thankfully, she has the decency not to draw out this conversation in front of Yenta the Matchmaker. The last thing I need is for the two of them to get attached to Graham. It will only make things worse when I have to explain his disappearance.

"I'm going to check in on the kids," she says, holding up her phone. When she disappears around the corner, my mom collapses back against the back of her chair. It's then that I notice how frail she looks, how the lines in her forehead became more prominent overnight.

"How about a bottle of water?" I ask her. "You should really hydrate."

My mom shoots me a grateful smile. "That would be great," she says.

I give her hand a squeeze, pleased to finally be the one who can offer her something. Then I start walking down the corridor, in search of any signage directing me toward the cafeteria.

But five minutes later, I'm no closer to locating it than I was when I started, the mazelike hallways continuously directing me in circles. Frustrated, I collapse onto a bench, drawing my knees to my chest and pressing the heels of my hands into my eyes.

"Fuck," I whisper into my hands.

"Hey, are you okay?"

Dragging my hands off my face, I squint, blurry-eyed, at the figure approaching me.

"Graham?" I ask. "What are you still doing here?"

He sets down a half-empty cardboard drink carrier on the bench beside me. "You think I was going to abandon you?" he asks. "I just went to get you something to eat."

Heat spreads across my chest. "Oh," I say. "I went to get some water for my mom but, um . . . I got lost on my way."

He smiles reassuringly. "Not to worry. I got a few coffees and bottles of water from the marketplace. I went back to the lounge where I left you and your parents took some of it off my hands. They said you'd gone for water, so I came to look for you."

He lifts a foil-wrapped package out of the drink carrier and hands it to me. "I got you an egg and cheese on a bagel. Not exactly NYC quality but the best I could do under the circumstances."

I stare at him, open-mouthed, my eyes tracing over every detail of him—the fathomless blue of his eyes, the soft petulance of his bottom lip—and it occurs to me that everything I thought I knew about romance was wrong. Up until now, I thought romance was about grand gestures and heartfelt confessions. I thought the most romantic thing that had ever happened was when Jake performed "Till There Was You" for Lexi during New Year's Rockin' Eve, or any time Shawn Mendes and Camila Cabello took a walk together on a beach. But it turns out the true definition of romance is sticking around to bring someone an egg and cheese sandwich while they're waiting in a hospital lounge. And just like that, I burst into tears.

Graham's eyes go wide with panic, and he leans forward, clasping my elbow.

"Oh God, I'm sorry. I tried to tell the man behind the counter that New Yorkers don't toast their bagels, but he was rather insistent."

I let out a watery sob. I've done everything in my power to make this just about sex, to tell myself that what Graham and I have is nothing more than a physical attraction. But despite my best intentions, I've cracked the doorway to my heart and allowed Graham to slip inside. Despite knowing that he is not mine, and that he never can be, I have let myself fall for him. And that terrifies me. Because there is nothing scarier than falling when you aren't sure that you'll be caught.

Grabbing Graham by the front of his sweater, I pull him toward me, pressing his lips to mine. He slides one hand up to my cheek, cupping my face, and lifting it toward his. I let out a full body sigh when his mouth starts to move against mine. The comfort it evokes spreads over me like a warm blanket.

"Fuck," I say when we finally break apart. "I really like you."

Graham's lips curl into a smile. "I really like you too, Ali."

I sniffle as I take a bite of my bagel. The combination of everything spice, warm egg, and melty cheese is the perfect elixir. Graham offers me the paper coffee cup and I take a long, fortifying sip. I feel better already. When I finish, Graham gathers my trash, tossing it in a nearby can.

"Should we head back to your family?" he asks when he returns.

"See if there's any news?" I nod, and we walk side by side back to the family lounge.

"There you are." My mom jumps to her feet when she sees us. "We just spoke to the doctor."

My heart hammers against my rib cage. "What did they say?"

From his spot on the sofa, my father harrumphs. "They said there's nothing wrong with her. It's just heartburn."

"Oh," I bark out a relieved laugh. "Alright, then."

"The doctor said we can see her now," my mom says. "I was just waiting for you to come back."

"I'll wait for you here," Graham says softly, taking a seat on the lounge chair across from my dad. But my mom shakes her head.

"Please, come in. She'll be thrilled to see you," she insists. Graham's face turns bashful, but nevertheless, he follows us into my grandmother's room.

"Hey, Mom," my mom says when we walk through her doorway. "How are you feeling?"

"Eh, I'm fine," Bubbie says. She straightens up in her bed, peering at us through her fogged-over glasses. Despite the circumstances, her hair hasn't deflated an inch.

"The doctor tells me it's just heartburn. Which makes sense since I had Edna's latkes during our canasta game last night. That old bat can't cook for shit."

"Bubbie!" Sarah protests.

Bubbie shrugs, nonplussed. "I'm telling you, she reuses her frying oil. It's a miracle I'm not dead." Her eyes travel over my shoulder to Graham.

"Well, hello!" she says gleefully. "I sure am glad to see you again."

Graham blushes.

"Here I thought I was going to die before I saw our little Ali walk down the aisle. But maybe there's hope for her after all!" I roll my eyes.

"Good lord, I'm not even thirty yet," I grumble. Bubbie ignores me, her eyes still fixed on Graham's.

"Anyway, I couldn't die before tomorrow night's Hanukkah party. Ali's latkes are to die for. You'll be there, right?"

I open my mouth to protest, but before I can say anything, my mom turns to Graham.

"We'd love to have you, if you can make it," she says.

Graham presses a hand into my shoulder, giving it a light squeeze. "I wouldn't miss it," he says.

The atmosphere has shifted during the drive to pick up my car from Trudy's house. There's been a seismic shift between us over the past twenty-four hours, and I know I'm not the only one who feels it. Graham and I are playing a dangerous game, one that has the potential to hurt the people we care about. Not to mention how much we stand to hurt each other. A knot of guilt forms in the pit of my stomach.

"Graham," I hedge. "I think we should talk."

Graham releases a low sigh. "I know," he says. "What we're doing right now isn't fair to anyone, and it isn't sustainable. I want to be with you, Ali. I want to come to your parents' house for dinner as your real boyfriend. No more sneaking around."

I bite down on my lip. "What about Claire? We can't keep going behind her back."

Graham's features tighten. "I know. I will talk to her when she's back from New York. We will figure something out. But I need to talk to her in person. It's only right."

A long-dormant sense of hope flutters in my chest. A few weeks ago, a future with Graham seemed impossible. But everything is different now, and I'm ready to take the next step forward.

But when we pull up to the house, there's a familiar figure standing in the front yard, wrapped in a quilted navy coat, and clutching a dog leash.

Graham's brows knit together. "My grandmother is home," he says slowly. "She wasn't supposed to be home until tomorrow."

My stomach bottoms out. *Shit.* The idea of coming clean to Trudy about our relationship is one thing. Actually doing it is another.

"Maybe she didn't see me," I offer. "I can hide in the car until you're both inside the house. I can easily fit under the glove box."

Too late. Trudy's brows knit quizzically as she stares at us. Then she raises a hand to wave.

Graham presses his lips together as he waves back. Then he turns to me.

"Look, I will have to tell her the truth at some point. But not until I speak to Claire. It wouldn't be fair not to tell her first."

I know he's right. And yet.

Hesitantly, I follow him out of the car and up the paved walkway.

Trudy's eyes light up as Graham makes his way toward her. Then she turns to me and a look of confusion flits across her features.

"Ali," she says. Her voice is pleasant but questioning. "What are you doing here?"

I paste on a smile, trying my best to ignore the hollow, fluttery feeling in my stomach that comes from being put on the spot. *Think, Ali.*

"I, uh . . . had a meeting with Graham and he mentioned you have a cake server that you'd like to use for the reception. I hear it's a family heirloom." It's not quite a lie—Graham did mention that his grandmother wanted him and Claire to cut the cake with the same knife she and her late husband used at their wedding.

Trudy's expression softens. "Oh, dear. That would be lovely. Why don't you come in? I'll fetch the cake server and then you can update me on all the wedding plans over a cup of coffee."

"Oh, that's so kind of you, but I really don't want to impose."

Trudy waves a hand. "Nonsense. It's freezing outside. The least I can do is offer you a warm beverage."

Wordlessly, I follow Graham into the kitchen, taking a seat at the now-familiar wooden table. Already, my throat feels tight, my heart beating too quickly in my chest. As much as I want to be with Graham, the less-than-ideal circumstances of this situation are triggering a stress response. A decision to call off the wedding comes with collateral damage, and the thought of hurting anyone makes me feel sick to my stomach.

"Ali, I haven't had a chance to thank you for all you're doing to make this a special day for Claire and Graham," Trudy says, as she pours coffee into a mug. "I know how hard you've been working. I mean, you're even making trips here on the weekends. I am so thrilled that my grandson and future granddaughter found you."

My stomach dips like I'm on a roller coaster. I wonder if Trudy can read the guilt on my face, if it's etched into my features. But when she hands me a steaming cup of coffee with a placid smile, I know I must be doing a sufficient job of masking my anxiety.

"Graham, darling?" she says sweetly. "Why don't you go fetch the cake knife? It's in the dining room breakfront. Third drawer on the left."

Graham disappears through the doorway and Trudy turns back to me. When her eyes lock on mine, there's a mischievous twinkle behind them.

"You know, just between you and me, dear, I was a bit surprised when Graham told me that he had proposed to Claire. They've known each other for years, and they've always just been friends. But I guess sometimes friendship blossoms into something more."

She's eyeing me carefully, like she's trying to gauge my reaction to her observation, and my breath catches. Has she guessed that this is a sham wedding? And if so, is she going to suggest pulling the plug?

I clear my throat, choosing my next words carefully. "It's not uncommon for couples to start off as friends first. They say friendship is the basis of any strong relationship."

"Hmm." Trudy purses her lips, and I get the sense she's disappointed with my answer. But when she slides into the seat across from me, her shoulders deflate, and I sense an immediate shift in her mood.

"It hasn't been that long since I lost my Bernard. He'd been my sweetheart since we were children. We spent our whole lives together. We built a business together, raised a family. I suppose in a way, he was my best friend." Her eyes grow damp, and she dabs at them with a napkin.

"Lately, I've felt like I had nothing to smile about. But this wedding is bringing me a sense of joy I haven't felt in months. On the days when I'm struggling, the idea of my grandson getting married at the hotel Bernard and I built together fills the hole in my heart. It gives me a reason to get out of bed in the morning. You know, my late husband and I were married there almost sixty years ago."

I give her a small smile. "Graham told me. He just made a reel for the hotel's Instagram account, showcasing your framed wedding portrait in the hotel lobby next to an invitation for his own wedding. People are loving the connection between past and present."

And just like that, inspiration strikes. I'm about to go way off script. But it wouldn't be the first time and it certainly won't be the last.

"Mrs. Dyson, I don't mean to overstep—"

"And yet I sense you're about to."

But the twinkle of amusement in her eyes belies the harsh tone of her words, giving me the confidence to continue.

"I couldn't help but overhear your conversation about selling the hotel. And I wonder if you'd consider waiting to decide until after the wedding. Graham's been working so hard, and I think there's a real possibility that the buzz surrounding the nuptials will reinvigorate interest in the hotel."

Trudy tilts her head to the side and gives me an appraising look. "You care about him," she says. It's a statement, not a question.

"Yes," I manage. "I mean, I care about them both. Him and Claire. It's my job, after all, to assist with making their day perfect."

A sound from the doorway steals the air from my lungs. Graham is lingering there, the color draining from his face.

"I found the cake server," he says hoarsely. *Shit. How long has he been standing there?*

Trudy shifts her attention to her grandson. "Darling, I've been thinking a lot about our earlier discussion about the hotel. And you are right. Perhaps I have been hasty."

Graham's mouth drops open, but it takes a full beat before he says anything.

"What do you mean?"

"You were right. You've worked so hard to rehabilitate the hotel, and I would hate to make you feel like your efforts are not valued. Check-in rates are not where I'd like them to be, but they are higher than they were a few months ago, and our financial troubles seem to have plateaued, at least for now. So how about this: I will wait until after the wedding to see if things have changed. If your social media efforts are successful and things have turned around after the wedding, then . . . I will consider staying on for a few more years. See where things take us."

Graham's eyes go wide.

"Are you sure?" he asks softly, and for a second, I can see the little boy he once was. My heart turns to Jell-O.

Trudy's smile is the most genuine I've seen yet. "I believe in you. I always have."

As much as the moment warms me, I can't help but feel like I'm once again intruding.

"Well, thank you so much for the coffee," I say quickly. "But I really should head out. I have a few more errands to run."

"Of course," Trudy says warmly. "Thanks so much for stopping by."

I don't look at Graham as I stand, and he makes his way over to where his grandmother is standing.

"I'll walk Ali to her car," he mumbles, pressing his lips to his grandmother's cheek.

He doesn't look at me as we walk side by side through the corridor, my hand wrapped tightly around the cake server's intricate handle. The cold air whips across my face as I step outside, instantly drawing tears. I swipe them away angrily. God, why do I always do this? Once again, I've been impulsive and overstepped, offered my feedback where it wasn't sought. And now Graham is angry. As he should be.

Once we reach the sidewalk, Graham grabs me by the hand, spinning me around to face him. He frowns as he takes in my tear-streaked face. He cups my face with both hands, using his thumbs to brush the moisture away from my eyes.

"Why are you crying?" he murmurs.

"It's nothing," I say, shrugging him off. "It's just the wind."

Graham shakes his head slowly. "God," he whispers. "You really are something else."

Shame snakes its way up my spine. *When am I going to learn to stop being so reckless?*

But before I can say another word, his mouth is on mine, capturing it with a searing kiss that sets every limb on fire. He slides his hands from my cheeks to the base of my neck, adjusting the angle for a deeper kiss. Every fiber of self-doubt evaporates as I fist the fabric of his sweater, pulling him closer.

I'm breathless when he finally pulls away and presses his forehead to mine. From the corner of my eye, I think I see movement in

Trudy's window, but I'm too consumed by the heat of Graham's ragged breath against my cheek to be certain.

"You're not angry?" I ask wearily.

A wrinkle forms between Graham's brows.

"Angry?" he asks. "For convincing my grandmother to give the hotel one more chance? Ali, no one has ever done anything like that for me. I don't know how to thank you."

I weave a hand through the soft strands of his hair. "She believes in you. We both do."

Graham lets out a contented sigh as he covers his hand with mine.

"I think I can do it," he says softly. "I think I can pull it off. All of it."

I smile as I trace the stubble on his jawline and try my hardest to ignore the growing bubble of dread in the pit of my stomach. Things will be okay. They have to be.

21

The doorbell rings a little after 5 P.M. the following day. I can't imagine it's Graham already—dinner doesn't start for another hour—but when I pull the door open, he's standing there sheepishly, clutching a bottle of wine.

"Hey," he says. "I know it's terrible manners to show up early. But I went to buy kosher wine and then I was worried that if I went back downtown, I'd just have to turn back around as soon as I got there."

"It's fine," I reassure him, taking the wine out of his hand to inspect it. "Wow, nicely done. I'm very impressed that you didn't show up with a box of matzah or those watermelon jellies."

"Matzah?" Graham looks perplexed. "Isn't that for Passover?"

"Sure is. But it doesn't stop grocery stores from trotting it out for every Jewish holiday. Anyway, come in."

I take Graham's coat (only sniffing it the slightest amount) and hang it in the hall closet before leading him into the kitchen.

"Wow, it smells amazing in here," Graham says. My mom looks up from her own project, where she's assembling marshmallows and Hershey kisses to look like dreidels, and grins.

"That would be Ali's brisket," she says with a grin. "You're in for a treat."

"Not only that," I say, sweeping a hand across my various workspaces. "I'm rolling out a rainbow latke platter this year. I've got zucchini, beet, and carrot varieties, plus I'm debuting a sweet potato version with a maple syrup dipping sauce." Graham's eyes go wide as they sweep over my makeshift latke factory.

"Wow, these all look amazing."

"Thank you. I do believe 'looks amazing' will be the key phrase here, since my family will exclusively eat the regular potato ones."

"What can I say? Our family appreciates tradition," my mom says.

Graham beams at me as she leans in to kiss him on the cheek. She inspects the bottle of wine he's brought and nods approvingly.

"Excellent," she says. "This kind doesn't make Howard fart."

Graham bites back a grin. "Anything I can help you with?"

"Here," I say, extracting a maroon box from the freezer and handing it to him. "You can make these pizza bagels for Sarah's kids. Despite those bento box lunches she's so fond of posting on social media, they're just as picky as every other kid I know."

"Pizza bagels?" Graham asks, inspecting the package. "Are they like pizza rolls?"

"They're a hundred times better than pizza rolls," I say, setting them down on the cooktop. "Pizza rolls could never."

"And what, pray tell, makes a pizza bagel superior to a pizza roll?" Graham asks.

"I'm so glad you asked," I reply. "Allow me to enumerate the reasons."

I hold up a finger. "First, they are open-faced, which means they don't get too hot on the inside the way pizza rolls do. So, you get all the flavors without burning off your taste buds."

Graham nods sagely. "That is the risk one runs with pizza rolls."

I stick up a second finger. "Two, they are delicious at every temperature. Fresh out of the oven? Yum. Been sitting on the counter for a while? Even better. Straight from the fridge the next day? Put it in my mouth."

Graham chuckles.

"Third," I continue. "They are versatile depending upon your level of hunger. Pizza rolls are always a snack, but pizza bagels can be either a snack or a meal, depending on how many you make."

Graham purses his lips. "You have convinced me. But I think I'll need to taste test, just to be certain."

By the time Bubbie, Sarah, Jordan, and their kids arrive forty-five minutes later, our feast is ready.

"Hanukkah sangria?" my mom asks, offering Sarah a glass of the Manischewitz-based punch that she makes every year.

Sarah wrinkles her nose. "No thank you," she says. "I'm off sugar."

"A perfect holiday for that," I deadpan.

"I'll have a glass," Graham volunteers. My mom beams as she hands him the gold-trimmed plastic cup.

"I know what you're thinking. How will you ever drink wine that isn't seventy-five percent corn syrup again?" I whisper in his ear.

Graham snorts before taking a hearty sip. He winces before suddenly handing the cup back to me.

"Is it time to open presents yet?" Olive and Emme suddenly appear side by side, like Generation Alpha's version of *The Shining* twins.

"First, dinner," my mom says firmly. She glances around the room. "Is everyone ready?"

"Ugh, I'm stuffed," Jordan laments, glancing around the table.

"For real. I can't eat another bite," I say. Bubbie belches loudly before stuffing another latke in her mouth.

My eyes trace over the remnants of our spread: brisket, *sufganiyot,* sweet noodle kugel, two varieties of homemade applesauce, and of course, the latke platter, which, predictably, is cleared only of the traditional potato ones. And of course, the true star of the show: the pizza bagels.

"Is it time for presents?" Olive asks. There's a smudge of powdered sugar in the corner of her mouth.

"Yes," Sarah tells them. "As soon as you help us clear the table. And no more gelt for either of you."

"Speaking of which," Graham says. "I know they aren't made of chocolate, but I thought you might like to receive another type of currency." Reaching into his pocket, he extracts a handful of coins, handing one each to Olive, Emme, and Jackson.

"Sick. Is this British money?" Jackson asks.

"Yup," Graham says. "See how the Queen is on the front? Ten pence for each of you."

"So cool," Emme breathes. "Way better than anything the tooth fairy brings us."

"If you ever go to England, you'll be all set to buy something," Graham says.

The kids are staring at him with equal parts awe and admiration, and I find myself sharing the sentiment. It's the second time I've noticed how smoothly Graham fits into my family. And more so, how much I love the way he does.

But what surprises me most of all when I glance across the table is the soft way in which Sarah is staring at him. Her lips are pressed together as she studies him, in that way she does when she's evaluating something. I usually see this face when she's scrutinizing a potential online purchase on her laptop screen, not a human. But before I can thoroughly read her expression, she's turned her attention to stacking empty plates and carrying them into the kitchen.

* * *

I'm not surprised when she approaches me half an hour later, while I'm washing dishes at the kitchen sink.

"So," Sarah says under her breath, as she grabs a serving platter and douses it with dish soap. "Graham has been spending a lot of time with the family lately. Remind me how you met again? You said you were planning a wedding together?"

The sponge slips through my fingers. *Shit.* I recognize that tone. It's the one she always uses when she's realized I've done something wrong and no one else knows yet. I glance at her out of the corner of my eye and try to keep my voice calm.

"Mm-hmm. Why do you ask?"

Sarah pointedly clears her throat. "I started following the Black-Eyed Susan on Instagram after the Bar Mitzvah. I've seen reels about how the owner's grandson is getting married there. But there weren't any pictures of this mysterious groom until yesterday, when he posted a photo of himself in the grand ballroom. And wouldn't you know it? He looked a lot like *that* guy."

We both turn to look at Graham, who's just set the mostly empty platter of pizza bagels on the counter. He lifts his head to meet my gaze, a guilty smile spreading across his face as he furtively pops a piece of bagel into his mouth.

"You were right," he says with a shrug. "They're perfect at every temperature."

He glances back and forth between the two of us. Then, seeming to sense he's interrupted something, excuses himself to finish clearing the table.

"You didn't know Graham was Mrs. Dyson's grandson?" I whisper once he's left the kitchen.

"I thought he was just the events manager," she whispers back. "How was I supposed to know? They have different last names. And don't change the subject. What the hell is going on?"

I clear my throat. "It's kind of a funny story," I say. "You're going to laugh when I tell you."

Despite the prickle of anxiety in my chest, there's also an immediate sense of relief the moment the words leave my mouth. I've been keeping this secret for so long and the prospect of telling my big sister the truth feels like an enormous weight has been lifted off my shoulders.

Sarah, on the other hand, seems less amused. "Tell me you're joking, Ali. That you're not having an affair with a man who's engaged!"

"No! It's not like that," I say, attempting to recalibrate. The metaphorical weight drops again, crushing me beneath it like a Looney Tunes character.

"I mean, yes, he's engaged to someone else, but they aren't really together. She's just a friend who needs a green card, which by the way you seriously can*not* repeat. He's hoping the wedding will help generate buzz for the hotel, because it's been struggling recently and needs a boost. And I haven't even told you the wildest thing. We didn't just meet. We actually—"

"Oh God, Ali," Sarah says, cutting me off. "This is just like you."

Now it's my turn to frown. "What's that supposed to mean?"

"It means that you always charge headfirst into a situation without pausing to consider consequences, or the wreckage you're leaving behind. I mean, have you ever thought about how this will affect his fiancée? What if Jordan had done this to me?"

My face grows hot. "I told you, they aren't really together," I say tightly.

Sarah shakes her head. "That doesn't make it right. This is her wedding you're planning, and you're fooling around behind her back. Imagine how humiliating this will be for her when she finds out."

My stomach roils. I hadn't really thought about how this would affect Claire. After all, it's not like Graham is cheating on her. But Sarah is right; there's more than one way to violate a person's trust.

"I mean, how do you ever expect to settle down and get married if you keep chasing after unavailable men?" Sarah continues, interrupting my train of thought. "Don't you want to be happy?"

I give her a pointed look. "You mean as happy as you are?"

She colors at this, but brushes off the comment, refusing to be redirected. "Tell me you haven't slept with him."

I cross my arms and smirk, answering the question for her. She shakes her head.

"Seriously, Ali," she sighs, like this conversation has completely drained her. "When are you going to grow up? You've got to get it together."

Anger starts building inside me. "Yeah, well, guess what? I'm never going to 'get it together' to your satisfaction. I'm never going to be able to live up to you, to be as perfect as you are."

Two pops of color form on Sarah's expertly contoured cheekbones. "I'm not . . . I never said I was perfect," she sputters. "I just want you to be happy."

"Has it ever occurred to you that I *am* happy? Just because my happiness doesn't look exactly like yours, that doesn't mean it isn't valid."

"So, what? He's going to call off his wedding and you're going to ride off into the sunset together?"

"Of course not," I retort. But suddenly, cold realization is starting to set in. What *do* I think is going to happen? Graham promised to tell Claire the truth, but they're still intending to get married. Then what? Our current situation is temporary. And it's about to come to an end.

"You don't have to worry," I mutter. "His wedding is in a few weeks and then he'll be back in New York, and this whole thing will be over." It's not possible for Graham to stay in Baltimore, even if he wanted to. As he mentioned, one of the conditions of his green card marriage is a shared home address.

For the first time since this conversation started, the fight leaves Sarah's shoulders. The disappointment melts from her face and is slowly replaced by a trace of sympathy. She rinses the platter under the faucet, then slides it in the dishwasher. "Look, you know I'm just trying to protect you."

"You're always trying to protect me." The words come out in a low hiss, much harder than I intended them to. Sarah flinches and I feel a pang of remorse. I take a deep breath, recalibrating.

"Sarah, you've always been like a second mom to me. And I love you, but you've got to stop babying me. I'm not a little kid anymore. I need to live my own life, make my own mistakes." The irony of my words is not lost on me, because Sarah doesn't know how right she is. Graham might be the biggest mistake I've ever made.

Sarah bites her bottom lip. "I know," she says slowly. "I know I just said this, but I just want you to be happy." She sighs. "And honestly, I don't think I've ever seen you look as happy as you do with him."

Her words roil in my stomach like acid. Deep down, I know she's right. Graham does make me happy. As hard as I've tried to deny it, my feelings for the man are growing by the day.

I thought that I'd been in love with Dev. But the way I felt about him doesn't begin to compare to the way I feel about Graham. If Dev was a candle in the darkness, Graham is the stadium lighting that brightens an entire arena. So isn't it just my luck that when I've finally met someone who makes me feel illuminated, he's not a man I'll be able to keep.

After everything's cleaned up, I take Graham upstairs, making sure to heed my mother's instruction of keeping the door open a crack. Some things never change, no matter how old you are.

I follow Graham's eyes as they take in every detail of my room: the turquoise walls covered in cutouts from *Teen Vogue* and a poster of a prepubescent Justin Bieber, with his swoopy hair and baby face. The faux-fur rug that I was obsessed with and is now stained with nail polish in one corner. The collection of chunky necklaces that I once considered the height of fashion.

His eyes settle on my unmade bed, the tie-dye comforter bunched in one corner of the mattress, before traveling to my face, the unspoken question evident in his expression.

"I'm not having sex with you in my childhood bedroom. Besides," I say, looking pointedly at the cracked door. "No one ordered dinner and a show."

Graham makes a faux-innocent look. "Who said anything about sex?"

I give him a playful shove and he topples onto the edge of the mattress before pushing back toward the headboard. I slide in beside him and we both lay back against the pillows. We roll onto our sides, facing each other. His fingers drift into my hair, his thumb stroking over the shell of my ear. But as I lean into his touch, it's impossible to ignore the echo of Sarah's words rolling around in the back of my head. *There's more than one way to violate a person's trust.*

"Everything okay with your sister?" he asks, as his hand moves down to my cheek. "It looked like you were having a pretty intense conversation in the kitchen."

"She's fine," I say. "It's just hard for her to sit down due to that giant stick up her ass."

Graham breathes out a laugh. His hand slides down the back of my neck, pressing his fingertips into the small of my back. My eyes flutter closed as his lips brush against mine and I sigh contentedly into his mouth. I fist his shirt in my hands as I pull him closer, closer. His hardness presses between my legs and he makes a low noise in his throat when I use my other hand to palm him over the fabric of his pants. His growing excitement beneath my touch melts away my lingering hesitation. Maybe Graham and I don't have a future together. But it doesn't mean we can't have fun right now.

Graham's eyes darken.

"I thought you said no sex," he rasps.

"I was referring to penetrative sex. Obviously."

Then I unhook his belt and slide my hand inside his jeans. His kisses turn harder, sloppier, as I take him in my grip, sliding my palm over his length as my thumb grazes the tip of him. His hand skims down my collarbone and over my breast, pausing to shape it in his hand before moving down to the waistband of my pants. His fingers travel languidly inside my underwear, brushing lightly over my skin, and I clamp my hand down on his wrist, digging my nails into his skin. A smirk spreads across his mouth.

"Can I help you?" he whispers.

"I certainly hope so," I whisper back, as I position his hand exactly where I want it. He cups me gently, his movements slow and teasing, until I let out a groan of frustration. Graham lets out a low breath of laughter as his finger slides into me.

Graham's hips press into me, his tongue following the same beat as his fingers as they slide into me over and over. I move my own rhythm over his shaft, matching his pace as we start to move faster, our foreheads pressing together, until he lets out a strangled noise and pulls back.

"What is it?" I ask.

"I just . . . I want to concentrate on you first. I'm going fuzzy."

His eyes are burning into mine, his blown-out pupils like two dark embers as he fixes me with his full concentration. The pressure in my center builds and I start to ride his hand, his thumb circling my clit as his rhythm quickens.

"That's it," he murmurs, his voice low and breathy against my ear. "Come for me, Ali."

His words push me over the edge of the cliff. I clap a hand over my mouth to muffle my cry as my thighs tighten around him. He bites my bottom lip as he slowly extracts his fingers. When I lift my head, I see that he's wrapped a hand around himself, stroking slowly. I cover his hand with mine, mimicking his rhythm before taking over completely.

Graham's eyes flutter shut, his breath coming out in short, labored bursts and I find myself unable to look away. There's something unbearably sexy about watching him come undone. Of witnessing this tightly wound man unravel at my touch.

I want to give him more, so I slide my lips around him. He lets out a half moan, half gasp of surprise before weaving his fingers through my hair, gripping it tightly as his body tightens and then releases with a soft expletive. His head drops back, and I lift my eyes to drink in the sight of him, watching the rise and fall of his chest. Then he dips his head forward, kissing me deeply, urgently, and I know now for sure that what I'm feeling for him at this moment extends beyond the physical, beyond lust. And I'm worried it's too late to turn back now.

Graham rolls onto his side again to face me. His brows pinch as his eyes drift over my face.

"What is it?" he asks, his voice low and husky.

"I'm starting to feel guilty," I admit. "You promise you'll talk to Claire? When is she coming back?"

"Tomorrow," he says, brushing a strand of hair from my face. "I promise I'll talk to her. We'll figure this out, Ali. Together."

I'm not sure what to say, so I just nod. Graham leans forward, pressing his lips against my forehead. And I close my eyes, allowing myself to soak up the moment, not knowing how many more we will have.

22

"You're invited!"

I glance up from my phone to see Claire standing in front of the conference room table, a bright smile illuminating her face. Asha and I are meeting with her and Graham this morning, but I'm so engrossed by the latest message in an email exchange that I don't hear her come in. A lighting technician has double-booked himself for next weekend, and I've spent the past two days trying to convince him to stick with our account. At this point, I've promised him everything except nudes and homemade sourdough.

"What's this?" I ask, closing my laptop and glancing down at the colorful piece of cardstock she's extended toward me. The words "One Last Hoe Down!" are scrawled across an illustrated pair of cowboy boots.

"It's a joint bachelor/bachelorette party!" she chirps. I must look befuddled because she quickly adds, "For me and Graham."

"No, I know who it's for," I say quickly. "It's just . . . not required to invite the planners to these types of things. You shouldn't feel obligated." What I don't say is that wedding planners are supposed to keep a professional distance from clients, not fraternize with them outside of work. Not that I've been particularly successful in this endeavor thus far, given that I spent last night with the groom's head between my thighs.

"We want you there!" she insists. My mind scrambles as I try to think of a sufficient excuse, but nothing comes. I scan the invitation quickly before noticing the date on the bottom. It's for this Saturday night, a week before their wedding. *New Year's Eve.*

The events of last New Year's Eve flash across my mind's eye. Lexi, Chloe, and I racing to Times Square so that Lexi could confess her love to Jake before he left the city for a world tour. I feel an ache of longing for the two of them. And suddenly the perfect excuse rolls off my tongue.

"You know what?" I exclaim a bit too loudly. "I just realized I can't make it. My two best friends and I have an annual tradition of celebrating New Year's together. They're coming to Baltimore to celebrate."

My chest tightens as I say the words out loud. I can't think of anyone I'd rather spend the holiday with than Lexi and Chloe. And up until last month, I'd assumed I would. Even though we're currently living in different cities, I'd figured it was a given that we would reunite to celebrate. But when I brought it up on the group text last month, Lexi said she was planning to spend New Year's on tour with Jake, and Chloe mentioned going to L.A. to hang out with Riley. I can't imagine she'd be willing to abandon her new girlfriend on arguably one of the most romantic nights of the year to come hang out with me and my engaged situationship.

"Bring them!" Claire insists. "Seriously, the more, the merrier."

I open my mouth again to protest, but she holds up her hand to stop me.

"Listen, you don't have to let me know right now. But we'd love to have you there. I know you and Graham have gotten to be close while I've been away."

Guilt tugs at my heartstrings. *If only you knew* how *close,* I think.

Even though I know Graham and Claire aren't romantically involved, she's easily my favorite client, and lying to her is starting to weigh on me. I know that Graham wanted to be the one to tell Claire the truth about us, but she's been in town for days and he keeps coming up with fresh excuses to put it off. And now I feel like I can't keep this secret a moment longer. If Graham isn't willing to come clean, then I will.

"Actually, Claire, there's something I need to tell you."

"Wait, before you do," she says. She slides her chair a bit closer and dips her head forward so her eyes are level with mine. "There's something I want to tell you too." She takes a steadying breath, and my pulse quickens with apprehension.

"As you know, I like you a lot. Graham does too. And he trusts you. Which means *I* trust you."

My stomach roils as I take in her open, earnest expression. I'm not sure where she's going with this, but I've never felt less deserving of a person's trust than I do of hers. I cross my arms tightly across my chest, hoping she can't read the shame etched across my face.

"The truth is," she says. She glances around the room quickly, confirming that we are truly alone, then drops her voice to a whisper.

"Graham and I aren't really *together.* He's marrying me as a favor, so that I can keep my job in late night."

My mouth falls open. That . . . I didn't see coming. I'm so taken aback by the unexpected confession that I don't even need to feign a look of surprise.

Two pops of color appear on Claire's cheeks, and I realize she's misreading my genuine look of shock as disapproval.

"Please don't think any less of me," she says quickly. "I would never ask someone to marry me for a green card. This isn't like, a Sandra Bullock movie. But Graham suggested it, and once he did, it felt impossible to say no. I mean, getting a job like this is a once-in-a-lifetime opportunity. A pipe dream at best, but even more so if you're a woman. I'm one of two on the twelve-person writing staff as it is."

My shoulders relax as I nod sympathetically. I know what it's like to work in a male-dominated industry. Even though half of my graduating culinary school class were women, only a fraction will ever become head chefs in restaurants. I've watched friends spend years stuck on garde-manger while male colleagues with less experience worked their way up the line. At the end of the day, the culinary industry is still a man's world. And I know comedy is the same way.

"I don't think I'll get another opportunity like this," Claire continues, and it's the first time I've ever heard her voice sound anything less than confident. "The fact that I landed this job in the first place is a small miracle. I can't go back to being sexually harassed as a waitress. I can't go back to the world of promoters refusing to book me on a stand-up show because they've 'already got a woman,' and after all, 'if women were funny, wouldn't there be more female comics?'" She shakes her head despairingly. "It's exhausting."

I straighten my shoulders, feeling a new surge of protectiveness over Claire. She has worked her butt off to get where she is, and despite the odds stacked against her, she's making her dream a reality. And suddenly, I want nothing more than for her to succeed.

"You're probably wondering why I'm having a bachelor party for a fake wedding," Claire continues, tucking a strand of red hair behind her ear. Honestly, I was so taken aback by her confession that I hadn't really registered it. But now that she's mentioned it . . .

"When Trudy suggested having the wedding at the Black-Eyed Susan, I knew I could sort of repay Graham for this enormous favor by helping promote the hotel. I have a respectable following on social media and so do a lot of my comedy and writing friends. My friend Dana says bachelorette party content gets a ton of traction. I figure the more opportunities we have to post about the wedding and tag the hotel, the more I can help to raise its profile." She smiles faintly.

"Graham comes off as a bit of a curmudgeon, but no one has a bigger heart. He would do anything for anyone. The least I can do is try to do something good for him."

She leans a bit closer and grins conspiratorially. "Also, I've been seeing this girl. A party in Baltimore is the perfect excuse to see her again."

"You're dating someone?" The surprises just keep on coming. At this point, I'm half expecting Oprah to materialize in the doorway, and announce that everyone on staff is also getting a brand-new car. "Does Graham know?"

Claire nods.

"To be honest, I think he's been seeing someone too. He's sporting a massive hickey on his neck that he keeps trying to pass off as a razor burn. Won't tell me a thing about it, though. Not that it's out of character for him. He's never been one to kiss and tell. He is British, after all."

Heat floods my cheeks as I remember the exact moment I gave him that particular love bite. I hope it isn't written all over my face.

She leans back in her chair and crosses her arms. "Graham has never been into relationships. It's one of the reasons he insisted this wedding would be no big deal. He kept saying he has no plans to date anyone seriously, and that I wouldn't be putting him out in the least. The man thinks he's protecting himself by being so anti-romance. I just hope that one day, he'll let go of all his hang-ups and allow himself to fall in love. Graham is the best guy I know. If there's anyone who deserves to find their soulmate, it's him."

Despite the kindness of her sentiment, it evokes a nagging sensation in the pit of my stomach. Graham keeps insisting that he has no interest in a serious relationship. But his words never seem to match his actions when we're together. Is it really that inconceivable that he'd let himself fall for me?

There's a larger issue at hand, though. If Claire finds out that we're seeing each other, she's not going to want to go through with this wedding and stand in the way of his happiness. And I can't let that happen. I can't be someone who ruins a wedding because she's sleeping with the groom. Claire's dream can't be destroyed because of me.

Still, there's another question plaguing me.

"Why are you telling me this?" I ask. "You could have just gone on with the wedding and never said a word."

Claire presses her lips together.

"The thing is," she says slowly, "as the wedding date approaches and the reality of what we're doing sets in, I can't help but wonder if I'm making a huge mistake." Her eyes are wide and glassy as they search mine.

"Tell me the truth," she says softly. "Am I doing the wrong thing marrying Graham?"

My mouth turns to sandpaper as I struggle to think of a reply. But before I can utter a word, I hear a rustling sound behind me. Turning, I see Graham and Asha standing in the doorway of the conference room.

"Oh good, we're all here," Asha says. She slides into one of the upholstered chairs, patting the seat beside her to indicate Graham should sit. "I can't believe this is one of our last meetings."

The wedding is only two weeks away, and today we're finalizing the seating chart. After this, we'll mostly be working on final behind-the-scenes details that won't require too much interaction with the bride and groom. *The bride and groom*. The placeholder term no longer feels appropriate. Claire and Graham aren't just a faceless couple: they're two people who have inadvertently become vital parts of my life. Claire isn't the only one who's starting to unravel in the face of the soon-approaching reality.

Once we've finished the chart, ensuring that Claire's handsy uncle will be seated far away from the bar, and her two friends, an on-and-off again couple with a tendency to sleep together at weddings and have a blowout argument afterward, are sitting on opposite ends of the room, Asha excuses herself to take a phone call, leaving me alone with Graham and Claire. As soon as she leaves the room, Claire turns to face Graham.

"I've invited Ali to the bachelor party," she announces.

Graham's eyebrows shoot up. "I thought we agreed that wasn't a good idea," he says slowly.

"Well, you've been overruled," Claire replies. "Now tell her she has to come."

Graham's eyes are wide as they swing to mine, and I can tell he's searching my face for a reaction. But before he can offer any further words of protest, I give him a reassuring smile.

"No one loves a party more than I do. I wouldn't miss it."

I'll give it to Claire: PBR, the Western-themed bar that's smack in the middle of the Power Plant entertainment complex, practically screams "Ideal Bachelorette Party Destination." The only directive the interior decorator must have received was "cowboys and beer," since the walls of the bar are decorated with Corona ads, antlers, and cowboy headshots. Claire asked the guests to come dressed in "Wild West chic" attire, even though this place is about as authentically Western as a Texas Roadhouse. Still, I've gamely accessorized my black party dress with the bedazzled pink cowboy boots I purchased for the Eras Tour and haven't worn since.

Claire's the first person I see when I step through the doorway of the bar. She's standing in the center of the dance floor, wearing a knockoff white Stetson with an attached veil and pretending to gallop on one of those horses on a stick. I swear, this woman is a national treasure. Once again, I feel a pang of guilt for sleeping with her fiancé, even if their romance isn't real.

She squeals when she sees me, dropping the stick horse and throwing both arms around me.

"You made it!" she says. "I'm so happy! Let's go get you a drink."

She leads me over to the bar area, where Graham is leaning against the scuffed wooden bar top, nursing a beer and looking ridiculously sexy in a worn denim shirt and red tie, topped with a gray vest and a brown felt cowboy hat. There's a star-shaped pin that reads "Sheriff." The grumpy expression on his face is only serving to enhance the overall look.

"If you're here, who's minding the saloon?" I ask.

Graham grunts. "Claire chose my outfit."

"And he loves it!" Claire laughs, nudging him with one shoulder, and he gives her an indulgent half smile. I can't believe I didn't notice their sibling-like body language earlier. At the same time, I can't help but wonder how no one here has taken note of the fact that they never kiss. The days leading up to a wedding are usually when couples are at the peak of their PDA threshold.

Even though he hasn't said a word about it, I'd expected he'd talk to Claire before tonight. At this point, I'm not sure what he's waiting for. But based on the casual, if slightly glazed way she's looking at me, it's clear she's still totally in the dark.

Claire hands me a shot of whiskey before tapping her own shot glass against mine.

"Cheers!" she says, then throws hers back with a grimace. I toss the whiskey down my throat in one swift motion, barely noticing the way it burns going down.

"I'm going to do a round and say hello to the guests," she tells me. "Try and get him to socialize?" I give her a smile, following her with my gaze as she flits off. I order myself a drink, then turn back to Graham.

"You still haven't told her?"

Graham's face darkens.

"I'm going to tell her. I'm just . . . waiting for the right moment."

I let out an exasperated sigh.

"And what moment is that? When you're walking down the aisle?"

I pull on one of my curls, twisting it around my finger. This can't go on much longer. I know this isn't the time or place, but I wish I understood why Graham was dragging his feet.

Speaking of Graham, a quick glance around the room confirms my suspicions: almost everyone here seems to be Claire's guest. I temporarily shove my frustration aside and change the subject.

"Didn't you invite any of your friends to this blessed event?"

He shrugs. "Most of them are back in London. But a few of the lads will be in for the wedding."

I give him a wry smile. "Will I be reuniting with Alfie?"

Graham's mouth rises in a half smile at the mention of his former roommate. "Believe it or not, we haven't kept up." He takes a small sip of his beer. "Are you still close with the women from your sorority?"

I pull a face. "Eh. I've been to more weddings and bachelorette parties than I can comfortably afford, but past that, we don't really keep up much outside of liking each other's social media posts. Plus, I've had to block a few girls who tried to recruit me to their MLMs."

Graham chokes out a laugh. "What about your friends from New York? I thought you told Claire you were bringing them tonight?"

My face falls. God, what I wouldn't do to share a round of margaritas with the other two musketeers right now.

"It's . . . possible that was a tiny fib," I say. "They're otherwise engaged this evening." I bite my bottom lip as the poor choice of words slips through my mouth. Mercifully, the bartender hands me the Jack and Coke I ordered, and I shove the frosted glass into my face before I can say anything else I'll regret.

I stare up at him, suddenly noticing the swollen purple crescents beneath his eyes. "Are you okay? You look exhausted."

Graham shrugs. "Between trying to manage the hotel and working my day job, I've been burning the candle at both ends. The social media attention from Claire's friends has certainly brought new followers to the hotel's Instagram account. But most of them aren't local, so I doubt any of that is translating into actual guests." Poor Graham. He's trying to do it all, and from the looks of it, it's killing him.

He blows out a sigh. "We gave it our best. But I'm starting to think it might all be too little, too late." His face looks so morose. Before I can overthink it, I wrap my arms around him.

"It's not too late," I whisper into his ear. "I see what you've put into restoring the hotel. You're amazing. You've got this."

Graham pulls away to study me, his eyes shiny behind his glasses.

"I appreciate your faith," he says quietly. "But the sooner we all face reality, the better off we'll be." He presses his lips to my forehead, and then disappears into the crowd.

23

Half an hour later, I'm slumped against the red sofa on the far end of the room, nursing a beer and wondering how much longer I need to hang around before it's socially acceptable to leave. I'm cycling through my mental Rolodex of exit strategies when I hear a familiar voice.

"Is it me or is that the saddest cowgirl you've ever seen?"

"Truly pathetic. I haven't seen her look this depressed since James Corden nixed the idea of a One Direction reunion special."

I lift my head slowly, not sure I can trust my ears. But there they are, the pair of them standing right in front of me like some kind of magical apparition.

"Shut up," I breathe. "What are you doing here?"

My two best friends in the world exchange a grin.

"You honestly thought we wouldn't come down here after you told us your sad-ass plans for the evening? What kind of friends would we be if we didn't show up at the bachelor party of the man you share a secret tattoo with, are currently sleeping with, and happens to be the groom of a wedding you're planning?" Chloe deadpans.

I bite down on my bottom lip as tears fill my eyes.

"That's the stupidest sentence any person has ever said, and I don't even care because I'm just so happy to see you guys," I say, throwing my arms around them. Lexi squeezes my waist and whispers in my ear, "We would never let you go through this alone. One for all, and all for one, remember?"

The threatening tears spill over, soaking the scratchy fabric of Lexi's dress. I pull away to study her outfit. She's wearing a belted denim dress with a red kerchief knotted around her neck. And Chloe looks flawless per usual, in a fringed, black leather miniskirt paired with studded cowboy boots.

"Damn," I sniffle. "You even dressed to the theme. That's true friendship."

Claire and Graham materialize behind them.

"You must be Ali's friends!" Claire says. "So glad you could make it!" She throws her arms around Chloe, either not noticing or not caring that my friend, who is generally not a fan of hugging, has gone ramrod straight, her own arms tightly at her sides, before moving onto Lexi, who graciously hugs her back.

"I'm Claire, the bride!" Claire announces as she straightens, a huge smile on her face. "Oh, and this is the groom, of course." Graham cringes almost imperceptibly at the title, and I can tell by the way my friends' heads snap to him that they don't miss it. Lexi and Chloe exchange a knowing glance.

"You're just in time," Claire continues. "The bunnies are about to go on."

I raise my eyebrows. "The bunnies?"

Just then, a country song I don't recognize pours through the overhead speakers, and a trio of women in cropped tees and assless chaps mount the bar top in front of us. In perfect synchronicity, they start line dancing. Claire dashes toward them and one reaches forward to help her up onto the table so she can join in.

"What in the Coyote Ugly . . . ?" Lexi asks.

Chloe's eyes go wide. "I think I like Baltimore," she murmurs.

Graham turns back to my friends. "Let me buy you both a drink," he says. "What's your poison?"

"A whiskey sour for me," Lexi says. "Chloe typically drinks the tears of reality stars after crushing their dreams of launching a namesake vodka brand. But if they don't have that, a Jack and Coke will do."

"I'll see what I can rustle up," Graham says. "I'd hate for you to have to lower your standards on our behalf."

Chloe grins at him. "Thanks for being an ally."

When he departs, Chloe turns to look at me with a pleased twinkle in her eye.

"Don't even think about it," I warn her. "You are not allowed to like him."

"Too late," she replies as she reaches for my beer. "I'm completely charmed. Which means everything because I am an excellent judge of character." She grimaces as she lowers the bottle.

"Ugh, what is this shit?" she asks, scowling at the foamy liquid.

"Natty Boh. It's locally brewed. Not exactly Baltimore's finest accomplishment, unfortunately."

"It tastes like urine and unfulfilled dreams."

"Remind me not to offer you a shot of Old Bay vodka."

Chloe shudders.

Graham returns a moment later, clutching two drinks. He hands one to each of my friends.

"So," Lexi says, lowering her voice as she leans toward him. "What are your intentions with our friend? Be aware that if you hurt her, I have mafia connections." She puts on her best "I could kill you" face as she says it, which makes her look as ferocious as a Pixar kitten. I raise an eyebrow, because as far as I know, her closest connection to the mafia is that she and Jake once ate at a Little Italy restaurant where a scene from *The Godfather* took place. For a week afterward, Jake walked around the apartment saying, "Leave the gun, take the cannoli."

"Way to cut to the chase, Lex," Chloe murmurs.

Graham's face softens. "I know the situation is less than ideal. But I promise you, I care about Ali. And I would never hurt her."

His words curl through my chest, warming me. But the cold grip of reality quickly replaces it. Because no matter how hard we try, there is no way either of us is going to emerge from this unscathed. It's just too complicated.

"Let's not do this here," I say, my eyes darting around the room in search of potential eavesdroppers. Thankfully, we seem to be in the clear; between the music pouring through the overhead speakers, the clanging of glass bottles, and the dozens of overlapping voices surrounding us, it doesn't seem likely that our conversation will be overheard. Still, I can't risk having this discussion right now, in a space filled with guests who think Graham and Claire are madly in love.

And speaking of which, Claire sidles up to us. She's ditched her stick horse, and her cowboy hat is now sitting slightly askew.

"Heyyyyy," she crows, and I can tell by the slight slur to her words that she's already tipsy. "What do you guys say to a game of shuffleboard? I'm dying to get to know Ali's friends better."

And that's how we end up stationed at the shuffleboard table in the opposite corner of the room. Graham and Chloe are on one team and Lexi and I are on the other, with Claire playing referee. But since teammates face each other, Graham and I are standing next to each other. Naturally. The smell of his cologne is intoxicating, his signature scent filling my pores. Attempting to get my head on straight, I narrow my eyes at him and put on my best game face.

"You're going down," I tell him.

Graham smirks at me. "I've heard that one before. But you've yet to deliver."

"You guys have played shuffleboard together?" Claire asks. We both whip our heads around to look at her. Her forehead is crinkled in confusion. I really need to do a better job of regulating my conversation. Those two drinks I had have gone straight to my head.

"Oh . . . I just meant . . . ," I stammer. Luckily, Chloe jumps in. Bless her heart.

"Claire, are you sure you don't want to play?" she asks. "You can take my spot."

Claire grins, then shakes her head. "I've actually got a better idea," she says. "I thought we'd spice this game up with a round of Never Have I Ever. I'll list the deeds, and if you're guilty, you drink. The best way to get to know each other!"

"Those aren't exactly the rules," Lexi hedges, and Chloe rolls her eyes.

"The only person who's going to be sober at the end of this is Lexi," she deadpans.

"Um, rude," Lexi replies.

"Come on, it'll be fun," Claire protests. My insides churn. I've never thrived during a game of Never Have I Ever, and I'm not keen on having personal secrets revealed to a client. Especially not one engaged to my . . . whatever he is. At the same time, I'm not trying to rock the boat, and I'm certain that too much protestation on my end will look suspicious.

"You got it, Claire," I say gamely. "But you're playing too."

She grins. "I knew you'd be down!" she says triumphantly. She begins scrolling through her phone in search of a question list.

"Okay," she says. "Let's start off easy. Never have I ever . . . played hooky from school." Chloe and I exchange a smirk as we raise our drinks to our lips.

"Oooh, *spill*," Claire says excitedly.

"It's not that scandalous," I say. "During Senior Ditch Day in high school, a few of my friends and I went to the movie theater to see *Neighbors*. I was going through a major Zac Efron phase in 2014."

Claire nods sagely. "Pretty sure everyone was going through a Zac Efron phase in 2014." She clears her throat, then scrolls down.

"I didn't participate in Senior Ditch Day," Lexi sniffs.

"Shocking," Chloe and I reply simultaneously.

Claire giggles. "You guys are fun." She returns her attention to her phone. Her eyes light up when she finds one she likes and she grins devilishly at Graham.

"Here's a good one for you. Never have I ever gotten a tattoo."

Graham chokes on his beer.

Lexi sighs. "You guys were right. This is a boring game for me." Chloe shakes her head as she takes a sip of beer. She has a tiny heart tattoo on the inside of her wrist. It's subtle and adorable. I'm kind of obsessed with it.

Claire's face lights up when I also raise my glass. "Oh, fun!" she says. "What sort of tattoo is it? Or do you have multiple?"

"Just the one. And it's hideous," I say. "I'll skip the details to spare you the trauma."

Claire snorts. "It can't be any worse than this tattoo Graham got in college."

"You might be surprised," Chloe deadpans. I shoot her daggers with my eyes from across the shuffleboard table.

I glance over at Graham, whose cheeks have turned a violent shade of crimson.

"You're up," I say.

He swings his gaze toward me. "What?" he asks hoarsely.

"It's your turn. At shuffleboard," I say.

"Oh. Right." He rolls his shoulders backward, then swings a puck across the board. Claire lets out a hoot before it crosses the "2" line.

"Foul! You crossed the foul line." She smirks at Graham. "Better luck next time, Teddy Bear."

She clears her throat as she glances down at the list of prompts on her phone. "Okay, let's see. Never have I ever performed karaoke in public."

"Yes!" Lexi thrusts a triumphant fist into the air as she takes a long sip of beer. "Making a comeback."

Claire grins. "Okay, this one is meh. Never have I ever lost a bet."

This time, it's Lexi who chokes, and Chloe claps her on the back.

"Careful there, cowgirl."

At first, no one dares to take a drink. But then, with a resigned slump of his shoulders, Graham reaches for his glass, and I follow suit.

Claire's eyes are gleeful. "Ali, I'm sure you ultimately served justice. But Teddy? You're too straitlaced to make a bet you can't win. Tell us the story."

Graham's eyes drop to the ground, and he bites his bottom lip.

"Graham!" Claire says, a bit harder. An uncharacteristic edge has creeped into her voice now and I can tell she's bothered that he's kept this from her. "This evasiveness has now fully sparked my curiosity. Spill, dude!"

I fully expect Graham to make up a story, but when he lifts his eyes to reveal the tortured look etched across his face, my stomach bottoms out. He wouldn't dare.

Would he?

"I never told you the full story about the tattoo," he says quietly. From across the table, I can hear my friends' sharp intake of breath.

"I got it after losing a bet to a woman I met in a bar."

Claire leans forward, propping her chin. "Shut up. I can't imagine you doing something like that. She must have been wild. And beautiful."

Graham turns to look at me. "She was the most beautiful woman I had ever seen."

My heart thunders against my chest as my body turns cold. This is it. It's really happening. I wanted Claire to know the truth, but now that the moment is upon us, I'm horrified by the prospect. The timing, the setting. Everything about this is wrong.

"Graham," I say hoarsely. But before I can say another word, a man with a dark head of curls bounces over and throws his arm around Claire's shoulders.

"It's almost midnight!" he announces a bit too loudly. He grins at Claire. "Everyone's looking forward to seeing the almost newlyweds ring in the new year with a kiss."

Graham blanches. Despite their decision to hold their engagement party on New Year's Eve, I don't think it has occurred to him until this moment that everyone would expect the holiday's requisite PDA.

"Oh! Jake's calling," Lexi says, offering a blessed interruption as she stares at the vibrating phone in her hand. She taps on her phone to accept the FaceTime call and Jake's dimpled face fills the screen.

"Jake!" Lexi says happily. "How are you calling me right now? Aren't you in the middle of a concert?"

"I'm backstage before my encore," he says breathlessly. "But I had to see you at midnight. It's kind of our anniversary."

Lexi's eyes fill with tears as she nods. "I guess you could say that."

"Holy shit. Is that Jake Taylor? Wait . . . oh my God. You're *that* Lexi?" Claire leans over Lexi's shoulder, staring slack-jawed at the phone screen in Lexi's hand. Not that Lexi seems to notice. She and Jake are grinning at each other like a pair of lovesick teens in a John Green novel.

My heart twists as I watch my best friend and the man she loves. As much as I've tried to deny it, this is what I truly want: a man who loves me wholly and unequivocally. No sneaking around or subterfuge; just two people who only have eyes for each other and aren't afraid to let the world know it. And my heart twists a little when I realize Graham and I can never look at each other like that. Not in public at least. The thought turns my stomach to lead.

There's a deafening roar of fans chanting Jake's name.

"I've got to go," he tells Lexi. "But I love you, Lex. Always."

"I love you too," she whispers, pressing her lips to the screen before disconnecting the call.

"One minute until midnight!" someone calls.

A crowd gathers around me, jostling Graham and Claire together. The air around me starts to feel too hot, the bodies around me too close.

"Ready to smooch, lovebirds?" someone teases.

Graham and Claire are standing next to each other now, Claire playfully throwing her arm around his neck in preparation. Even though I know it's not real, that there's nothing romantic between them, I can't help but feel jealous. And hurt.

Despite my best intentions, I have fallen head over heels for this man. And the truth is, I want what Lexi and Jake have. To be the rising sun on someone's horizon. To be loved boldly and openly. To not have to hide the way I feel.

Graham turns to me, and I know he can read it all on my face. The helpless look in his eyes threatens to crack my heart in half.

"Ten, nine, eight . . ."

I turn on my heel, heading toward the door. I'm on the street before they ever reach one.

24

"Ali, wait!" I hear my friends calling as their footsteps echo behind me, but I don't stop until I'm outside, stumbling across the cobblestones. The frigid winter air whips across my face, forcing mascara tears from my eyes. I brush a hand across my face as I shove through the crowd. When I reach the water fountain at Power Plant's entrance, I collapse onto the stone ledge, drawing my knees to my chest and burying my face in them. Somewhere in the distance, there are fireworks blasting, intermixed with the screams and loud whooping of college kids with fake IDs. It's a grim, if fitting, soundtrack to my misery.

"Hey." Lexi and Chloe settle on either side of me, and then my friends are wrapping their arms around my shoulders.

"I'm such an idiot," I mumble. "I knew this was a horrible idea, and I let myself fall for him anyway. And now look where it's led me."

"You're not an idiot," Lexi says. "You're just . . ."

I lift my head and glare at her. "Don't you dare say it."

Footsteps approach and I see a pair of shoes on the pavement. Lifting my head, my gaze settles on Graham's face. The purple lights of the fountain reflect across his features, which are twisted in agony.

"Can I talk to you?" He glances behind him at the line of honking cars looping through the traffic circle. "Maybe somewhere quieter?"

"We'll give you guys some privacy," Chloe says, as she and Lexi stand. Lexi shoots me a sympathetic glance over her shoulder before the two of them disappear back into the crowd.

I glare at Graham. "What are you doing out here? Shouldn't you be kissing your fake fiancée at your fake bachelor party?"

Graham's face collapses. "Please. Five minutes. That's all I'm asking."

Reluctantly, I follow him down the sidewalk until we're off the main drag. He finds a bench, dropping down onto it. I sit down beside him.

Graham blows out a sigh as he stares into the distance.

"I know that must have really sucked for you," he says quietly.

My eyebrows shoot up to my hairline.

"It must have really *sucked* for me?" I repeat incredulously. "Now there's the understatement of the century. Everything about this situation sucks, Graham." He opens his mouth to say something else, but I cut him off.

"The worst part is that I don't even recognize myself anymore. I wasn't like this before I met you. I was the human embodiment of joie de vivre. I lived in the moment. After the way things ended with Dev, I never let things get too serious or allowed myself to fall too hard again. And you know what? It was working out just great for me. But I'm not that girl anymore, because you have ruined me. You've ruined me but in the best possible way, and now I don't want to go back to being the person I once was."

I take a fortifying breath as I try to calm my racing heart. "Falling for you has made me remember that I want love. Genuine, passionate, all-consuming love. And I'm not willing to settle for whatever this is."

Graham reaches forward to grab my arm.

"I want to be with you, Ali," he says quietly. "More than I've ever wanted anything. We can figure this out and find a way to be together."

Frustrated, I yank my arm away. "How? You're going to call off your wedding to Claire and we're going to just ride off into the sunset on horseback? And even if you did, then what? Claire will be screwed, the hotel will fold, and I'll lose my chance to get a promotion and prove that I'm not just some flake."

As much as the truth hurts, there's no point in denying reality. It's impossible not to consider the collateral damage that would come with our decision to be together. And then there's the other elephant in the room.

"You lied to me," I say quietly. "You promised you would tell Claire the truth, and you didn't."

"Because telling the truth won't help anyone!" he yells.

His eyes pinch shut, and he blows out a ragged breath.

"If I tell Claire about us, she'll insist on calling off the wedding. There's no way she would go through with it if she knew how I felt about you. I know she'd want to put my happiness first. But if she calls off the wedding, I lose the opportunity to convince Granny to hold off on selling. And it's not just me I'd be hurting. If we cancel, you lose your opportunity for a promotion. And my grandmother. She keeps telling me how much joy this wedding brings her. This would crush her."

Graham's head drops back as he stares morosely at the night sky.

"This is an impossible situation. No matter what I do, I let someone down."

The reality of his words hit me like a dodgeball to the chest, sending the air whooshing from my lungs. Because he's right. And we both know it. Even if he managed to make things right with Claire, there's no way I'd get the full-time gig that Antoine is offering. Most likely, he'd fire me all together. No sane person would retain a staff member who broke up a client's wedding because she slept with the groom. Not to mention it would tarnish Asha's impeccable career. Once word got out about what happened, I have no doubt that clients would be apprehensive about working with her. Worst of all, it would prove my parents right. That I'm not a person to be taken seriously.

Graham stands up and starts to pace back and forth on the sidewalk. Then he pauses, turning to look at me with a look of renewed optimism.

"How about this? I can go back to New York with Claire for a few months, get her set up, and then I'll come back here. I'll tell my grandmother that it didn't work out with Claire. We can be together for two years until I can file for divorce, and then you and I can do whatever we want."

His eyes are pleading, and my resolve threatens to crumble. But then I shake my head. Despite the way I feel about Graham, I know in my heart that this isn't right. And I'm not willing to settle.

"No."

Graham's shoulders collapse. "You don't want to be with me?" he asks, his voice strained.

I blink rapidly, desperate not to let my own tears fall. "Of course I want to be with you, Graham," I manage. "But not like this. I don't want to be your mistress."

Graham recoils at the word, his eyes filling with hurt.

"My *mistress*?" he chokes out. "How could you even say that?"

I level my gaze at him. "You're proposing the idea of marrying another woman and keeping me as your side piece. That's the literal definition of a mistress. Sorry to be blunt, but those are the facts of the situation."

Graham's face darkens and I know I've hit a nerve. "Those are not the facts," he says through gritted teeth. "You're not going to be my mistress. You're the woman that—" He pauses, running a tongue over his lips. When his eyes meet mine again, they are resolute.

"You are the woman that I love. I love you, Ali."

My heart drops to my stomach. I open my mouth but discover that I've been rendered speechless. So, I just stand there, gaping at him. His fathomless blue eyes narrow as they search mine and I wonder what he's able to see in there. If my own eyes reveal my innermost thoughts, which are screaming that I feel the same way. That I love him too, so much that the thought of it terrifies me. The words bubble up from my chest, tickling the back of my throat.

But then I swallow them down quickly. I can't let the feelings I have for Graham cloud my judgment. Because the reality is that continuing down this path will only lead to heartbreak. And based on the way I feel about Graham, I'm not certain I could survive it.

I let out a resigned breath. "It's not enough though, is it? The way we feel about each other. None of it matters if the timing isn't right, and let's face it, the timing couldn't be worse. We can't be together, and we both know it."

Graham's face is twisted in an expression of pure agony, but he doesn't argue with me. I'm right and we both know it. It's the push I need to finish this.

"You're getting married next week," I tell him. His brow furrows as his eyes snap back to mine, undoubtedly confused by my sudden shift back to a professional tone. "Asha and I will make sure the day goes off without a hitch, that the wedding is so spectacular that it's all anyone talks about for weeks. That it brings so much positive attention to the hotel that your grandmother is forced to reconsider selling it. And when it's over, you will go to New York with Claire, I will accept my new job, and we will move on. This thing between us was never going to last and the sooner we can accept that, the better off we'll be."

"Ali, please," he says, his voice low and strangled. From the corner of my eye, I see Chloe and Lexi emerge from the shadows. The sight of my two best friends is like an elixir. It fills my veins with strength, giving me the resolve I need.

"Goodnight, Graham," I say. Then, I brush past him, walking toward them. It takes every ounce of strength not to look back.

25

“Serious question and please do not lie to me,” Chloe says. “Am I incredibly high or is that doll staring at me?”

Lexi and I follow her gaze up to the ceiling of the Papermoon Diner, where a disembodied doll head surrounded by a wheel, a wooden chair, and an overturned piano gaze unseeingly back at us. Every inch of this place is eclectically decorated, from the nude, Crayola-hued mannequins in the garden to the collection of Pez dispensers in the lobby. It’s trippy even when you haven’t just popped an edible.

I shrug and stuff a sweet potato fry into my mouth. “I think it’s a combination of the two.”

Lexi shudders before turning her attention back to me. She pushes her half-eaten plate of banana custard French toast aside and then rests her elbows on the table, her eyes softening around the edges as she stares at me. “Do you want to talk about it?”

“There’s nothing to talk about,” I say. “This whole thing was a mistake from the beginning and it’s my own fault for letting it go on for as long as it did. But I’ve finally come to my senses and put a stop to it. Next week, Graham will marry Claire and then he’ll fuck off to New York and I’ll never have to see him again.”

Lexi’s eyes go puppy dog–round with sympathy. “It’s fine,” I say, tearing my own eyes away from her. "I'm fine. I just want to drink my milkshake and disassociate. Then we can go home and have a Bob Barker marathon."

I take a long pull of peanut butter–laced dairy that will undoubtedly tear my stomach to shreds in the next twenty-five to forty minutes since I forgot to refill the Lactaid stash in my purse.

Lexi and Chloe exchange a look. My eyes narrow as they dart back and forth between the two of them, trying to parse out the unspoken conversation that's currently taking place.

"What?" I finally ask. "What is it that you two so desperately want to say?"

Chloe purses her lips. "It's just interesting that you haven't made the connection."

I narrow my eyes. "What connection?"

"You're constantly telling us that Graham has the personality of a senior citizen. Meantime, your lifelong crush is quite literally an old man."

I freeze, my straw halfway to my lips. Dear God, how have I not noticed this before? In all the time I've spent teasing Graham about his impending AARP membership, I've failed to recognize how much he reminds me of someone I've loved for half my life. The irony is too much to bear. I push my milkshake to the side, no longer hungry.

Lexi lets out a low sigh. "Are you sure you guys can't work it out?"

I roll my eyes. "You really have gone soft since Jake," I say wryly. "And didn't the two of you just give me a lecture about how I shouldn't ruin my career over a man?"

"That was before," Chloe says.

"Before what?" I ask.

Chloe levels her gaze at me, her features arranged in her trademark, no-bullshit expression. "Before I saw the two of you together. Before I watched him look at you like you hung the goddamn moon."

She leans forward, pressing her elbows into the table. "Before he told you that he loved you."

My stomach cartwheels the same way it did when I first heard Graham say those words, the effect of it undiluted. A watery image of his face swims in front of my eyes, his expression a tormented combination of agony and desperate hope. My heart twists as I remember the way his face fell when I didn't say it back.

Chloe leans back in her chair and crosses her arms. "And you know what else? I think you love him too."

I open my mouth to protest, but ultimately decide against it. I know better than to lie to the two people who know me best.

"Okay, fine," I admit. "You're right. I love him. I love his stupid Mister Rogers cardigans and his dorky glasses and his soothing BBC accent. I love his ridiculous, messy hair that is totally incongruent with the fact that the rest of him looks like a human spreadsheet. I love that he feels like my fated mate, which sounds so corny I could die, but how else do you describe a connection you have to a man with a matching tattoo? I love everything about him and it's fucking terrible, because we can't be together. Are you happy now?"

Lexi lowers the hand that's crept up to her mouth at some point during my unhinged monologue.

"Holy shit," she whispers. "Ali, you have to tell him how you feel."

I throw up my hands in frustration. "Why? What would that accomplish?"

"I don't know!" she says. "But it's got to be better than this! Sitting here drowning your sorrows in a freaky ass diner."

I pop another sweet potato fry into my mouth. "How dare you? This place is iconic. Name one place in New York that has a superior collection of Pez dispensers."

Chloe is staring at the ceiling again. "I'm telling you, this fucking doll just winked at me."

"So, that's it?" Lexi asks. "After all the hellish first dates you've been on, you finally found real love and you're going to walk away from it?"

I grab an untouched chicken tender off her plate and take an enormous bite. "Do you have a better suggestion?"

Lexi opens her mouth to speak, but then closes it again. Because that's what this all boils down to, isn't it? It's a shitty situation but there's nothing to be done about it.

Chloe shakes her finger at the ceiling. "Wink at me again, harlot, and I'll come up there and cut your eyes out."

"How many gummies did you have?" Lexi asks.

"Three," she replies. "I had a second since the first was so good, and then you didn't want yours, and I wasn't going to let it go to waste. They were peach-ring flavored, for Christ's sake."

I wave to the waitress to signal for a check. "Think it's time to get Snoop Dogg out of here. Mind if I stay with you guys tonight?"

Lexi reaches across the table to squeeze my hand. "A sleepover, just like old times. Sounds perfect."

Spotify is blasting the angriest Rage Against the Machine songs I could dig up, though I can barely hear over the sound of pots and pans slamming against the countertop. Every available surface is littered with produce—carrots, mushrooms, celery, onions, and garlic—all of which I'm dicing at a rate even I find borderline dangerous. But I'm in my element and it feels good to be back in the kitchen, a place where I feel in control. I've just dumped half the vegetables onto a baking sheet and slammed the oven door when my mom pokes her head through the doorway.

"Is it safe to enter?" she asks cautiously. I shrug.

"It's your house."

She purses her lips, like she's trying to bite back a retort, before stepping inside.

"Smells good in here. What are you making?"

"Rage ragu," I say. "Served with a side of self-loathing."

My mom nods. "Are you making pasta to go with it?"

I gesture to the handmade pappardelle that I've just rolled out and cut into strips.

"Can't have a pity party without carbs."

Her face breaks into a cautious grin. "That's my girl."

She settles onto one of the kitchen stools and watches me closely. "Do you want to talk about it?"

"No." *Yes.*

She tilts her head to study me. "Is this about Graham? Did you two have a fight?"

I grab a large skillet from one of the kitchen cabinets and coat the bottom in olive oil.

"No fight," I say. "Just came to my senses. It was just a mistake to get involved with him." Now there's the understatement of the century. The entire affair is what my family would call classic Ali: short-lived and impulsive, with no thought to the long-term consequences. I'm nothing if not true to form.

I switch on the burner, allowing a minute for the oil to preheat, before tossing in a handful of sliced cremini mushrooms. I'd uncorked a bottle of red wine for deglazing, but when I turn back around, my mom is pouring some of it into two long-stemmed glasses. She slides one of them toward me, and I reluctantly take a long gulp.

My mom traces her fingertips around the rim of her glass as she gives me an appraising look.

"You miss cooking," she says. It's more of a statement than a question and I nod silently. Lately, I've felt a pull toward the kitchen, a place where I can harvest my creative energy, and use it to bring joy to others. It's a high that's incomparable to anything else. It's what I regret most about leaving my previous job in New York.

"I do," I admit. "I like wedding planning a lot, but . . . I do miss working in restaurants."

"Have you ever thought of going back?"

My head pops up. "You mean changing careers *again*?" I genuinely cannot believe what I am hearing right now. I know I'm seen as the family flake. At this point, the only way I can top my own flakiness is going back to a career I've already left behind.

My mom shrugs. "Why not? Life's too short not to follow your passions." Well, that's rich, coming from her.

"You mean like you did?" I ask, unable to keep the bitterness out of my voice.

My mom frowns. "What's that supposed to mean?"

I fling a dish towel over my shoulder. "You were trying to make a career for yourself as an artist when you met Dad. But you gave up painting to have kids and settle for a nine-to-five job in a soulless, corporate field. You're not exactly the poster child for chasing one's passion."

My mom sighs.

"Oh, Ali. I didn't give up a career as an artist because I abandoned my dream. I gave it up because I found a new one. Raising you and your sister has been the best experience of my life. And as for working in the nursing home, I was surprised as anyone to discover how much I loved it. But that's the thing about life. Sometimes it takes you in unexpected directions."

"I guess that's my problem," I lament. "I don't have direction." I give the mushrooms a final stir. They're browned now, so I add in the tomato paste and minced shallots, plus some oregano and red pepper.

The savory aroma of the combined ingredients fills the kitchen and I take a gratuitous inhale. I might be a grade A fuckup in every other aspect of my life, but at least I can still conjure culinary magic.

I turn back to my mom before finally sharing a truth I've been reluctant to admit to anyone, including myself.

"Everyone in my life is settled. Lexi has her new business and her relationship with Jake. Chloe's always had her shit together, and now she's in love too. Sarah came out of the womb with a day planner and a ten-year plan. And then there's me, the perennial screw-up."

My mom reaches forward to squeeze my hand. "Baby, you are not a screw-up. Do you have any idea how proud you make me? It takes guts to change careers, let alone to move cities at the same time. You had to start all over again when you ventured into wedding planning, and I've seen how hard you've worked without complaint. If wedding planning is your life's passion, then you have my full support. And if you want to quit and go back to being a chef, then I'll support that too. Just promise me you won't be so hard on yourself. Not every path to happiness is linear. I just hope that when you find the thing that is right for you, you aren't afraid to accept it."

Her words uncoil the knot that's been slowly forming in my chest. Circling the counter, I throw my arms around my mom's neck, burying my face in her shoulder. She rubs reassuring circles into my back as she hugs me close for longer than she has in years.

Later, when we're enjoying the ragu, I reflect on what she said. When *was* I the happiest and most fulfilled? The answer comes to me almost immediately, the mental image of working with Graham at the murder mystery party. That was the best of both worlds: getting to work as both a chef and event planner. But as wonderful as that day was, it was a one-off. Without the perfect setting or people to vouch for me, who would trust me to both cook and plan? Trudy is still planning to sell the hotel after the wedding and Graham will be moving back to New York. All these silly dreams—of the perfect career, romance, and happy endings—are leaving with him. Wedding planning might not be perfect, but it's a commitment that I made to myself, and I need to see it through. I'm going to put my best foot forward and finish what I've started. And that means making sure Claire and Graham's wedding goes off without a hitch. No matter how much it hurts.

26

I manage to avoid Graham for the rest of the week, volunteering to confirm pickup times with vendors and do final checks with the florist, and leaving Asha to handle any tasks related to Graham, Claire, or the Black-Eyed Susan. She doesn't seem to notice, already in the zone in the way that she always is right before an event. And before I know it, it's Saturday afternoon, the day of the wedding.

I step into the hotel's gilded lobby, pausing to smooth a hand over the black satin wrap dress that I nabbed from the petite section at the Loft. Since my mother and her opinions are not in attendance, I've skipped the heels, instead finishing off the outfit with a comfy pair of black flats.

The ceremony doesn't start for another three hours, but the lobby is already buzzing with activity. A florist brushes past me, directing two assistants who are wheeling a cart of centerpieces toward the ballroom. I spot two people wearing laminated press passes sitting in overstuffed chairs and realize with a flutter of excitement that they've come to cover the wedding. Today is everything Graham and his grandmother had hoped it would be. I just hope it will be enough for Trudy to change her mind.

The crowd parts, and there he is, leaning against the front desk.

My pulse trips over itself at the sight of him. He looks obscenely handsome in a half-done tuxedo. The black pants are slim and stylishly cut. He's wearing his white button-down without the bow tie or cummerbund, the golden locks of his hair mussed as always. He's chatting amiably with the man standing behind the reception desk. But then he turns, as though he can feel me staring at him. He swallows hard as he pushes his glasses up his nose, and then he's walking toward me.

"Ali," he says, his voice a low scrape. He reaches a hand forward to cup my elbow. "Can we talk?"

I take a step backward and remove his hand from my arm. "This isn't a good time, Mr. Wyler. I was just about to head back into the kitchen to check in on preparations. Perhaps Asha can assist you."

His eyes widen a fraction at my formal tone. Hurt is written all over his face, and it takes every ounce of willpower to maintain a neutral expression.

"Please," he implores softly. "Five minutes."

Murmuring a curse under my breath, I grab him by the wrist and drag him over to the maintenance closet, slamming the door behind us.

Placing my hands on my hips, I tip my chin upward to glare at him.

"What? What is it that you so desperately need to say?" I intend for my voice to come out harsh, but the effect is lost when it cracks a bit on the last word. I take a shaky breath, forcing myself to calm down. The last thing I need is to lose my cool right now. Not on a day my career hinges on.

Graham takes a step forward, closing the space between us, and I feel my breath hitch as his blue eyes run across my face.

"Ali," he says, his own voice shaking. "I can't . . . I don't know what to do. Tell me what to do."

I feel myself deflate as the fight leaves my body. I drop my head against his chest, and he wraps his arms tightly around me, pulling me close. A treacherous tear escapes my eyes, and he must feel it dampen his shirt, because he tightens his grip. My eyes fall shut as I savor his warmth, the feel of his heartbeat beneath the starchy fabric of his shirt. It's probably the last time he will ever hold me like this.

We stand there for a few moments, locked in an embrace, neither of us speaking. But then I force myself to pull back. I swipe my index fingers beneath my eyes, wiping away any smeared eyeliner. Lifting my chin, I force myself to breathe, force myself to look at his face. His own eyes are damp, his expression tortured.

"There are two members of the press sitting in the lobby," I say, my voice somehow steadier, more assured than I feel. "One from *The Sun* and one from *Baltimore Weddings.* Antoine also has contacts at Style Me Pretty who should be here soon. Photos from this wedding are going to be everywhere, and once the public sees them, it's going to be huge for the Black-Eyed Susan. Your grandmother will change her mind about selling. Everything you've wanted, everything you've been working for. This is the day it all comes to fruition."

Graham reaches forward, pressing the pad of his thumb to my lips. His expression is miserable.

"What if I no longer want those things?" he whispers. I stare up at this man, this man that I love, who loves me. And I remember every memory he's ever shared about the Black-Eyed Susan. About helping his grandfather oversee reservations. About going into the walk-in fridge with the kitchen staff to learn safety procedures. About ensuring that guests were happy and had what they needed. This hotel means everything to Graham.

I think about myself. The sacrifices that I've made, giving up my life in New York to pursue a new dream, standing up for myself and working to prove that I'm strong and capable. And it occurs to me that maybe there's more to love than getting what you want in the short term. That maybe love is about making sure the people you care about never lose the things they hold dearest.

I reach forward, pressing a hand to his cheek. He closes his own hand over mine, his eyes fluttering shut as his fingertips stroke my skin.

"Today is going to be perfect," I whisper. "For your grandmother, for Claire, even for you. And everything will be as it should." I can't meet his eyes as I brush past him, grasping the doorknob and yanking the door open. I freeze when I come face-to-face with a startled Asha.

Asha's mouth drops open as her eyes travel over my shoulder to look at Graham. I can only imagine the thoughts that must be going through her mind right now. Then her eyes narrow a fraction, and I watch in horror as she mentally assembles the pieces.

"Mr. Wyler, uh . . . needed a Band-Aid," I fumble. "And there weren't any left in the emergency kit, so we went looking for some."

Asha's eyebrows shoot up to her forehead. "In the utility closet?"

"Yup," I say, nodding quickly. "But it looks like they're fresh out."

"That's interesting," she says slowly. "Because I checked the emergency kit before I left this morning, and the Band-Aids were fully stocked."

She flicks her gaze over to Graham. "Mr. Wyler, you should probably head back to the groom's suite. The photographer wants to do some getting ready shots."

He nods contritely and slides past her, pausing to glimpse back at me over his shoulder before disappearing down the corridor.

Asha rotates back toward me, arms folded across her chest.

"Asha, it's not what you think," I say.

She cocks her head to the side. "Are you sure about that?" Her voice is hard and cutting, and my cheeks instantly flood with shameful heat. *Shit.*

The worst part is the look of disappointment in her eyes. In all the time I've spent worrying about losing my job, I'd neglected to consider how much it would hurt to lose Asha's respect. It hurts like hell.

I'm still fumbling with what to say next when a head of fire-engine red curls rounds the corner.

"Heyyyy," Claire drawls, and it's clear from the way the final vowel drags that she's already cracked open the bottle of champagne we've left in the bridal suite. Her face lights up when she sees me.

"Ali! You're going to help me get ready, right?"

"Actually, I—" But before I can tell her that I was on my way to check on things in the kitchen, Asha cuts in.

"Yes, Ali will be with you for the rest of the afternoon," Asha says smoothly.

"But I—" I try again, but Asha shakes her head.

"Don't worry about the food," she says. "I can check on it before heading over to the groom's suite." She levels her gaze at me.

"We have a job to do today," she adds meaningfully. "It's our responsibility is to make sure things go as planned." I don't miss the intended innuendo. That my promotion is very much on the line and if I want it, then I will need to see this wedding through. I press my lips together and nod.

Which is how, ten minutes later, I find myself in the bridal suite with Claire, three of her giggly, tipsy bridesmaids, and a sole bridesman.

Claire presses a flute of champagne into my hand before raising her own into the air.

"A toast!" she says. "To old friends." She turns her head toward me and smiles. "And new ones." At her words, my stomach drops to the floor.

Numbly, I take a small sip before placing the glass on a nearby table. I may not have been the epitome of professionalism thus far, but I've made a commitment to myself to do better from here on out. And that starts with keeping a level head today.

"Just one sip? That's not the fun-time gal I know! Come on, drink with us." Claire is slurring her words as she takes an unsteady step toward me. I realize too late that she's way drunker than I initially thought, because a second later, she stumbles on her heels, and the contents of her champagne flute come hurling toward me. We both watch in horror as the bubbly gold liquid sloshes across the front of my dress.

"Oh, shit," Claire mumbles, reaching for a napkin and dabbing furiously at the fabric.

"It's fine," I say, placing my hand over hers. If there's one thing I've learned from event planning, it's how to treat champagne stains. I pull the dress away from my body, inspecting the wet blotch. It's visible but not too egregious, thanks to the dark fabric. As soon as the ceremony starts, I'll cut into the kitchen to treat it with dish soap.

"I'm so sorry," Claire mumbles, and I can tell she's on the verge of tears. "I can't believe I did that. Now you're soaked. Why don't you borrow one of the bridesmaid's robes?"

I pause my dabbing to look at Claire's face. For the first time, I notice her pale pallor and the purple crescents beneath her eyes, which her makeup is only just managing to hide. I've seen my fair share of nervous brides, but this is something else entirely. Claire looks absolutely wrecked.

"It was an accident. Seriously, don't sweat it," I reassure her.

Still, the liquid has started to soak through the fabric, raising goosebumps on my skin. I grab another handful of napkins and dab at it, but it's not doing much to stop the cold wetness on my belly.

Quickly, I untie my bow on the front of my dress, so that I can pat the stain from the inside. But the minute I feel the cold air against my exposed skin, I realize my mistake. Cold dread pricks over my body as I stand there, frozen in place. And even though I'm still looking down at the plane of my stomach, I can feel Claire staring at me.

Slowly, reluctantly, I lift my head to glance at her. Sure enough, she's frozen in place, mouth hanging open, her eyes glued to a tattoo that I know with absolute certainty she's seen before. The temperature in the room drops ten degrees.

"Everyone," she says in an eerily calm voice I haven't heard before. Her eyes still haven't left the ink on my body. "Can we have the room? I need a minute alone with Ali."

Claire's friends exchange confused looks, but nonetheless follow her directions as they file out. I watch them as they leave, murmuring quietly among themselves, and no doubt wondering what kind of private exchange Claire needs to have with her wedding planner minutes before she's due to walk down the aisle. I doubt any of them know the truth about Graham and Claire, so they probably think she's about to chide me for my lack of professionalism. After all, I did just practically strip naked in the bridal suite. If only they knew how unprofessional I've actually been.

When my gaze travels back to Claire, I notice her eyes are filled with tears, and my chest goes tight.

"Claire," I say hoarsely. "I can explain."

Her eyes are still fixed to my tattoo, her bottom lip trembling slightly, and I realize that I'm still holding the front of my dress open, leaving myself fully exposed in more ways than one. It isn't until I begin hastily retying it that she finally drags her gaze upward to look at me.

"You're her," she says hoarsely. I open my mouth to speak but she holds a hand out, stopping me. "Is this why you took us on as clients? To get back with him?"

"No, of course not!" I say, my voice pleading. "I would never do something like that. I swear, I had no idea that Graham was your fiancé when we first met."

"Have you been seeing each other again? While I've been away?" she asks quietly.

My heart drops to my knees, but I can't manage to say a word. Still, my silence is confirmation enough.

Her face darkens. "I can't believe this. I thought we were friends."

"We are!" I protest. "Claire, I never meant to hurt you."

Claire gives me a tiny smile that somehow manages to be completely heartbreaking.

"Then why have you been sneaking around behind my back? You've had nothing but opportunities to tell me the truth and you never said a word. I've poured my heart out to you. I asked you point blank if you thought going through with this wedding was a bad idea, and you said nothing."

"I thought I was doing the right thing," I say softly. And I did. But now that I'm looking back on it all, reconsidering all the reasons I told myself that it made sense to keep the affair to ourselves, those reasons do not, collectively, add up. This has all been a mistake of epic proportions. And now it's too late.

Claire starts pacing again.

"I can't marry him," she says, her heels clacking against the floor. "Not when I know it would keep him from being happy."

Graham was right. Claire's instinct is to sacrifice her career for his happiness. But calling off this wedding won't do either of us any good now. I bite my bottom lip, my brain scrambling as I try to figure out how to salvage this situation.

"Claire," I say pleadingly. "Please reconsider. I would never forgive myself if I messed this up for you, if I cost you your visa or career. Working on late-night TV is your dream, and I can't let you give that up because I made a bad choice."

I bite down on my bottom lip.

"Some things are more important than love."

Claire's eyes go round.

"Oh my God," she says softly. "You *love* him?"

Shit.

"Shit," she says. "I need to go talk to him. This has been a terrible mistake. There has to be another way."

"Claire, wait!" I reach forward, grabbing her wrist. She stares down at her wrist, mouth ajar, before flicking her gaze back to me. The sense of betrayal in her eyes evokes a wave of nausea.

"Please," I say hoarsely, my voice cracking. "We ended things. It's over between us. Don't throw everything away based on our bad choices."

Claire bites down on her bottom lip and I can tell she's wavering. But then there's a knock on the door and Asha pokes her head through the doorway. Her eyes widen a fraction as she takes in the looks on both of our faces.

"Everything okay?" she asks tentatively. My heart is hammering in my chest as I watch for her response. But then she gives Asha a tiny smile and nods.

"Just some pre-wedding jitters," she says, and I start breathing normally again.

Asha looks visibly relieved. "Totally normal," she reassures her. "We're actually getting ready to line up. You ready?"

Claire turns back to me, the question in her eyes, and I give her a small, reassuring smile. I can feel Asha turn her head toward me, but I can't meet her eyes. Instead, I busy myself adjusting the train of Claire's dress.

"You look beautiful," I tell her softly. She looks over her shoulder at me, her eyes a storm cloud of mixed emotions.

"Are you sure?" she whispers. I nod and she presses her lips together, resolute.

"Okay," she says. "Let's do this."

I can already hear the violinist playing as we make our way down the carpeted hallway, every long, slow note of Canon in D seemingly mirroring my footsteps. We arrange the bridesmaids in a tidy line outside the ballroom doors. A quick peek inside confirms that every inch of the interior has been styled to perfection.

When the last bridesmaid has made her way down the aisle, the music changes again, this time to Claire's pick: "Another One Bites the Dust," by Queen. It seemed funny when she'd first suggested it, but I'm having a hard time summoning amusement now.

The guests rise, turning to look back at Claire. My breath catches in my throat as I look past her to see Graham standing at the end of the aisle. But unlike everyone else in the room, he isn't looking at Claire. Instead, he's staring straight at me.

I turn backward, pressing myself against the doorframe. I close my eyes as I tip my head back, willing my breath to steady itself.

"Hey." I jump at the sound of Asha's voice. My eyes pop back open as she presses a hand into my shoulder. "Are you okay?"

I stare at her, blinking back hot tears.

"No," I manage. "No, I'm not okay." The admission shakes the floodgates loose and my vision blurs as hot tears begin to fall. It's the first time that I've really admitted it, to myself or anyone else. *I am not okay.*

I swipe a fingertip underneath my eyes, undoubtedly smearing my carefully applied eye makeup.

"Go home," she says quietly.

I gape at her in disbelief.

"I can't leave," I say after a beat. "Antoine is here. I'll never get the job if I walk out now."

Asha's face twists with emotion. Disbelief, exasperation, and one more thing I can't quite identify.

"You're never going to get the job if Antoine finds out you're sleeping with the *groom.*"

Her words hit like a gut punch; the impact sends me stumbling backward.

"Go home," she says again, softer this time. "You are clearly in no state to work. I will handle Antoine." Her words break my heart all over again. I've let down so many people today. Graham, Claire, myself, and now Asha. She took a chance on me and now she's down a partner and left cleaning up my mess. My vision blurs as a fresh wave of tears burns the back of my eyes.

"I'm sorry," I choke out. And then I push past her, fleeing toward the lobby without daring a glance back.

27

At first, I'm not sure if the knocking sound is coming from behind my bedroom door or my computer. I'm curled up in bed, where I've been burrowed like a gopher since fleeing Graham and Claire's wedding two days ago. My laptop is open in front of me, currently streaming my 7,000th consecutive episode of *The Price Is Right.*

Bubbie was retired from her job at the library by the time I was in elementary school, so when I was home sick, she was the one who would babysit me while my parents worked. It was there, curled up on the couch together, that I discovered the joy of daytime television. *The Price Is Right* was my grandma's favorite, and so it became mine as well. Watching it now brings me right back to the warm, childhood memory. Or at least it did, before I realized that my adoration of the host has carried over into my love life.

A contestant has just guessed the exact price of a scooter, a talent he's attributed to watching the show every single day. Normally this episode makes me smile but today I'm just feeling bitter and envious. What I wouldn't do to go through life with that kind of certainty.

The banging sound returns, more insistent this time. I hit pause and call out, "Seriously, Mom, I am not interested in reading chakra!"

The bedroom door cracks open and a beautiful head of glossy black hair pokes through the doorway.

"Can I come in?" Asha asks. I sit up abruptly, suddenly self-conscious of my surroundings, which look very much like I'm cos-playing Depression Barbie. I'm dressed in the same fuzzy pajama set I've been wearing for forty-eight hours that may or may not be from Delia's circa 2012. My hair is even more disheveled than usual, and my bed is covered in crumbled tissues and half-eaten packages of gummy bears. I brush the remnants of my Nutella and banana sand-wich off my pajama shirt, slide the empty plate onto my nightstand, and then gesture for her to come in.

My stomach somersaults as she takes a seat on the edge of my bed. I've been avoiding her calls and texts since yesterday, not interested in hearing about how badly I've screwed up, how I've let her and everyone down. I'm still mortified that she sent me home. The thought of disappointing Asha has sent me down a shame spiral from which I may never emerge.

I never should have left the wedding. I should have pulled it together and acted like an adult. But now it's too late, and I've come to accept that I will never be leaving my bed again. I'm going to live out the rest of my days here, like the grandparents in Willy Wonka.

"Hey, champ. How are you doing?" she asks carefully.

I choke back a laugh, incredulous.

"Seriously?" I ask. "That's your first question? Aren't you furious at me right now?"

Asha gives me a sympathetic smile. "Listen, I can't say I would have behaved any differently if the man I loved was getting fake married to someone else."

My jaw drops. "You knew? Did . . . did Sarah tell you?"

Asha shakes her head. "I found out right before Claire walked down the aisle. She asked where you were and when I said you weren't feeling well, she told me everything."

Hot tears hit the back of my eyes. I blink them back rapidly. I never should have kept this from Asha in the first place. I thought keeping this secret was the best way to protect everyone. And in the end, it achieved the complete opposite.

"Asha, I'm so sorry. I ruined everything. You put yourself on the line for me, and I let you down."

Asha slides up closer to me on the bed. She reaches a hand forward to squeeze my legs through the sheets.

"You didn't ruin everything. But I do wish you would have told me what was going on from the beginning. I've known you since you were in training bras. I thought we trusted each other."

I cover her hand with mine and give it a squeeze.

"Of course I trust you. I was just so embarrassed, and I didn't want you to think less of me. I wanted you to see me as a reliable partner, not your best friend's impetuous little sister who needs to be dug out of another catastrophe."

I shrug. "Not that it matters now. I've destroyed my chances at any future in event planning."

Asha's expression is unreadable. "You really haven't checked your phone," she says under her breath. "Well, let me fill you in. Even after her confession, I managed to convince Claire to go through with the wedding. I promised her that I would talk to you, that we would figure something out, that they could always annul the marriage if they decided that was what was right. But also, that my job was to make sure this wedding went off without a hitch and I intended to do so."

A heaviness settles over my limbs as my rib cage goes tight. I knew that Graham was no longer mine. But somehow, hearing about it from Asha hits different. I feel my eyes well up with tears again as I nod numbly.

"Hang on there, Juliet," Asha says, as she hands me a fresh tissue from my night table. A trace of amusement creeps into her features, and she pauses for a dramatic beat before continuing. "Even though it's mostly been faded out of modern ceremony scripts, the preacher who was officiating asked if anyone objected to the union. He was right in the middle of his 'speak now' moment when someone stood up. I swear, it was like we'd all been teleported into a Taylor Swift music video."

The hair on my forearms rises. "Who objected?"

A slow grin spreads across Asha's face. "Trudy."

Of all the names that Asha could have thrown at me, this was the last one I ever expected to hear.

"Trudy . . . objected to the wedding? On what grounds?"

The smile on Asha's grin widens. "Apparently she said she couldn't abide her grandson getting married when he was in love with somebody else." My stomach bottoms out.

Trudy . . . knows about us? For how long? What must she think? My mind flashes back to our last conversation in her kitchen, the curious way she was studying me. The rustle of curtains in her window after Graham kissed me on her front lawn. She couldn't have known what was going on between us. *Could she?*

But before my thoughts can continue down this path, Asha starts speaking again.

"And *then,*" she continues. "Another guest stood up and said she objected too. Because apparently, she is in love with Claire? Turns out she's a waitress you all met in a restaurant one night and the two of them have stayed in touch."

A memory stirs, conjuring the mental image of our waitress from the night of our accidental double date. The way Claire grinned at that waitress, the one who she insisted looked like Zendaya.

"Oh my God," I moan with a laugh. "This is some made-for-TV movie shit." Then a thought occurs to me, and the amusement melts off my face.

"Hold on," I breathe. "They didn't go through with it? But . . . the hotel." The whole reason I pushed Graham to go through with this was to show Baltimore that the Black-Eyed Susan is still a premier destination for weddings. That it should not, under any circumstances, be turned into condos.

Asha bites her bottom lip.

"Funny you should say that. Because while it may not have played out quite the way you intended it to, the evening certainly succeeded in portraying the Black-Eyed Susan as one of the most romantic spots in the city."

I raise a questioning eyebrow. "What do you mean?"

"The press who came to cover the wedding?" Asha hesitates, like it's obvious. "They had a field day with the story. It was the lead story on *Baltimore* magazine's homepage."

She grins. "Also, it seems one of the guests filmed the entire thing and uploaded it to TikTok. A home organizing influencer with a huge following reposted it and it went viral overnight." She gives me a knowing smirk. *Sarah*. That little she-devil.

"They even played a clip of it on the *Today Show*," Asha continues. "Apparently, there's a growing waitlist of guests who are desperate to host events at The Second Chance Romance Hotel. There's no way Trudy is going to sell now. Seriously, have you not been online at all?"

She glances over at my computer screen, where the frozen image of Bob Barker stares back at her. His mouth is still halfway open, poised to remind everyone to spay and neuter their pets. "Oh, I see. So online, but not during this decade."

"I'm sorry, can we back up?" I ask. "Antoine must be furious with me. I've certainly blown my chance at that promotion." The irony is almost too much to bear. I pushed Graham to go through with the wedding, not just to save his family's hotel, but also my own career. And in the end, I blew it all up anyway.

"Don't you worry about Antoine. I've handled him," Asha says, brushing an invisible piece of lint off her pant leg.

"You've handled him," I say slowly. "Handled him how?"

"I told Antoine that you came down with a sudden bout of the stomach flu. You know how much puke freaks him out." I nod slowly. During my second week at the office, one of the receptionists, who, unbeknownst to anyone else, was pregnant, threw up in the trash can under her desk. Antoine shut the entire office down for three days and even had a professional cleaning crew come through to disinfect everything. Apparently, his anxiety rooted back to a childhood projectile vomiting incident at Disney World.

"I also told him that you knew that Graham was in love with someone else. That it's why you were spending so much time with him, to convince him to head down the aisle. That they never would have made it to the big day without you. That you knew the identity of this woman and kept that secret." She gives me a conspiratorial smile. "All of which is true."

My mouth falls open. "How long did you know?"

She shrugs. "I had an inkling that was confirmed when I found the two of you in the broom closet." She smiles. "Now what are you going to do about the sad British export that's currently pacing your living room like a puppy who's lost his favorite ball?"

I straighten up. "Graham's here?"

Asha nods. "Your dad has asked him several times to pace elsewhere because he's trying to watch Monday Night Football and can't concentrate." Well, that tracks.

"I told him he needed to wait for me to talk to you first," Asha continues. "Seniority and all that." She smiles at me. "Plus, I wanted you to have all the facts before you made a decision."

She rises to her feet. "I know you haven't been taking Antoine's calls either. I've told him that you were still stuck with your head in the toilet. But give him a call back today. He wants to offer you a full-time position."

"Asha?" I ask. "What would you do?" I'm not even sure what I'm asking: if I want her advice about the job or about Graham. But she just shakes her head.

"Only you can answer that," she says. "But no matter what, I'm proud of you, kiddo."

The sentiment brings an unexpected prickle of tears to my eyes. I was so worried that I hadn't realized how desperate I was for her approval until she gave it to me.

"Thank you," I choke out.

She gives me a small smile before disappearing through my doorway. A moment later, a familiar head of blond hair pokes through. The sight of him sends a storm of conflicting emotions through my chest. Apprehension, anger, sadness, longing, and perhaps most distressing of all, a flicker of joy.

"Hey," he says tentatively. "How are you doing?"

I gesture to my surroundings.

"Thriving, clearly."

He gives me a small smile that doesn't reach his eyes.

"I've been calling you," he says.

"Yeah, I guess I've forgotten to charge my phone for the last two days." I tip my chin toward my phone, which is lying on my nightstand like roadkill.

"May I sit?" he asks. I nod again, numbly as I gesture to the spot that Asha just vacated. Apparently, I'm having open office hours today.

Graham pushes his glasses up the bridge of his nose.

"I guess Asha told you about the wedding," he hedges, his eyes carefully searching my face for a reaction. He won't find one though; so many feelings are flooding through me at once that I've emotionally flatlined.

I nod again, and Graham, seemingly drawing confidence from the fact that I haven't yet asked him to leave, slides closer to me, and takes my hand in his.

"Ali," he says, his voice urgent now. "It's over. We can be together. We can go back to New York. You can find a planning job there and we can . . . we can be together." His voice trails off at the end as he studies my face, seeming not to find the reaction he was hoping for.

I bite down on my bottom lip as I weigh his words. He's finally saying everything I've been wanting to hear for months. But suddenly, I can't summon the joy I had anticipated.

A long beat passes, and then another.

"No," I say quietly.

Graham's mouth drops open. "No . . . you don't want to be with me?" he asks.

I shake my head. "Of course I want to be with you," I say. "But I don't want to be your backup plan. Your default second option now that your original choice fell through. I know that we were in an impossible situation, but this still doesn't feel like the right ending. I don't want to play second string. I want to be someone's first-round pick, you know? I wanted to be chosen."

"Ali." His voice is thick now, his words coming out strangled. "I choose you. Why do you think I'm here? I want to be with you. I love you."

"I love you too," I say, and the words cause a physical ache in my chest, because the moment I hear myself say them out loud, I realize how true they are. I swallow the lump in my throat, soldiering on.

"I thought I'd been in love before, Graham. But it's not possible, because what I've felt in the past can't even hold a candle to the way you make me feel. My whole life, I've felt like no one takes me seriously, like I'm just a good-time gal. Loved, yes, but not your first call when something goes wrong. Not someone people feel like they can count on. But you. You see me the way I see myself, the way I wish everyone else would see me. You make me feel like I should be someone's first choice. And now, I don't think I can settle for anything less. I want to be someone's first choice."

Graham shoves his glasses up his forehead, digging the heels of his hands into his eyes.

"Fuck," he whispers. "I fucked everything up. I was so determined not to let everyone down and I've lost the one thing that really mattered."

"That's just it, Graham," I say. "You have lived your entire life trying to make everyone else happy. Have you ever stopped to ask yourself what would make you happy? Do you even want to go back to New York?"

He opens his mouth, and then closes it again. A dark storm cloud passes over his features.

"It's a good job," he says quietly, tightly. "It's the reason I spent so many years studying. It's what I worked for. It's flexible, it pays the bills. There's no reason to leave it behind."

"There's one very good reason to leave it behind," I argue. "It doesn't make you happy. For once, do something because you *want* to do it. Life is too short to just get by. To live without passion, without doing the things that fill you up inside."

"Ali," he tries again. "*You* fill me up inside."

"I know that you love me, Graham," I say softly. "But you can't expect someone to spend their life with you if you haven't figured out how you want to live life for yourself."

Graham presses his lips together, then nods slowly.

"And what about you?" he asks after a beat. "Are you going to take the planning job? Stay in Baltimore long-term?"

It isn't until he poses the question that I realize I know the answer.

"No," I say softly. "I don't know what I'm going to do next. But I'm going to follow my heart."

"But your heart doesn't lead you to me?" Graham's voice is strained.

What a ridiculous question. My heart has belonged to him since the moment I pulled that cookbook out from under his car seat. But telling him the truth only sets me up to be hurt again. It's time to let him go, once and for all.

"I'm sorry," I say quietly. "I really hope you find what you're looking for."

"You too," Graham says. He rises stiffly from the edge of my bed and heads toward the door. Before he leaves, he turns to look back at me, and his expression is so shattered that I consider taking it all back. But before I can, he disappears through the doorway, shutting the door behind him.

28

I swore I wouldn't be that woman who wallows after a breakup. And this wasn't even a breakup. How can you end things with someone when you were never really together?

And yet, I wallowed. After a few weeks, my mom started sending me on errands, assigning me chores like a kid again. I knew she was just trying to help get me out of the house. And it did help, a little. Gave me a reason to change out of pajamas and brush my hair. Hit more than two hundred steps a day.

Today's task is a grocery run. When I turn down the street on my way home, I see my sister's minivan parked in my parents' driveway. I don't remember my mom mentioning that they were visiting today, but the past two weeks have been a blur and it's possible that it slipped my mind.

I press my hands to the window, peering inside the van. At first glance, I don't see anyone. But then I hear a rustling sound from the back seat and spot the reflection of a blond mane. I pull open the passenger door, and truly nothing could prepare me for the sight before me. Sarah is sprawled across the floor, her back slumped against the opposite door. Her normally immaculate hair is unbrushed and her clothing is rumpled. Most shocking of all, she's surrounded by fast-food wrappers and nibbling on what appears to be a fried chicken sandwich.

I blink twice, not sure I can trust what I'm seeing.

"Sarah?" I ask tentatively, since I'm not certain the woman in the car is really my sister or some kind of lab-made duplicate. Like the time the government produced a Will Byers body double on the first season of *Stranger Things*. She locks eyes with me before peeling back the paper wrapping and taking an enormous bite of her sandwich.

"Are you okay?"

"Yep," she says through a mouthful of food. There's a mayonnaise-soaked piece of lettuce stuck to the corner of her lips. "Never been better."

"Hmm. That's interesting," I say as I crawl into the van and attempt to squeeze my butt into one of the tiny booster seats. "Because last time I checked, you had strict policies against processed foods. And eating in the car, for that matter."

She takes a long sip from her enormous soda cup before letting out a loud belch. "Doesn't ring a bell," she says.

"Sarah." I reach into one of the grease-soaked paper bags on the floor and extract a french fry, popping it into my mouth. "What's going on?"

She lets out a defeated sigh. "I think I'm having a nervous breakdown."

I survey the interior of the van. Admittedly, if Sarah was going to have a psychotic break, this is what it would look like. It's sloppy and out of character, but still contained and relatively unobtrusive. Only Sarah could do a nervous breakdown responsibly.

"Do you want to talk about it?"

Sarah groans, burying her face in her hands.

"Jordan took Benny to get a haircut."

"And that's a bad thing?"

"I'm always the one who takes him. But I double-booked myself this morning because the twins were doing a lemonade stand to raise money for gymnastics, and I hadn't finished baking the cookies yet, and I couldn't be at both places at once, so Jordan took him. Only . . . he went rogue."

She reaches into her purse, scrolling through her phone for a moment before handing it to me. There's a photo of Benny on the screen, wearing a barbershop apron with a dinosaur print. But instead of his usual classic cut, the sides of his head have been closely shorn, the remaining curls on the top of his head styled into a mohawk.

"Well," I say, cocking my head as I study the photo. "It's a look."

Sarah lets out a watery sob.

"It's a *disaster.*"

"It's not a disaster," I reassure her. "*Mean Girls 2* was a disaster. This is just a haircut. It will grow back."

Sarah hiccups.

"I know everyone thinks I'm a control freak."

I raise an eyebrow, but don't say anything. Still, she takes my silence as confirmation. She sniffles as a fat tear rolls down her cheek.

"It's true. I *am* a control freak. But it's only because I feel like I have to be. Everyone is counting on me all the time. I can't let go of the helm because steering the ship is the only thing that keeps me from sinking."

I study her for a moment, flabbergasted by this confession.

"Sarah, you can't put that kind of pressure on yourself. You can't let the whole world rest on your shoulders. It's not healthy."

Sarah's gaze drops to her lap. "Welcome to my entire life. Sometimes the pressure feels like it could crush me. But I never want to ask for help or tell people when I feel stressed out because I don't want them to worry about me. I never want to let anyone down."

A lightbulb goes off in my head as I make a connection. As sympathetic as I am to Sarah, I've punished Graham for doing the same thing. I've been furious with him for allowing his obsession with not letting other people down interfere with his own choices. Too blinded by my own pain to notice how much he's like my sister, who I am so much more willing to forgive.

She lifts her eyes to look at me. "But I feel like I've let you down."

"Me?" The thought is incomprehensible. Sure, she can be an insufferable perfectionist, but I've never felt like Sarah's let me down. Sarah never lets *anyone* down. It's kind of her thing. Although now I can see how the weight of that role is starting to crush her. Heavy is the crown and all that.

"Sarah, you have never disappointed me. You've always been an incredible sister."

She sniffles again. "I let you down with Graham. You trusted me when you told me about him, and I made you feel awful about it. I let my own insecurities get the best of me instead of listening to what you were saying and showing up for you. And now you're depressed and lonely and I'm poisoning myself with phosphates, and my baby looks like Mr. T and everything is a disaster!"

She lets out another loud sob, and I slide to the floor, putting my arm around her. She leans her head on my shoulder, her tears soaking through the neck of my T-shirt. After a moment, her tears die down. She grabs a tissue from the cupholder and blows her nose.

"I think I was jealous," she hiccups. "That's why I discouraged you so much."

I would have been less shocked if Sarah had sprouted wings.

"Jealous?" I manage. "Of *me*?"

She sighs. "Mom and Dad wanted another kid so badly. It took them years, and when they finally had you, you were a *lot*. They were exhausted and overwhelmed, and I didn't know how to help other than to be a perfect angel, to do everything right and never give them any trouble. And that became my role. I was the responsible one, the one who didn't rock the boat, the one who made everyone happy and never asked for anything. But you? You always got to be a kid. You got to try new things, make mistakes, scrap plans and reboot. You don't think I would have loved to run off to New York for a few years, go on endless dates and try out a new career?"

"The dates weren't really that enviable," I point out. "But you could have gone to New York. You're the most capable person I know. You can do anything."

Sarah shakes her head morosely.

"I was always trying to set a good example for you, steer you on the right path, because Mom and Dad wanted me to. But you were never interested in anyone else's path. You've never wasted a second worrying about what other people think. You live your life for you. You've always followed your passions and charted your own course. I wish I could be that fearless."

A confusing mix of adoration and sadness washes over me. Sarah has always been like a second mother to me, and I've spent my whole life looking up to her. But I placed her on such a high pedestal that I never imagined she'd feel envious of me.

"You know I've always admired you," I say. "But our relationship doesn't have to be a one-way street. I'm back at home now, and I'm here to help you in any way you need. I can babysit and make you meals, or just hang out with you and be your friend."

Sarah looks up at me with watery eyes. "I would love that," she sniffs. "I would love to be your friend. You're the coolest girl I know."

I give her shoulder a squeeze, and a feeling of contentment washes over me. After spending my life being the wild child, the hippie, the directionless little sister, the idea of Sarah relying on me for once feels *good*.

"So, I say this not as your big sister, but as a friend," Sarah says, putting emphasis on the last word. "I think you made a mistake letting Graham go."

"No, I think you were right about that one," I say. "It's time for me to grow up and stop chasing unavailable men. I feel like I finally know exactly who I am. I don't need a man to make me feel whole. But when I am ready for a partner, I don't want to play games. I want to be someone's first choice."

I can tell Sarah wants to say something else, but to her credit, she doesn't, stuffing another fry in her mouth instead.

"Okay," she says after a beat. "I have to clean all of this up before I go home. My kids will turn feral if they smell saturated fat."

"Counter idea," I say. "We hide the evidence, but instead of going home right away, we go out for pedicures together."

Sarah gives me a watery grin. "I'd love that."

As party planning goes, I do believe that Bubbie's ninetieth birthday celebration is my best event to date. I've transformed my parents' living room into a replica set of *The Price Is Right,* complete with a Contestant's Row. Sarah helped me recreate the bidding lecterns with construction paper–covered shoeboxes and dry-erase boards. After lunch, we're going to play a simulation game, where contestants will guess the price of household items from 1935, the year Bubbie was born. We've even hired a Bob Barker impersonator, who, according to my time check, is currently running late.

I find Bubbie over by the buffet table, nibbling on a potato chip from a bowl I labeled Plinko chips. All the party guests are wearing yellow sales tags with their names printed across the front, just like contestants on the show.

"Hey, birthday girl," I say as I sidle up to her. "Are you having a nice time?"

Bubbie's face lights up as she reaches forward to squeeze my hand. Someone must have cleaned her glasses, because for once, both of her lenses are clear. Her gray-blue eyes sparkle behind them.

"Ali, I'm having the time of my life. Everyone that I love is here. What more could I ask for? And the very cute party planner has outdone herself."

I grin back at her. "The best is yet to come. We're going to start playing the game in a few minutes. Although my dad might be running it if our hired host doesn't show up soon."

Bubbie gives me a smile and a conspiratorial wink. Before I can read into it, Sarah comes over and squeezes my shoulder.

"Fake Bob Barker just arrived. I set him up in the kitchen," she says. "You ready to get started?"

I grin. "Let's do this."

Turning back toward the living room, I cup my hands around my mouth. "Attention contestants! If you would please take your seats, our game is about to begin!"

The small group of guests titters as they head back to their folding chairs. It's not a huge crowd: my family, Sarah's kids, Bubbie's sister, Great Aunt Betty, a few of Bubbie's neighbors, and the members of her mah-jongg league. Once everyone is seated, I dim the lights, then nod to Sarah. She grins back at me before pressing her lips to the karaoke machine microphone we borrowed from her twins.

"Barbara Rubin, come on down! You're the first contestant on The Price Is Right!" she calls gleefully into the mix. My mom practically bounces from her chair as she makes her way down to Bidder's Row. "Jackson Goldfarb, come on down!"

Jackson thrusts a fist into the air before sprinting over to the second space in Contestant's Row.

"Elaine Reiser, come on down!" Bubbie's face lights up and the unbridled joy in her expression makes my heart swell. We are so, so lucky to be able to celebrate her today.

Sarah clears her throat theatrically before calling the next name. "Last but not least: Ali Rubin, come on down!"

I freeze, my water cup halfway to my lips. I wasn't supposed to be a contestant until the next round. My dad was meant to be the fourth player. I turn to Sarah, eyebrows raised, but she just smiles and waves me toward the front of the room. Shrugging, I head over to the empty chair next to Bubbie. She squeezes my hand as I slide into the seat beside her.

"And now, here's the host of The Price Is Right: Bob Barker!"

There's a long beat as the room goes quiet with anticipation. Sarah pulls back the tinsel curtain covering the entrance to the kitchen and whispers behind it. A moment later, a figure shuffles through the doorway, and my bones turn to jelly.

Because the man cosplaying Bob Barker in a white wig, pinstripe suit, and a goddamn pocket square is none other than Graham Wyler. He's clutching a long, thin microphone that's a perfect replica of Bob's, and I notice it's trembling slightly in his grasp. His eyes meet mine and my stomach bottoms out.

Speechless, I swivel my head toward Sarah. She gives me a small, triumphant smile before disappearing into the kitchen. That little sneak.

Graham is still standing motionless, his eyes locked on my face, seemingly oblivious to the crowd's applause. It's clear that he's completely out of his comfort zone, and I can't help but love him for it. But also, what the actual fuck?

"Welcome," he says, "to The Price Is Right. Who's ready to get started?"

"Graham!" I hiss as I leap to my feet. "What the hell are you doing?" I fold my arms across my chest. "Oh my God. Are you trying to grand gesture me?"

"Of course I'm trying to grand gesture you," he whispers back. "Now, would you kindly take your seat so I can get on with it?" Then he takes a deep breath, steadying himself, and plasters on an enormous smile. Slowly, I lower myself back into my chair. My heart is beating so hard I'm afraid it will burst out of my chest.

"Here is the first item up for bid today," he declares.

Bubbie squeezes my hand. "You know, I've always been a sucker for a British accent," she whispers. She gives me a knowing smirk and my mouth drops open. *Was every member of my family in on this?*

With a flourish, Graham lifts the cover of the silver cake dome I'd arranged on a folding table on our makeshift stage. When I'd set it up earlier, there was a five-pound bag of sugar underneath, its twenty-five-cent price hidden behind a yellow tag reading 1935. But now, the sugar has been replaced with a cookbook. Even from a few feet away, I can make out the title. *Jewish Festival Cooking.*

Graham sweeps his arm theatrically across the book.

"Straight from one of Hampden's most charming used bookstores, it's a cookbook with the ability to rekindle a decade-old love affair. Use it to prepare tried-and-true holiday classics like charoset and Hamantaschen, or gift it to a loved one. But whatever you do, don't hide it in your car like a coward."

"Graham!" At this point, my face is burning with mortification. "Seriously, get down from there. You've made your point."

"I see the young woman in the front is eager to start the game," he says. "But let's start the bidding in the order our contestants were called."

He turns to my mom. "Barbara, what do you bid?"

My mom pretends to mull this over. "I'll go with two hundred dollars."

"What?" I squawk. "You know that's way too much!" My mom shrugs with a grin. "Whoops."

Jackson is up next. "I don't know, bruh? Six dollars?"

I shake my head. I can't believe my own flesh and blood is doing this to me.

When it's Bubbie's turn, she grins conspiratorially at Graham. "Pass."

I gape at her. "You can't pass! This game is for you!"

She smiles at me. "This game is for *us,* Bubbeleh. And right now, it's your turn."

Graham/Bob looks at me expectantly. "And what's your bid, young lady?"

I let out a resigned sigh. Looks like we're really doing this. "Thirty-five dollars."

Graham removes the label covering the book's price. But underneath, instead of a figure, there's just one word: "Ali."

"Come on up," he says gallantly. "You're the next contestant on The Price Is Right!"

I rise tentatively, coming to join him on the stage. I lean close to whisper to him.

"Seriously, what are you doing here?"

He gives me a placid smile, holding himself steady, but his eyes, brimming with emotion, give him away.

"What does it look like?" he whispers back. "I'm choosing you." His words hit like an arrow, and my vision blurs as tears prickle behind my eyes. *He's choosing me.*

Then he straightens and gestures toward the homemade Plinko board that Sarah and I constructed.

"Okay, ma'am," he says, slipping back into Bob Barker mode. "Would you like me to review the rules for our audience?"

"Graham," I try again, more urgently this time. I blink rapidly to keep the unshed tears from falling. "We should talk outside."

"Let's finish this round first, shall we?" he replies. "In fact, why don't we see what we're playing for?"

He takes a step backward and throws out his palms with a resigned sigh.

"The final prize is me. All of me. I know that we were never supposed to fall for each other, but we did, and it was the best thing that ever happened to me. So, I'm offering myself, a man who is desperately in love with you and wants to give you every part of himself. After all that's happened, I understand if you don't want anything more to do with me, and if you want me to leave you alone, I will. But I came back here because I think you might feel the same way about me as I do about you. And I'm just wondering if you would consider being with me, out loud, in public, all the way? Because I sure as hell want to be with you."

I stand there, staring at him in disbelief, and for the first time since he took the stage, it occurs to me how vulnerable he is. The man has spent his whole life avoiding a misstep and now here he is, risking a public rejection. For once, he's going after something that's just for him, even though there's a possibility that he'll walk away empty-handed. I'm proud of him.

The dam finally breaks. I let out a shuddering sob as streaks of hot tears cascade down my cheeks. Graham reaches forward to brush them away with his thumb.

"Either way, I'll be staying here in Baltimore. So, I just wanted to give you a heads-up, in case we happen to run into each other in line for coffee." His voice is softer now as he stares at me, his eyes searching mine.

I stare back at him, thoroughly confused. "What are you talking about?"

One corner of Graham's mouth rises. "I'll admit you're not the only old love keeping me here. The Black-Eyed Susan is the second most important lady in my life."

A thousand chaotic thoughts are swirling through my head. That can't be right. I look around for Ashton, because surely, I'm being punked. "But I . . . I thought it was sold to a developer."

"That was the plan. But he was outbid." A smile tugs at the corner of his lips. "The new manager has rudimentary business experience. He's doing all he can to manage the financial aspect of things and has just enrolled in an online degree program for hospitality management."

My mouth falls open. "You bought the hotel?" I ask slowly. It's such an out-of character move that I can hardly wrap my mind around it.

"Back up," I continue. "The Graham I know wouldn't just give up his career. What changed?"

Graham shrugs. "A very brave person once told me that I shouldn't live my life always picking the safe choice. I wished I could be more like her, to stop living in fear of making a mistake and just pursue my dreams. So, I took a leap of faith. Running the Black-Eyed Susan is my full-time job now. It looks like I'm going to be hanging around here for a while.

"Although," he adds. "Given the hotel's recent success with themed events, I *am* in search of a partner with culinary and event planning experience. Someone who can enact my vision for a successful rebranding."

My brow furrows.

"Wait. Is that why you've come here? Because you want me to be your *business partner*?"

Graham shakes his head. He takes a step forward, closing the space between us.

"Of course not," he says. "I could hire another partner. Sure, they'd probably make very dull charcuterie boards, and neglect to stock the freezer with Bagel Bites, but I'd make it work. That's not what this is about."

He takes another step closer, lowering his head until his face is inches from mine.

"I came here because I want you. Every part of you. I don't want to live another day without you. You're the key to my lock, Ali."

I bite my bottom lip, weighing his declaration. But already, I feel the pull of my body toward his, the magnetism of our undeniable bond.

"Oh, honey, kiss him already!" Bubbie hollers from her chair.

I turn to the kitchen doorway and see Sarah grinning at me. "You know what they say about the sage advice of your elders," she says with a shrug. "And it is her ninetieth birthday, after all. It would be wrong to deny her wishes."

I roll my eyes. My family could power a football stadium with the energy of their guilt.

And then, without further ado, I grab Graham by his tie, yank him forward, and press his lips to mine.

In the background, the crowd has erupted into thunderous cheers, but I barely hear them. I'm hardly conscious of anything at all, aside from the weight of Graham's hands circling my waist and the way his lips are molding to me.

When he finally breaks the kiss, he drags his fingers through my hair, tucking a rogue curl behind my ear. His thumb brushes my cheekbone as he stares into my eyes.

"I love you, Ali," he says. "You're it for me."

"I love you too, Graham," I say. "Now what do you say we make this commitment official with a second tattoo?"

Graham smirks as he presses his forehead to mine.

"Don't bet on it," he whispers.

Epilogue

"For goodness' sake, Lexi, will you stop it already? Your dress is fine."

Lexi huffs as she reluctantly tucks the lint roller back into her clutch. "Sorry, I just need a distraction. Otherwise, I'm going to start crying again." She takes a deep breath as she pats a finger delicately beneath her eyelid, careful not to smudge her professionally applied makeup. "I'm just so nervous."

"There's nothing to be nervous about," I assure her in my best wedding planner voice. "Everything is going to be fine. Right, Chloe?"

I turn to my other best friend for backup, but her eyes are just as glassy.

"God, not you too. You're supposed to be the stoic one."

She sniffles. "I can't help it. We've all come so far."

Despite my teasing, it's hard not to get choked up myself. Chloe's right: this year has been a whirlwind. For the past twelve months, Graham and I have been running the newly relaunched Black-Eyed Susan, with a focus on the hotel's capacity as an event space. Slowly but surely, we built up our clientele (thanks in no small part to Chloe, who we hired as our social media manager), and I'm proud to say that the hotel is firmly back on its feet.

Claire landed on her feet too. After featuring the story of her and

Graham's failed wedding on *The Cash Castillo Show,* which became one of its most popular episodes, the network was more than happy to secure her a work visa. She also launched a new podcast called "The Time I Almost Committed a Felony." It's not only hilarious and chart-topping, but it's also brought new voices to the conversation around immigration. Best of all, her friendship with Graham has continued to thrive. And that's what matters most of all.

As for me, in my dual capacity as the hotel's head chef and special events coordinator, I've never been happier. Every day is a new adventure, the perfect amount of unpredictability to satisfy my restless spirit. But Graham is my anchor, allowing me to ride the waves without ever getting lost at sea. And now, we're about to embark on the next chapter.

"I never thought I'd see the day we'd be marrying you off to a finance bro," Chloe says, shaking me out of my daydream. "But here we are."

"Former finance bro," I correct her. "Current hotelier."

The three of us turn to stare at our reflection in the floor-length mirror. Two women in matching, ivory bridesmaids' dresses are flanking another in a white bridal gown. Me.

The door to the bridal suite flies open as a flurry of motion and giggles explodes through the doorway. Benny is in the lead, looking like a baby model in a pint-sized tuxedo. His twin sisters are on his heels, flower petals flying behind them as they chase their little brother. Sarah trails in last, shaking her head. I can tell she's fighting the urge to pick up every fallen petal and return them to their rightful baskets, and I'm proud of her for instead allowing herself to go with the flow and just live in the moment. Then she meets my eyes, and her face relaxes.

"Oh, Ali," she sighs. "You look beautiful."

"I just saw you ten minutes ago," I laugh. "Seriously, everyone needs to calm down."

Nevertheless, she closes the space between us, wrapping her arms around me, firmly but gently enough not to wrinkle my dress.

"I'm so proud of you," she whispers in my ear.

I give her a squeeze back. Then there's a soft knock at the door, and we turn to see Asha standing there, holding a clipboard and looking chic as ever in a balloon-sleeved blouse and cropped leather trousers.

"It's time," she says.

Then she organizes us into a line, with my nieces in the front, followed by my two best friends in the world, and at the very end, my first friend. Sarah.

The music has already started playing, the low notes of the piano and cellist duo echoing through the walls. We chose to walk down the aisle to "Can't Help Falling in Love." Classic yet fitting. Because no matter how hard we tried to fight it, somehow this ending has always been inevitable. And I wouldn't change a thing.

One by one, the women I love disappear through the doorway, making their way down the flower-lined aisle, until finally, it's just me, standing between my parents. I'm faintly aware of my mom's soft sniffles, but then I see him at the end of the aisle, and everything else fades into the background. Our eyes lock, and once again, I hear the single word that's been echoing in my brain. *Mine.* At last.

Asha's voice comes up behind me and it's only then that I realize I'm crying.

"Are you ready?" she asks softly. I take a deep breath and nod, because truthfully, I've known the answer to that question for a long time. Since Graham asked me to be his partner—in business, in life. Or even back when he invited me into his London flat all those years ago. I just wasn't ready to admit it yet.

My mom gives my hand a tiny squeeze, and I squeeze it right back.

And then, I put one foot in front of the other and take my first step forward.

Acknowledgments

Acknowledgments are one of my favorite parts of writing a novel, because publishing is a team sport, and now I get to thank everyone who made this book possible.

I'd first like to thank my agent, Melissa Edwards, whose continued guidance, tireless support, and wry sense of humor make publishing such a joyful experience. Thank you so much for championing my writing. I can't wait to publish more books together!

I immediately connected with my editor and fellow Baltimore native, Sallie Lotz, while on submission with *Till There Was You*. The only thing more fun than writing all my favorite places into this novel was having an editor who knew exactly where Snoasis was located and agreed that chocolate with marshmallow syrup is the elite flavor combination. Thank you for all your thoughtful edits, which shaped this story into its best possible self. We should celebrate with a trip to Ocean City. You're going to love it, Melissa! (You will hate it.)

Once again, I want to thank the St. Martin's Griffin team, including my terrific publicist, Meghan Harrington; excellent marketing team, Kejana Ayala and Brant Janeway; and thorough copyeditor, Lani Meyer. I also want to thank Olga Grlic and Petra Braun, who are such thoughtful collaborators and once again produced a jaw-dropping cover that exceeded expectations.

I'm so lucky to have met Ellie McDonough and Haylie Swenson in Jennifer Close's writing workshop. Having beta readers (and treasured friends) who've known Ali since she was first conceived in 2021 made all the difference when it came to revising this book. Thank you for loving Ali and bespectacled men in cardigans as much as I do.

I want to extend my gratitude to everyone who read early drafts, including Holly James, Sierra Godfrey, Ambriel McIntyre, Melissa Liebling-Goldberg, and Andrew Knott. A special thanks to Clare Blackwood, who inspired the character of Claire after venting about the lack of late-night shows in Canada. She deserves to be in a writer's room!

I am so thankful for my online and real-life friends, especially my Harrisburg girls, who show up for me in all the ways. #TeamMelissa offers daily guidance, support, and laughter, and I'm so lucky to know you. Thank you to Honey Nails and Spa in Harrisburg, who provides me a biweekly space to read and also keeps my book in their window. I also want to give a shout-out to my local indie, Cupboard Maker Books, who has been so incredibly kind and supportive and painted my book on the side of their building?! You ROCK!

I am blessed to have a loving family with whom I shared Shabbat dinners every Friday night as a child. Thank you for your love and support and for inspiring some of the characters and scenes in this novel.

I'm forever grateful to the backbone of my publishing team, my daughter, Jordana, who refuses to leave a bookstore until she has hand-sold every copy of TTWY in stock. You are the coolest girl I know. And to sweet Ezra, my little prince, whose green glasses and tiny cardigans inspired so much of Graham.

Finally, I want to thank Avi, my best friend and the love of my life. I'm incredibly lucky to have a partner who is loving and supportive, who moves mountains to foster my career, and whose extensive knowledge of industrial freezers is the gift that keeps on giving. You are the best and I'll love you forever.

About the Author

Leslie Gilbert

Lindsay Hameroff is a writer, humorist, and former English teacher raised in Baltimore, Maryland, and based in Harrisburg, Pennsylvania. Her writing has been featured in *McSweeney's Internet Tendency, The Belladonna, Weekly Humorist,* and fan letters to Harry Styles. She is also the author of *Till There Was You,* her debut novel.